Changing

and

Labradors

A Novel

By

Helen Aherne

Warmest wishes,
Helen Aherne

Copyright © 2017 by Helen Aherne

All rights reserved. No part of this book may be reproduced in any form or by any means, electronic or mechanical, including photocopying, recording, or by any information storage and retrieval system, without permission in writing from the author. Exception is given in the case of brief quotations embodied in critical articles and reviews. This is a work of fiction. Names, characters, places, and incidents either are the product of the author's imagination or are used fictitiously.

ISBN: 978-1975941123

Published by CreateSpace

Dedication

To

My lovely husband, Richard, for his love and encouragement during the writing of this novel – and for living on pizza when I forgot to cook.

My wonderful son, Charles, of whom I have always been immensely proud, and his amazing family – Aja, Leila Realtán and Donovan Oisín.

Colm and Chris, for innumerable jokes, some worse than others!

And Annest, my lovely step-daughter, for introducing me to the music of Seasick Steve.

Chapter One

Jack's phone pings, stopping him mid-sentence, as we lie back in the throes of post-coital pleasure. I smile smugly to myself, pleased that it wasn't a few minutes earlier, when it could have been *coitus interruptus* - a real passion killer. The sun, shining through my bedroom window, warms my skin as I fleetingly ponder the phenomenon of modern communication – mobile phones. Don't you hate them having the power to interrupt the most intimate, saddest or even the happiest of life's moments. I stare as he snatches his mobile from the bedside table, scanning the brightly lit screen.

'Sorry, sweetheart, it's the States. I need to phone them,' he says over his shoulder, one leg already out of our bed.

'Now?' I say, a little taken aback that he can switch in seconds flat, from hot, passionate lovemaking to the cold world of business and finance.

'Come on, Rachel, you know how it is – this

Bedford project we're working on? We've had nothing but problems with the client. You wouldn't believe the crap they come up with – anything to push the price down.'

'*Another* new one? I thought it was the Seattle account you were on? Your new boss is really piling on the work, isn't she?'

'Yeah, I know …what can I do?' he says, rubbing his thumb tenderly along my cheek. 'I'll just make a quick call … need to pop to the loo.'

I watch his strong, tanned back and neat hips as he walks away from me and, not for the first time, revel in the fact that this attractive, successful man and I have been blissfully happy together for the last two-and-a-half years. The only downside is his numerous trips away, which are starting to annoy. They seem to be more often and longer recently, due to some discontented client in the States. Still, I remind myself, you can't expect to have the financial rewards without putting up with some of the inconveniences. And Jack's job is certainly well paid.

I listen to Jack's muffled conversation, hear the toilet flush, and feel the familiar fluttery feelings inside as he comes out, leaning half-naked in his Calvin Klein boxers against the bathroom door. But my joy is short lived because I know before he says anything I'm not going to like what he has to say.

'Sorry, Rache. Problems again. I have to leave right away for the States.'

§

An hour later I head into work at the veterinary clinic, arriving at my parking space just as Annie, my colleague, jumps out of a low-slung sports car with the roof down. The handsome blond driver reaches over, grabs her playfully by her T-shirt and practically drags her back in, kissing her passionately. Leaning in, she exposes shapely legs which seem to go on for ever and she's totally oblivious to the spectacle she's creating outside the bleak, grey-brick building, which serves as our place of work.

'Go, Annie,' I mutter to myself begrudgingly. I'm bad-tempered due to my conversation with Jack this morning. He was packing as I left the house for his business trip to the States. It's my birthday on Sunday and I was hoping he'd have something suitably romantic up his sleeve. At this rate, we won't even be in the same country, never mind the same restaurant. He'd better grab a quick moment to call though – that way, at least, I'll know he's gone to the trouble to remember, even if he can't be here. It's the most basic thing to do in a relationship – remember your girlfriend's birthday, don't you think? Surely, it's written *in blood* into your diary. I tell myself not to be so needy, and head into the office.

Annie skips up the steps beside me.

'Well, well,' I smile, nodding towards the car, 'Ricky – the IT genius? Justin – the car salesman?' I ask, looking back at the Adonis who hasn't managed to tear his eyes away from my gorgeous friend.

'Neither!' she teases slyly. 'Rodders – City boy – met him at The Spotted Peacock last night. Told you you should come with me. His friend was hot too.'

'Annie, Annie,' I laugh. 'You're impossible!'

The rest of the morning leaves no time to hear about Annie's new chap from The Spotted Peacock, as we're run off our feet. The veterinary practice I work for in Norebridge is extremely busy, and today especially. Later, as I sort through some files in the back office Annie rushes in, her fiery red hair bouncing around her freckly face and she's trembling with excitement.

'Rachel, you'll never guess who's in the waiting room! Doesn't have an appointment, but he's worried about his dog – Labrador, lame front paw,' she says as a matter of course, hands waving frantically around.

I've been daydreaming that Jack will turn up unexpectedly and whisk me off to a romantic dinner for my birthday (which I know is impossible unless he can time-travel). Or will at least have arranged for a massive bouquet to be delivered. 'Who?' I ask reluctantly, not particularly interested in our mystery visitor.

'None other than The Strop!' she almost screeches. 'Oh, my God – he's *soooo* gorgeous.'

§

Anton Wickers-Stroppton, known locally as The Strop, is our resident *cause celebre*. A hugely successful rock star, he moved to our village a year ago and, much as I hate to admit it, it's due to his presence in Norebridge that our town has been put back on the map. Every so often, when he's done something incredibly stupid, the media descends in droves, jockeying for position outside the wrought-iron gates of Mill House, his home, hoping to catch a glimpse of Wickers-Stroppton. And, to find out who the current beauty is, clinging possessively to his arm. He hangs out with names and faces we're only familiar with from television and the media. And, many a career has been made just through association with the famous man.

Besides being a brilliant musician he's famous for mooning his shapely backside up against the train window one drunken Friday night, on his way home from London last year. An elderly widow had a 'fit of the vapours,' collapsing out cold on the platform. Only his remorse and concern for the stricken woman kept him out of prison. It seems his minders escorted her to hospital, The Strop paying for a private room and everything else to boot. For some reason, she needed to stay in hospital for five days – for a *fainting fit?* He then covered the cost of a private nurse to stay with her in her own home for a month. The judge was well impressed.

However, lighting up a fag *in Church,* the one and only time he attended Sunday service didn't win him any favours among the gathered congregation. The Vicar, on the other hand, was surprisingly forgiving and it was later rumoured that the Parish Youth Club, the Community Hall and the Parish crèche had quite suddenly come into funds!

§

'I've never seen him in the flesh before,' Annie says excitedly as we head out to reception. 'I certainly wouldn't mind seeing a bit more either,' she says liciviously, a cheeky smile lighting up her pretty face. But she's totally incapable of dealing with The Strop and stands beside me, mouth agape, gazing adoringly at the man before us.

'How long has he been limping?' I ask, in what I hope is a business-like manner. I may be madly in love with Jack, but it doesn't stop me appreciating the handsome man standing at our reception desk. Hair, black as a raven's feather, flops over a deeply furrowed brow. Dark eyes are set back under thick, heavy eyebrows – a challenge, I'd say, to even the most competent beautician. And, giving him the look of a Victorian gentleman, is a set of sideburns, which frame a thin, sculptured face. He's dressed entirely in black and a large, double-breasted greatcoat envelops what looks like a tall, slim frame. To my astonishment I feel a strange attraction to this notorious stranger.

'He was fine yesterday evening when we went for his walk,' he says, worry etched on his face. 'It must have been this morning – he went off chasing a rabbit while we were out. But I didn't notice anything until we got home, when he started limping. Could it be a thorn or something? I've looked, but can't see anything myself.' He kneels down beside the animal, running his hands gently along it's flanks. I begin to wonder if it's pain, or sheer pleasure, eliciting the long, slow moans from the animal, who slowly rolls over offering its soft underbelly for rubs. And I hear a sigh from Annie next to me, who's rooted to the spot and I can only imagine what's going through her ever-fertile mind!

We call Henry, our boss, who takes The Strop into the consultation room. A short time later, much to Annie's disappointment, he despatches him with a very sad looking Lab, doing his best to lick his paw through his dressing. It seems the animal's cut through the soft pad very deeply, possibly on a rough stone, or piece of glass in the undergrowth. I notice the frown has disappeared from his owner's face and I feel a rush of affection for this person, who obviously adores Zebedee –brother to Lucius and who, The Strop informs us, will be waiting for them impatiently back home.

Chapter Two

'I'm not kidding you, Rache. He was amaaazing! Never mind his hands – you wouldn't believe what he can do ...'

We've just grabbed five minutes for a quick cuppa when Henry strolls back into reception, stopping at the front desk to pick up his post. 'You feeling OK, Rachel?' he asks me, full of concern. 'You're looking very flushed. Not coming down with anything, are you?'

Little does he know I'm red up to the eyeballs just from listening to Annie's account of her sexual shenanigans with Rodders the evening before. Talk about the Kama Sutra – I think they could write a version of their own. She's just regaled me with tales of ear chomping and toe licking (ugh, I can't bear anyone to touch my toes), and something about ... strawberries. My mind boggles as I wonder did he chop them first, and what exactly he was doing with them? I'm no prude

– but neither am I in the same league as '*Fifty Shades* …' This is so outside my sexual comfort zone even for, as I like to think of myself, a fairly clued-up, almost-forty-thirty-five-year-old! But, that's a throwback to a jokey reference of 'thunder thighs' by a teenage friend. Years later, at a school reunion, I was told she'd always been jealous of me. It seems she'd had her eye on the chap who asked *me*, instead of her, to the school disco. But, the barb struck home and never quite left, despite my lovely mother's numerous attempts over the years at reassurance. But, since then my body image has been the scourge of my life. That's why I'm all the more intrigued, and if I'm honest, *hugely* in awe of Annie's sexual gymnastics and total lack of inhibitions.

'Rachel. *Rachel!*' Suddenly, I realise Annie is trying to tell me something. 'Henry wants you in his office.' I look over and realise Henry is holding the door to his office open, waiting for me to join him.

'Sorry, Henry. Just thinking about … eh … the rest of today's schedule of appointments,' I answer lamely.

'Exactly what I wanted to catch up with,' he says. 'How are we fixed? Any possibility I could leave at four o'clock today? I … eh …just have something I need to do. Someone I need to see.'

I look at my boss as he seats himself behind his desk, and realise he is being a little evasive. Unusual for Henry. And it makes me wonder what's going on in the life of Henry Donaldson, Vet Extraordinaire.

§

It's four o'clock before I get time to grab a quick coffee and a sandwich. I've been dying to check my mobile, which I never do when I'm working. As Practice Manager I feel it's important to give good example, and that means banning personal mobiles during working hours. If I didn't, with Annie's love life she'd be on the phone non-stop. She's been very good about it though from the first day she started with us, and keeps it on silent and in the cupboard. *And,* she's managed to turn it into something positive – typical Annie.

'Well, the way I look at it is,' she'd said flippantly on that first day, 'if the guys can't get me anytime *they* like, it just makes them that bit keener!'

And it certainly seems to work for her. I've never seen anyone put so little of themselves into relationships, only to have men panting about her like dogs after a bitch on heat. Unlike me – I'm an all-or-nothing kinda gal - two weeks after meeting someone and I'm washing their socks and ironing creases into their underpants. I know – sick-making, isn't it? You'd think I'd have learned after numerous failed relationships.

'Your problem, Rache, is you give too much,' Annie often chides me. 'You're always available, always ready to cancel *your* arrangements to fit in with theirs. You're just too nice. You need to wise up,' she says with the wisdom of someone much older than her twenty-nine years.

Annie sits back in her white plastic chair in what serves as our staff room. It's a joyless room, but the best we can make of a small, airless cupboard with no windows or views. We've tried to decorate it a little but, really, there's very little we can do to cheer up the space, despite painting it the brightest shade of buttercup. Although Annie's rebellion at the male's fascination with the female figure is to stick up several posters of fit looking men – Aidan Turner of *Poldark* being our favourite. Especially the one of him in a field, naked to the waist, holding a scythe and making grass slashing into something sensual. He *does* cheer us up on our bad days.

§

And today feels like a bad day. Nothing yet from Jack, not even a text before he boarded his flight to say he's sorry he had to go again. I have texted him, but give him the benefit of the doubt that he's just too busy, sorting things out on the flight for his conference with his American client-from-hell. This is the third meeting in six weeks and I really hope he can solve whatever problems they're having so we can get back on an even keel.

'Well, any news from Boy Wonder?' Annie asks later, as we gather our things together to leave for the day. She's not Jack's biggest fan. We had a drink together one evening, shortly after we started going out together and, somehow, they seemed to rub each other up the wrong way. Annie thought he was too condescending towards me, Jack thought Annie too flighty. Too 'blonde' was how he put it – despite her red hair. I was furious with him when he said it – furious at what he was implying. Annie may look like a blowsy, revealing-a-bit-too-much-boob-and-bum sex goddess, but she's an intelligent, caring person. I think Henry and I are the only people who *do* get to see that side of her.

'No, not yet. He's still on the flight, doesn't land in

the States for another three hours,' I say in his defence, 'but I'm sure he'll ring tonight.' It sounds like I'm making excuses for him. And, if I'm honest with myself, that's exactly what I'm doing.

Chapter Three

Further south Aidan Milligan sighed quietly to himself, hoping it couldn't be heard on the other end of the phone. 'Yes, that would be nice. Just ... yeah ...let me get settled in first though, Vee. There's a lot I'll need to sort out, then you could pop down for the weekend, maybe? No, no ... sorry if it sounds like I'm putting you off. Really, I'm not, Vee. Actually, I think I'm just a little nervous, can you believe it?'

He was about to leave for Norebridge to finalise the details of his new job. A little later, having said his goodbyes, Aidan put the phone down, relieved. He wished Veronica wouldn't push so much. He'd already said she could come for a visit at a later date, but there were still things that had to be clarified. Worst case scenario was he could decide this new venture wasn't for him. He'd left himself a 'get out' clause of three months, feeling confident that at that stage he'd know for sure.

Grabbing his bulging hold-all he hesitated at the

front door, taking a last look down the hallway of his 4-bed semi. The house had been his statement of independence, once he'd left his parents' comfortable home some years ago. Too big for him on his own, he always harboured the hope it would be filled with kids, laughter and lots of love. That joy had eluded him up to now. But he didn't want to sell it and decided he'd let it out once he knew for sure if Norebridge was the place he wanted to spend the rest of his life.

§

He'd almost missed the advertisement in the *Norebridge News* six months ago. It wasn't a paper he'd ever seen before and noted it was from a town about two hundred-and-fifty miles away. Someone, probably a visitor to his home town, had left a copy on the table in his local coffee shop. Out of curiosity he'd picked it up and browsed through it as he drank his breakfast coffee. And there it was – on the second last page – a small 2 x 2 column offering part of a small, rural veterinary practice for sale. Two staff plus vet, it stated, and a varied list of clients. Small and large animal experience required. *Sounds like a bit of a one-man band. Too much work, on call 24/7 and possibly buried in the back of beyond, with little or no social life.*

'Perfect,' he heard someone mutter, and to his astonishment realised it was him. What was he thinking? No, no way - he had a good job which he enjoyed; a comfortable house, *and* he had a girlfriend of two years, Veronica, with whom he was in love and, who he knew for sure, was hoping they would take the next logical step and get married in the not too distant future. He was perfectly happy. Wasn't he?

But as he drove home he couldn't get the idea out of his head. He visualised brambly paths winding their way into lush woodland; clear, fast flowing streams bursting with fish; fertile fields abounding with wildlife and ... yes, probably, he admitted to himself, a few crotchety old farmers, suspicious of some 'townie' coming to their patch with some high-falutin' fancy theories about how they should be running their farms.

He pushed the idea to the back of his mind that evening, as he picked Veronica up. They were meeting friends at the opening of a new restaurant in town. *Guido*'s was considered the 'in' place to be seen and Veronica loved the fact that, as one of the three local vets, Aidan was usually on the guest list for most official openings that took place in their small town –

the new Art Gallery, the recently renovated cinema last month, a Cheese and Wine fundraiser for the local girls' school. While she enjoyed rubbing shoulders with those who considered themselves the leading lights of their community, Aidan hated it.

'You look gorgeous,' he smiled, as she came down the stairs of her rented cottage. Her red dress looked like it had been painted on, leaving nothing to the imagination, while exposing very little. Sexy black high-heeled shoes encased well-toned legs. She had the perfect figure, and she knew it. Aidan knew it was the result of her rigid discipline - she carried around a list of forbidden foods and never deviated from it, no matter what temptation she was faced with. Sometimes he wished she'd just relax and have a big wild cherry ice cream cone on their Sunday drives. At the same time, he was proud to have this beautiful woman by his side, and knew he was the envy of all his male friends and colleagues.

§

That night, at dinner in the new restaurant, as they listened to George Hardwick drone on about his and Marian's recent holiday to Dubai and their über-luxurious hotel, his latest brilliant round of golf and Marian's new black, granite-topped designer kitchen, Aidan made his decision. He was going for it! He was going to grab this opportunity which had, practically, landed in his lap. Otherwise, he could see himself dying of boredom before he was forty.

Chapter Four

How could I have doubted him! It's Sunday, and it's my birthday. A dozen red roses and a romantic card declaring his love (and an apology for being such a grumpy boots lately), have winged their way to my door. Still no phone call, and no reply to my texts, which is strange. But there's always tonight.

Unfortunately, I've agreed to go with Annie and Henry for a birthday celebration to The Spotted Peacock. Given a choice, I'd much prefer to sit at home with a nice glass of wine and wait for Jack's call. But Annie was insistent – no way would she allow me be on my own for my birthday. I agreed, sure that I would have heard from Jack before going out. Actually, I'm annoyed – he's had all yesterday to phone me – and most of today. Even a quick *'Happy Birthday. Missing You. Love you. Talk to you later'* text would have been fine.

The doorbell rings as I'm slapping on some tinted moisturiser – my nod to big girl make-up. 'Coming,

Annie,' I shout, taking the stairs two at a time while she keeps her finger pressed impatiently on the doorbell.

'Get a move on, woman. We're wasting valuable drinking time,' my friend chides me good-naturedly as she comes into the hall. Then she stops dead, her hand flying to her mouth, as she looks at me, horrified.

'You're not even ready – Rachel, *hurry*! We're meeting Henry in five minutes – we'll be late.'

'What do you mean I'm not ready? What's wrong with me?' I ask, puzzled.

'Well, for a start – where's your party dress? And is that a *scrunchie* I see on your head? Why aren't you wearing any make-up?' She shakes her head in disgust.

I look at her short, cerise tunic-style dress, tiny cut-outs displaying her slender shoulders. Long sleeves, cuffed tightly at her narrow wrists, give her a very feminine, almost vulnerable appearance. Nude tights and high-heeled cerise platforms belie her short frame, making her look tall, elegant and very sexy.

I look down at my classy trousers – black background with flowery detail – combined with a soft black, cashmere cardi with three-quarter length sleeves. The cardi's my sexiest piece, two mother-of-pearl buttons open, showing just a hint of cleavage. It's soft and warm, and the most expensive piece in my wardrobe. It's also practical, going with just about everything else. So, in moments of 'I don't know what to wear,' like tonight, it's a safe fall back. And, more importantly, I love it. Annie whips out her mobile and dials a number.

'Who are you calling?'

'Never you mind. Just get your bag and let's go,' she orders, pushing me towards the front door.

'Where are we going? I thought you were worried about being la...'

'Hi, Henry,' I hear her say. 'Are you at the pub? Oh ... OK. Listen, Rachel's had a slight ... no, make that a *huge* wardrobe malfunction. But, we'll be there as soon as possible. Sorry? No, no ... nothing you can do, thanks. Just have another drink. See you, yeah, yeah. Bye!'

§

'Why are we going to your house?' I ask, as we drive through the quiet streets. Annie's on a mission, and I know from experience when she's in this mood, there's no persuading her from her goal.

'Because you need some serious rescuing,' she throws at me. 'From *yourself,* woman!'

OK, I may not be the Kate Moss of Norebridge, but I've got my own style, which I'm happy with. I've never been a slit-to-the-thigh girl, but I'm not exactly Victorian either. We've arrived, and Annie is already jumping out of the car, opening the door to her parents' house. A quick 'Hello,' shouted to her mum and dad who are watching television in the sitting-room, and she's racing up the stairs to her bedroom. I follow, a little exasperated at all the fuss. It looks like she's been burgled when we go inside, but I don't say anything disparaging as I know her untidy habits from work. Annie's not lazy, she just can't see the point in spending time on something as mundane as tidying up, when there are so many other exciting things to do with her time.

Clothes are strewn everywhere – over a chair, hanging on the wardrobe door, and there are even several piles of multi-coloured things dotting the carpet. But it's also a very feminine, girly room and the last thing I would have expected from Annie. Floaty, sheer voile drapes a small bay window and the walls are painted a soft, matte white. Crisp, white bedlinen covers a brass-and-black wrought-iron bed which, to my surprise, has been made. Four giant, fluffy pillows are arranged neatly along the headboard, and a cotton throw of autumnal greens and browns is spread across the end. It all looks incredibly inviting. This surprises me, as I thought she'd make much more of an independent, woman-about-town statement – more modern, stark blacks and greys, perhaps.

'Right!' my friend puts an end to my perusal of her bedroom, as she flings open the door of her wardrobe. 'What have we got?' she mutters, and immediately grabs a hanger with a dress on it, throwing it on the bed. 'Try that,' she orders, 'and that,' she says flinging things haphazardly in my direction.

'Why?'

'Because I'm not letting you go out for your birthday in *that* outfit,' she says disdainfully, running her eyes up and down my carefully selected clothes. I know there's no point arguing. I won't get out alive, so I just give in, grabbing the soft mauve and pink thing she's catapulted at me first.

Reluctantly I undress, carefully folding my cardi and trousers and placing them on the bed. Then, pulling on the dress I've been given, I shake my head - 'No way, Annie, absolutely not. I'm not going out in this. *You* could get away with it, but not me!'

I look at myself in the full-length mirror on the

wardrobe door. There's way too much flesh on display – it just about covers my crotch. I'm sure if I bend down my old grey-white comfy knickers will be visible to everyone.

'Hang on, hang on,' she laughs, pulling it down from behind. It seems some of the material had become caught up in the lining. Aahh, yes, much better, I think, as it falls just above my knees and looks far less sluttish.

'Oh, right. But I don't think it's me, Annie. It's so …'

'Bright? Colourful? Flattering?' my friend teases. 'Rache, it's about time you realised you are absolutely gorgeous. Drop dead gorgeous, in fact. I'd kill for your freckle-less face and amazing skin. But you never show yourself off. Now, come on – hair and make-up next.'

'No, Annie, I'd rather not, if you don't mi…'

But she's already gently pushed me into the chair in front of her dressing table. Opening the top drawer reveals a collection of tubs, pots, tubes and brushes, plus an array of lipsticks of every colour and shade. There's a fortune in there.

She pulls all the hair back off my face and refastens it with the offending scrunchie. A vivid green jar is uncapped, and lashings of brilliant white cream smathered onto my face. Annie plucks a tissue from a box on the top of the dressing table, hands it to me, saying 'Rub it in, then wipe it off – quick!' Wordlessly, I obey, while she fumbles around in one of the other drawers.

'Right, hold your head back,' she instructs, as she lathers lotion onto my face, massaging softly around my eyes. Next, she dots foundation onto my forehead, cheeks, chin and the tip of my nose, which she then rubs gently, finishing with a flourish, drawing it all together across my cheeks. Her fingers feel like feathers on my skin.

'Close your eyes, Rachel,' she says and I feel her stroke my eyelids. I guess she's putting on eye-shadow, something I've never bothered with. Next comes mascara, after which she applies a coat of Vaseline – 'to give your lashes that shiny, silky look,' she laughs. 'Shut it,' she barks, as my mouth opens to protest.

'Now, nearly finished. Which colour?' she asks, holding up two lipsticks. One is a blowsy, fuck-me scarlet, the other a softer, peachy colour. No contest.

'That one,' I point to the delicate peach, which she immediately chucks back in the drawer. She proceeds to roll out the harlot-red and apply to my pouting lips.

'Annie, I said *that* one,' I screech.

'Yeah, yeah,' she laughs. 'Wait until we're finished, then if you really don't like it I'll use the other one. Right, hair and then we're off.'

She releases my hair and, before I can comment, grabs a huge, chunky paddle brush, sweeping it up and around my head. She takes a long, pointy tortoise shell hairgrip and secures it at the back of my crown. Grabbing a few dangly bits, she pulls them out here and there around my face.

'Don't worry, casually tousled is the look we're going for,' she laughs at my worried expression. 'Right, come over and have a proper look in the long mirror. If there's anything you're really not happy with we'll change it, I promise. Oh, hang on – shoes!'

She roots around in the bottom of the wardrobe, emerging with a pair of high, black patent sling-backs.

'Perfect,' she says, handing them over.

Chapter Five

I put them on, toddling over to the mirror like a balancing act in a circus, and gasp as I look at my reflection. My auburn mop no longer looks like I've been dragged through a hedge backwards. Instead, it's twisted up into a sophisticated chignon, surrounded by a mass of floaty bits, falling softly around my face. The mascara adds a touch of mystery to what I consider a pair of rather, small and insignificant eyes. I'm truly amazed, they look huge. She's gone for a pale grey eye shadow, which seems to highlight my green eyes, somehow adding light and a lively sparkle to them.

The dress, with its slashes of colour, hugs my figure and, I note delightedly to myself, diminishes my generous hips while emphasising my small waist. Fifteen denier *Barely Black* tights encase my legs, giving them shape and length. Who knew!

'Wow, Annie,' I say, not quite believing it's me in the mirror.

'Yeah, exactly,' my friend says, giving me a quick

hug. 'Now, go - out to the car, or we'll both be fired,' she pushes me ahead of her. A little unsteadily I trot down the stairs and out to Annie's car. Pulling out of the drive she throws a sideways glance at me as I sit in the passenger seat, trying to pull down Annie's dress, which has ridden up to a dangerous level, barely covering my thighs.

'Stop fidgeting, woman,' she laughs. 'For once, just enjoy being young, and attractive. I was going to say "young, free and single" - but there's Jack,' she says in that way she has when she mentions his name.

'Oh, Annie, I wish you'd give him a break. He's not the monster you think he is, honestly.'

'Has he called to wish you a Happy Birthday?' she looks at me with a knowing expression.

'I'm sure he's just been busy with the clients. They're being very difficult, you know, Annie. But he *has* sent the most exquisite bouquet of flowers.' I don't mention my unanswered texts and even to my own ears it sounds lame.

'Yeah, right.' Seeing my face, her attitude softens. 'Sorry, Rache. Tonight, Jack is off limits. Let's just enjoy the night out with Henry. I know he's no Aidan Turner, but we can always pretend.' And we both laugh out loud at the thought of Henry, our boss, being a hunky, sexy seething mass of masculinity.

'*But, he has a heart of gold!*' we both shout simultaneously. This only makes us laugh all the harder and Annie, momentarily distracted, swerves to avoid a set of red and white bollards alerting drivers to the presence of a broken wall.

§

I feel unsure as I step out of the car outside The Spotted Peacock. This is a totally different me – not the real me, I feel. But Annie, intuition on high alert, grabs me by the arm pushing me gently towards the door.

'No, I won't allow you to chicken out. Anyway, Henry is already here. We can't stand him up.'

'I just feel a bit … strange.'

'Well, you look amazing. Now, get in there and stop being such a Moaning Minnie,' she smiles. 'Remember – chin up, chest out!'

As we enter the pub through a pair of saloon-type swing doors I'm suddenly smacked back against Annie, by a figure emerging briskly from the dark depths of the pub. Luckily, I grab onto one of the doors, but Annie is not so fortunate. Having suffered the full brunt of my weight she topples back, hitting the wall and landing with a grunt across an empty beer barrel, positioned as part of the *olde worlde* décor in the hallway.

'I'm so sorry. God, are you OK? Are you hurt?' I hear someone ask anxiously.

Next thing I know a man's pulling me into his arms. They hold me firmly and I'm looking up into a pair of green-flecked eyes. 'Yes, I'm fine, really,' I reply. He smiles and the eyes crinkle up at the edges and a deep frown disappears as he realises I'm alright.

'And *I'm* OK too – in case anyone's interested?' I hear in the background. I realise it's Annie. I look over at her, he does too.

'Oh, Annie, are you alright?' I ask my friend. Handsome Stranger goes over and extends his hand to help her up.

'I'm really sorry, it was very clumsy of me. I was just trying to get outside to answer my phone,' he explains and it's then I notice the insistent trilling of a mobile he's holding in his hand.

'Well, I suppose you should answer it then, shouldn't you?' Annie says, crossly. We're still standing in the hallway. He's still looking at me and I'm feeling a little foolish.

'We're both fine, thanks,' I hear myself say. 'Let's go, Annie. Henry is waiting,' and feeling suddenly more in control I take Annie firmly by the arm, pushing her through the double doors. Outside, I hear him finally answer his ringing phone.

'Hello? Oh, hi. Listen, just a minute ... No, better still. I'll call you back?' I hear him say to the person on the other end. But it seems the caller is not happy to be fobbed off and I hear him reluctantly continue the conversation.

Glad of the opportunity to remove myself from the farcical, almost pantomime situation, I turn to my friend. 'Move it, Annie. Just *go*, for God's sake,' I hiss to a slightly crumpled Annie, who is craning her neck to look back at our handsome assailant.

§

Henry stands to greet us as we join him at a small table in the corner of the pub. 'Wow, Rachel. Is that really you?' he looks at me, astonishment clear on his slightly chubby face. 'I don't think I've ever seen you in a short dress before. Didn't even know you had legs,' he jokes, and he reddens up.

'Don't, Henry, or she'll head for the hills,' Annie

warns. 'You should've seen what she had on before. And on her birthday too!'

He kisses us both and asks what we'd like to drink. But before he heads to the bar, he coughs a couple of times, then clears his throat and says:

'Eh, Rachel, Annie ... there's, eh ... something I need to tell you. It's only been finalised today, but ... eh ... Oh, dear. I don't quite know how to say this.'

I feel sorry for Henry. He's an amazing vet and I have the greatest respect for him, but when it comes to anything personal he's absolutely hopeless. Then I suddenly think back to his strange evasiveness before lunch today.

'Oh, my God, Henry! You've got a woman – you're engaged – getting married, even,' I smile at him, clapping my hands with delight for this lovely man. 'I *thought* you were a bit edgy this morning.'

'Sly dog Donaldson,' Annie laughs. 'Good for you, Henry. About time too!'

'Come on, Henry,' I tease, 'bare all. Who is this mysterious person to whom you've pledged your troth? Why have we not heard of her before now?' Then I realise Henry's getting more and more uncomfortable as we persist, so I throw Annie a look that says *OK, let's hear what he has to say.*

'Sorry, Henry. We're just happy for you. But is that what you want to tell us?'

'Eh, no ... Actually, it's about the practice...' We're stunned into silence, a feeling of dread hanging in the air. Annie is the first to find her voice.

'No, Henry, no, *pleeeeease* don't say it's closing. I *love* my job! Please don't sell up. What would we do? Who else would put up with me?' Annie says, covering her face with her hands.

'Oh, no, no, Annie. Don't worry, the practice is not closing down. I'm so sorry to have worried you like that – and *you,* Rachel. No, it's actually better. Well, at least *I* think it's better... You see, I've decided to expand the practice, and to do that I've advertised for another partner. He's been for several visits, mostly at weekends, but I didn't want to say anything until we'd finalised everything, which we did today. He could easily have changed his mind and you would have been worried for nothing.'

'Who is he?' I'm curious to know about this person who is going to be our new boss, along with Henry. 'What's his background?'

'Well, he's very highly qualified. Has been partners

in a three-vet practice for the last eighteen years, has small as well as large animal experience. Deals mainly with the small variety though, but is anxious to get to grips again with a wider variety of larger patients. *And*, he's tired of city life and wants to move to the country. All round, he seems ideal.'

'Is he married/single/divorced/looking?' Annie asks, forever on the lookout for new conquests.

'Well, here he comes,' Henry smiles, looking over our heads towards the door. 'You can ask him yourself.'

We turn around to see the new arrival and I nearly fall off my stool. Walking towards us is the handsome stranger we bumped into on our way in. I get a better look at him now as he lopes towards our table. He's tall, his blond hair windswept and untidy. A casual navy jacket is open, revealing a blue and white button-down shirt over navy chinos. Sensible climber boots finish the look. The sleeves of his jacket and shirt are pushed up, as if he's about to inspect a cow's bottom, but before I have time to dwell on it, Henry introduces the newcomer.

'Rachel, Annie – this is Aidan Millington. Aidan, this is Rachel – Veterinary Nurse and Practice Administrator and Annie – Nurse and Practice Receptionist.'

'Aidan? *AIDAN?* Just like ...' I hear Annie screech, as if it's some sort of joke. I know exactly what she's thinking, and I get a flash of naked torso and a man slashing grass with a scythe in a corn-filled field in deepest Cornwall.

'Yes, *yes*, Annie, the same,' I laugh at my friend.

'It's an Irish name, isn't it?' I ask the new man, as he looks puzzled from Annie to me and back. 'It's OK,' I assure him. 'Just an inside joke. Nothing wrong with your name.'

'Well, perhaps, in time I'll get to see the funny side too?'

'I'm sure you will,' Annie replies, throwing him a saucy look. He smiles politely, turning to Henry.

'It's really nice of you to have me to stay with you, Henry,' he says warmly. 'But, really, I could stay in a local hotel? I certainly wouldn't want to put you out.'

'Absolutely not, Aidan, dear boy. It'll be nice having a housemate for a while. Until you get settled. Actually, for as long as you like,' Henry beams, his chubby cheeks reddening up in embarrassment.

You lovely, lovely man, I think. Why can't I fall in love with someone kind and caring like you. But I've got Jack. OK, he may not always be thoughtful lately, but I'm sure that's only down to work overload. Soon, I'm hoping, when this contract is sorted, we'll get back to where we were before all this U.S. work got in the middle. We'll find ourselves again.

As for our friend Henry – perhaps it's time for Annie and me to do a little matchmaking and bring some real joy into this sweet man's life.

Chapter Six

Norebridge may not have been the centre of the universe, but Anton Wickers-Stroppton loved his adopted home. Once a thriving textile-manufacturing town it consisted of one main street, from which several smaller streets and cobblestone lanes fed off, an Aladdin's cave for tourists during the summer. None of your big chain stores here – instead Norebridge boasted a wonderful blend of unique shops and businesses, some still run by descendants of the founders. Now sadly defunct, the textile industry had given the town its distinctive collection of picturesque buildings, dating back to when it was rich and thriving. Standing at the large drawing-room window of Mill House, overlooking the town, Anton could see lights from the houses twinkling like a thousand tiny stars, and as he looked into the darkness he wondered how he'd gotten himself into yet another 'situation' like the one he'd found himself in that morning.

§

He'd woken up, struggling to open his eyes which seemed to be glued together. Lifting his throbbing head from the pillow, he immediately regretted his action. This had to be the worst hangover he'd ever had – he felt as if he'd been hit by a mallet. Surely, he hadn't drunk that much the night before? Gently raising himself into a sitting position, he jumped as something moved next to him, under the covers.

Curiously, he raised the feather duvet and was astonished to see an exquisite female form stretched out next to him. Lying on her stomach her neat bum moved slightly as the cooler air reached her skin. A Marilyn Monroe platinum blonde head was turned away from him, so he couldn't see who it was, or if he knew her. Well, *obviously*, he must know her – and very well, by the looks of things. But he couldn't recall her name – had he ever known it? Where had she come from? He couldn't remember a thing.

Slowly, so as not to disturb his neighbour, he climbed out of bed, tiptoeing quietly over to the large bay window. Heavy, black-out curtains kept daylight out, but The Strop needed to see who his mystery guest was. With an effort, he pulled the curtains back, moaning as the sunlight hit his throbbing eyeballs, momentarily blinding him and causing him to reel backwards, into a round, mahogany table displaying a collection of sepia photographs. Several showed a happily smiling man and woman. And one, which seemed to have pride of place, showed the man in the act of throwing a young child into the air. It was obvious, from the child's face, he was thoroughly enjoying it, laughing down at the man who held him.

As if in slow motion, the table tilted, sending photographs and a vase of flowers crashing to the polished, parquet floor. The resulting noise startled his guest, who leapt up in bed.

'Huh? Who's there?' the blonde asked, turning round to reveal two full, heavy breasts.

'Good morning. Eh ... who are you?' asked The Strop.

'Chesney,' came the reply, accompanied by a slightly high-pitched giggle and a shrug of shoulders. From this angle he could see the sharp outline of collar bone and realised the girl seemed much thinner and younger than his first impression.

Oh, shit. How the hell had that happened?

'Eh, sorry ... don't mean to be rude, but who are

you? How did you get here?'

Again, the high-pitched giggle, as Chesney covered her face with both hands. Then, looking over at Anton, she said 'Don't you remember? Your friend – Jamesie? In the pub, last night? *They're* here too. You don't remember anything, do you?' And Anton couldn't help feeling that she was greatly amused by this. But, at least, hearing her voice made him realise she wasn't as young as he'd first feared. Despite the girlish giggle there was a slightly hard undertone and Anton heard himself exhale, relieved.

§

His last memory of the night before was going into The Spotted Peacock to meet his friend, who had come up from London for the weekend. He vaguely remembered Jamesie had two good looking girls with him. Their names were …? Well, Chelsea, obviously. But the other? Nope, he gave up trying. Nothing – a big, fat blank.

'Would you like some breakfast, Chelsea?'

'It's *Chesney*. Eh … yes, please.'

'Of course, eh … Chesney. The shower's through there,' he said indicating a door neatly concealed in the wood panelled wall. 'Get dressed and come join me in the kitchen. I'll go and find Jamesie and his … guest.'

As he descended the wide mahogany staircase he decided he would really have to knock the booze on the head – and soon!

Chapter Seven

Jack woke with a start as the Boeing 747-400 touched down with a bump at Gatwick. It had been a rocky ride from Seattle, lots of turbulence and crying babies. Raising the blind, he looked out his window onto the grey, uninspiring Sunday morning. Soft, misty rain hung in the air and ground staff, wrapped up against the inclement weather, scurried back and forth as the plane drew into its allocated spot.

'Ladies and Gentlemen, welcome to Gatwick Airport, London, England,' the pilot announced in his American drawl, 'where the temperature today is 11 degrees Celsius. We hope you have enjoyed your flight with us, and hope to see you again soon on Virgo Airlines. For those of you travelling further afield, we hope you have a safe and pleasant onward journey. Have a good day.'

No chance. Once they'd come to a stop Jack stood up, excusing himself as he slid past his fellow passenger.

Reaching up he opened the overhead locker, when a large, animal print cabin bag toppled out, hitting him in the face and landing with the sickening sound of clinking glass on the narrow aisle floor.

'Oh, shit,' he heard someone shriek. 'That's my goddamn bag you're knocking around there, buddy. You better not have broken my niece's wedding gift.' The person who had been standing in the queue, two passengers back, now pushed past them aggressively to reach the bag. Jack looked down at the short, white-haired female, pink scalp showing through short, wispy locks. A round, chubby face housed two small, glinting eyes, which made Jack think immediately of Danny DeVito. 'What the hell do you think you're doing?'

Before Jack could reply, the tiny dervish had turned to the other passengers, shouting 'Did you see that? He just yanked open the locker. I think he's smashed my niece's wedding gift.'

Embarrassed, they looked away in every direction but at Jack. One man smiled awkwardly at the little woman. Big mistake. The next thing the poor man knew he was being grabbed by the arm, as she shouted, '*He* saw him, didn't you?'

'Well, actually …' Too late. His newfound friend

was shouting for cabin crew to take control of the situation.

Oh, bloody hell. This is all I need. As if the day wasn't going to be bad enough already.

§

Two-and-a-half hours later Jack exited the airport. The hideous green glass statue, depicting a well-endowed Atlas-type character in a very suspect pose was not, in fact, smashed. It should have been, in Jack's opinion. Her niece would have been grateful to him. But he'd had to wait while the offending article was unwrapped, inspected in the presence of amused airline staff, and re-wrapped with infinite care at one of the concourse shops. This service was paid for, rather begrudgingly, by Jack. It was this or go through the very time-consuming process of completing an on-board incident report. Luckily, the DeVito lookalike was on a time schedule and had to be in Manchester for the famous niece's wedding, taking place later in the day.

There were twenty-two tired and weary travellers standing in the taxi queue, as Jack joined the line eventually. He'd be here for hours, he thought. Looking at his watch, he sighed deeply. It was almost lunch time and, at this rate, it wasn't worth his while going into the office, which is what he'd intended, even though it was Sunday. He felt wired, needing to work off some pent-up energy after the long flight. Maybe he'd just go home, then go for a run. But the thought of what lay ahead filled him with dread.

§

'Pardon me, but are you going straight into London?' For a moment Jack didn't realise someone was speaking to him.

'Sorry?' His mind was racing to the task ahead.

'Well, I was wondering if you'd like to share a taxi?' The person lowered her voice, adding 'you look less like an axe murderer than any of the others here.' Jack could hear the smile in the voice and turned around to address the speaker. She was stunning - slim and athletic looking, with shoulder-length blonde hair, cut in layers of big, bouncy curls with a choppy fringe over two heavily made-up eyes.

'London – are you going into the City? Maybe we could share?'

Jack grabbed the opportunity to reduce his waiting time and jumped into the taxi after the stranger. Her name was Kyla, she told him – PA to a Texan oil magnate, who had generously paid for her trip to England, including a week's stay at the Dorchester. Jack wished he had a boss half as good natured, instead of Gabrielle, who would have his guts for garters when he eventually showed up at the office tomorrow. But for the moment, he was passed caring, thanks to the rabid DeVito lookalike and her unfortunate niece's wedding present. He truly hoped she'd be shunned by her British relatives and would have the worst trip of her life.

§

Kyla's room at the Dorchester could only be described as sumptuous, with a bulging mini-bar, and a walk-in shower that could house an American football team. In answer to Jack's *'What the hell am I doing here?'* moment, he pushed any thoughts of Rachel out of his mind and basked in the admiration of this American girl, who considered his British accent 'real cute.' To ease his conscience he'd texted Rachel, making the excuse he'd been delayed. He couldn't face what lay ahead just yet.

Kyla was certainly not a shy girl and they'd made fast and furious love on the bed - giant sized even by

American standards - the minute they'd closed the door behind them. Their clothes lay strewn around the room, and they lay in thick, fluffy bathrobes, eating lunch of salad and rare steak.

'How long did you say you're going to be in London?' Jack asked, more out of politeness than interest.

'My trip is for two weeks, but I'll only be in London for three days. I want to travel round England and go to Scotland and Wales as well.'

What is it about Americans, Jack thought, *they think nothing of travelling a thousand miles a day and still call it a holiday.* He couldn't think of anything worse. His idea of a holiday was a beach, a sun lounger, sun shades, endless poolside cocktails and lazily watching any female talent around – unknown to Rachel, of course.

Rachel didn't share his idea. She found it boring, and on their first holiday together to Spain had taken to driving out into the countryside, which she immediately fell in love with. She'd made friends with a farming family and ever since she'd been sending and receiving Christmas cards and had, two years ago, entertained their daughter, Magdalena, for a whole month in her home in Norebridge, helping her learn English. He'd found it quite a drag.

'Maybe we can meet up while I'm here?' she looked at him seductively. *No way, José. These few stolen hours are madness enough.* But, God, those eyes – they were the most beautiful shade of blue. It was like looking into the sky. He turned towards his companion, slowly drawing on the belt of her bathrobe which fell open, revealing her curvaceous body and, before he could stop himself, they were lost in each other again, which for a little while at least, blotted out the car crash that was Jack's life.

Chapter Eight

Looking across at the man who is now our new partner in the practice I try to find something I don't like about this stranger, who has landed in our lives. I can't find anything – so far. But then it's only been two-and-a-half hours. He seems amused at Annie's very pointed flirting, even a little embarrassed, but to his credit takes it all in his stride. She invites him to 'bunk down' with her, if Henry's lodgings don't come up to scratch. He laughs good-naturedly, insisting that he's sure it'll be fine and is looking forward to a bit of male company for a while. Not missing a trick, Annie enquires if his company is mainly female? To which he replies, 'And how could any man have too much of that?' She looks over at me and, covertly, raises her eyebrows. I know she's dying to find out more about this man and already pity poor Henry who, I know, will be interrogated at length in the office tomorrow.

'Do you have any family living in the area, Rachel?' he asks. It takes me a while to realise he's talking to me, as my mind is elsewhere. Approximately five thousand miles away and I'm wondering if there's a message from Jack waiting for me on the answer machine at home.

'Sorry? Eh ... no. But my boyfriend, Jack, lives here in Norebridge too. He's away at the moment in the States. He'll be back on Monday.'

'Monday?' Annie says. 'I thought he was coming home today.'

'No, he texted. There's been some sort of delay,' I answer. Luckily, Aidan picks that moment to speak to Annie.

'And you, Annie?'

'Me? Yeah, I live with my parents and two animals of brothers, *still*. But, believe me, as soon as Henry gives me the raise – *that you know I'm entitled to, Henry Donaldson*' – she says pointedly, looking at our very embarrassed boss, 'I'll be down at the estate agent's as quick as you can say 'party flat.' Can't wait to get out and start living on my own.'

'Oh, I don't know, Annie. I think you'd miss being around them,' Henry insists.

'And how, Henry-who-lives-with-mummy, would you possibly know? I'm sure you go home every evening, have a sherry with your mum and relax. No shouting at anyone to get out of the bathroom, or fighting to get the telly remote so you can watch *The X-Factor*. You can watch what you want, eat what you want, and drink what you want without anyone accusing you of being selfish, a glutton, or an alcoholic in that order!'

'But Annie, living with one's mother at my age is ... eh ... not always what it's cracked up to be. Sometimes, it can be ... well ... a little ...'

'Ideal? Just you wait, Henry. Who knows? When I have enough money maybe it won't just be moving house, it might even be moving to the city. And, then, the world's my oyster.'

Smiling, I look over at Henry and am stunned to see the look of horror on his face. I realise in that instant, that our lovely boss is head over heels in love with the feckless Annie. Poor Henry, I think, excepting a miracle, or a complete u-turn in my friend's choice of men, he doesn't have a chance in hell of ever winning the hand of this particular fair maiden.

§

I drink the last drops of my champagne which Henry

kindly provided and feel I've done my duty. We've celebrated the whole birthday thing, complete with a giant cupcake and candle. The rest of the pub even joined in as they tormented me with a very off-key version of 'Happy Birthday.' But I want to make my excuses and leave, impatient to get home to check my answer machine and e-mail. Henry kisses me soundly on the cheek and is becoming very effusive, even for Henry. Annie hugs me warmly, instructing me to 'wear sexy gear more often and show off those legs.' Henry agrees, laughing and reddening up to the hair roots. The new man stands, offering to walk me out, but I assure him I'm fine. However, he insists he's paying a visit to the Gents and takes me gently by the elbow.

'I just wanted a word, Rachel,' he says as we come out into the car park. 'Please don't have any worries where I'm concerned. I'm not coming in to make sweeping changes or anything like that. I'm really very pleased, and grateful, that Henry chose me as his new partner. I feel this is the start of a whole new life for me and I can't wait to get stuck in. Perhaps I'll be able to take some of the load off Henry?'

'That would be great for him, Aidan. He works too hard, takes too little time off and really has no life outside the practice.' I'm touched that this stranger has taken to my boss, as I feel very protective of him. 'Henry is wonderful – both to work for and as a person. And, God knows, he's patient and kind. I mean, he puts up with Annie and me – he must be a saint!' We both laugh and I turn to leave. 'Well, goodnight then.'

'Where's your car?' Aidan asks, scanning the car park.

'Oh, it's OK. I'll walk home, it's only ten minutes. I'll be fine.'

'No, no. Wait, I'll walk you home. It's not safe on your own at this time of night. Let me tell Henry first,' he insists.

'Honestly, Aidan. This is Norebridge, for heaven's sake. Nothing is going to happen,' I laugh. 'I'll be fine,' I insist, as I start to walk away.

'Rachel, I wouldn't let any woman walk home on her own, I don't care how close it is. Hang on a sec,' he says, turning back into the pub. I can only laugh at his assumption that I'll wait for him outside as I turn and walk in the direction of my house. I'll be home before he comes back out. But I misjudge him and almost immediately hear footsteps running up behind me.

'What is it with you?' he laughs. 'Too strong

willed by half. I just want to see you home safely, the same as I'd do with any female in my company.'

'But, Aidan, you forget. I'm not in *your* company – you're in *mine!*'

Chapter Nine

Jack comes home today. I hug myself in anticipation and excitement. It's the tail-end of summer and I'm sitting on the bank of the meandering river eating my lunch. This is my favourite time, and I find Norebridge especially beautiful at this time of year - summer is not quite over, nor has Autumn yet begun its stealthy slide into cooler days. The park is still bursting with overflowing borders of vibrant, multi-coloured flowers and shrubs. A young mother and her little boy run excitedly to feed the ducks, bulging bag of bread at the ready. The warm sun bathes me in its heat as I look across the river through an old weeping willow, its fronds dipping in the flowing water, like fingers caressing silk. On the other side, I see tourists ambling through the narrow streets, perusing the shops for gifts for friends and families back home.

Birds dip and dive overhead and I look up at the young fledglings practising their aerial manoeuvres for their maiden flight to sunnier places. Each year the swallows build a nest over my front door. I don't mind the constant droppings as I remember my Irish grandmother telling me it was a good omen to have a swallow's nest under the eaves. I watch them every day and marvel at their antics as they venture out for the first time. How courageous they are to leave the safety of the nest, swooping bravely outwards and upwards into the unknown. Sometimes, like them, I wish *I* could be so brave in my own life.

I finish my sandwich and check my watch. Twenty minutes left before I need to get back to the practice. I can't resist, and lie back on the soft, sweet-smelling grass, closing my eyes for five minutes. I'm conscious of the sounds of life going on around me and feel a sense of peace and calm. It makes a welcome change to the turmoil of my mind lately, since Jack's departure for the U.S. He's been so edgy and sharp.

I've felt uneasy since he left, and Annie's constant sniping about him hasn't helped. We parted on an argument over this sudden trip, which I feel guilty about. I know it's his work, but he's become too available lately, ready to drop everything and jump on a plane in an instant. Unreasonably maybe, I feel a little jealous and wish he'd be so available to me. Spending my birthday without him – and not even a phone call, text or e-mail – has me worried. He's never done that before.

I'm wondering what it'll take to get us back on track, because I really do love Jack.

§

A cool breeze brushes my skin and I wake with a start. Oh, Lord, it's two hours since I closed my eyes! How did that happen? Jumping up, I gather the detritus of my lunch and race towards the main gate of the park. We have a busy appointment schedule this afternoon and now Annie will be on her own to handle a howling collie, a sex-crazed Russian Blue and a pampered Pomeranian, complete with its own YSL collar, encrusted with diamonds. Apart from the collie, who is sweet but heartbroken after losing his mate, I think the other two are just frustrated at the raw deal they've had, with the owners they've been given! Spoiled rotten, each as fat as the other, they look like they're about to explode. Henry has tried on numerous occasions to tell the owners – gently and diplomatically – they would both benefit from more exercise and less treats. Both he and I know he's mentally including the owners in this advice – but to no avail.

As I burst through the narrow wrought-iron gate I slam straight into someone coming through into the park. Accidently, he steps on my foot, sending a sharp, shock of pain up my leg. I drop my things, letting out a very unladylike 'Bugger!' as I do so.

'Well, well. You're in some rush,' I hear someone mutter.

'Yes, I know, I know, sorry. I'm so late getting back to work. I need to go.' He's already bent down to pick up my bag and litter. I stoop to help and suddenly find myself collapsed in a heap on the warm tarmac. My foot won't take any weight and I can't stand up.

'Ouch! Would you mind giving me a hand, please? I don't seem to be able to stand.' At this stage I look up at the stranger and realise it's none other than The Strop, who'd come into the surgery recently for the first time with his injured Labrador.

'Of course,' he says, extending his hand to help. 'Oh, hi, it's Rachel, right?' he says, smiling. And I'm astonished that he remembers my name. 'Where's your car? Although, perhaps you shouldn't be driving? That looks like it needs to be looked at fairly quickly. Maybe I should take you straight to A & E?'

I look down and can see my ankle is swelling as we

speak, and the pain is becoming more intense too. 'No, really. I have to get back. Annie will be on her own,' I say unreasonably, as anyone can see I'm going nowhere fast on this ankle.

'Right then, don't be ridiculous. I'll take you back, but you're not walking. No, no – don't even think about it,' he says, making a talk-to-the-hand gesture. And I realise he's right, I can't do this on my own. My ankle is already overhanging the straps of my lovely summer sandal, like you see on tired, elderly ladies, whose feet have swollen with the summer heat. He senses my reluctant agreement and holds out his arms as if he intends sweeping me into an embrace. And, suddenly, before I know it, for the second time in two days I end up in a strange man's arms as The Strop scoops me up before I can object further. All I can think of is he's going to get a hernia, or throw a disc in his back.

'Oh, careful,' I say.

'Ah, don't worry, I won't drop you. You're as light as a feather.' Again, that smiley tone. Is he being sarcastic?

'No ... I didn't mean that. I was just worried you'd hurt your back.'

'No fear. Champion weight-lifter, I am,' he says in

a funny and what I imagine is an exaggerated Welsh accent. And this time I know for sure he's joking. There are no bulging muscles, his frame is lean, but I can feel the reassuring strength in the arms holding me firmly. I look up into dark eyes and get a real close-up of this famous man. He smiles at me, and for a second I imagine I see a sadness in those lovely eyes. Then I brush the thought away as ridiculous.

'We'll take my car,' he says, 'I think it'll be easier to get you in without hurting your foot. I'll make sure to get your car back to you later. Happy with that?' he asks. And I am, thinking how nice it is to have someone else take charge, for a change.

I can see what he means, as he settles me gently on the huge back seat of an enormous, silver-grey Bentley, which luckily is parked quite close to the gate. I had visions of him crumbling under my weight, as he struggled across the car park, trying to locate his car. Having magicked a pillow from somewhere and placing it gently under my leg, he folds his long, slender frame into the driver's space and we're off. On the way, he tells me Zebedee is not quite back to his old self, is still limping slightly, but otherwise is doing well, and I marvel that this mega star is such a normal, down-to-earth person. If it wasn't for Jack, I tell myself amused, I could quite easily fall in love with this gorgeous man.

Chapter Ten

Thank God, the door to the practice is wheelchair-friendly and wide enough to let Anton through without too much manoeuvring. It slams back against the wall as we enter, and to my huge embarrassment, he shouts 'Coming through!' Everyone in the reception area stops what they're doing and stares at us, even Mrs. Carson's collie, Billy, for once shuts up, stunned into silence.

'Bloody hell,' I hear from behind the counter. 'What happened to you?' Annie asks, staring at my ankle which, due to Anton's height is right about eye level to her at the moment.

'You can put me down now, thank you,' I say, mortified.

'Not so fast, young lady,' he grins, 'not until I know you'll be looked after. I've brought you this far, I want to see this through. Hi, you're Annie, right?' he says, extending fingers from somewhere under my rear end. 'She' he looks down at me, 'was really worried about you being on your own. I think she'd have hobbled all the way back here, if she could. So, where do you want her?'

'I *am* here, you know,' I say, amused. But I might as well not be, as Annie looks up at Anton and asks 'Do you think she needs to go to the hospital?'

But I'm having none of it and jump in, 'No, no, I'm OK. Just a bad sprain, I'd say. I'll be fine. And,' I say, looking up gratefully at my saviour, 'he would have taken me to the hospital, but I didn't think it was necessary. Anyway, we're too busy. If I sit on the stool behind the reception desk I can check people in. But, you'll have to escort patients in to Henry, if you don't mind, Annie?'

'Already ordering everyone about, I see. Why does that not surprise me,' Anton laughs. 'Do you have an ice pack anywhere? That would probably help the swelling?'

'I'll sort it,' Annie says heading in the direction of the back room, where the fridge/freezer is. She returns seconds later with a frozen sac which Anton takes out of her hands.

'Here, I'll do it,' Anton says. '*You,*' he points accusingly at me, 'just hike yourself up on that stool and I'll strap this thing to your ankle.' And I do, without question. But the touch of Anton's hands as they gently move over my ankle sends a shock wave through me. I'm stunned, that I could react like this to another man, when I'm so madly in love with Jack and I find it difficult to look at Anton.

'I can look after her now,' I hear Annie say.

'And this lot too?' he says, gesturing at the mayhem which has resumed behind us. 'I don't think so. Who's next?'

I take a quick peek at the appointment list and gesture over at Mrs. Carson, who's Border Collie is trying, unsuccessfully, to hump his mistress' leather boot. Before either one of us can do anything, he's loping over to her, fondling the dog's silky black ears. Billy, looks up at him adoringly.

'Know exactly how you feel, mate,' Anton says sympathetically. Billy whimpers pityingly, placing a paw on Anton's knee, as he hunkers down beside the dog and its owner.

'Well, well, I don't believe it. Billy doesn't usually take to men, and a total stranger at that,' the 80-year-old lady smiles. 'He really likes you, and,' she lowers her voice seductively, 'I really believe animals, especially dogs, are great judges of character. Are you married?'

'Are you available?' he teases. The old lady slaps him playfully on the arm.

'When you're ready, Mrs. Carson,' I hear Annie say. 'If you can drag yourself away from this gentleman? Henry is waiting for you now.'

'Spoilsport,' Anton says to Annie, holding out his hand to Mrs. Carson, who allows herself to be helped up and escorted, arm in arm, down the corridor to Henry's consulting room.

'Are you really OK, Rache?' Annie asks anxiously.

'Annie, I'm fine. Let's get through the appointment list and then maybe you, or Henry, could help me get home and, I promise, I'll take it easy for the rest of the evening. Anyway, Jack's due home tonight. So, I'll be waited on hand and foot!'

'Mmm, OK, then.' But I know Annie's not convinced.

§

'Don't you think someone should stay with her until Jack arrives?' Henry was not at all happy leaving Rachel on her own, even though they'd tucked her up comfortably with a rug on the couch, and made sure she had a nice, hot cup of tea and a biscuit. The TV remote control was also close to hand.

'Henry, you worry too much. Rachel is sure it's just a slight sprain, she'll be fine. Anyway, when lover boy comes home he'll fuss over her a bit – hopefully.'

'You don't like him very much, do you, Annie? What's he done to deserve your lowly opinion of him?' Henry asked.

'Oh, nothing,' Annie says with a casual wave of her hand. But Henry was sure there's more to it than what she's saying. 'Just call it woman's intuition, Henry,' she smiled at him.

'Oh, well then – no arguing with that, is there!' He laughed. 'There's no better yardstick in the world. My lovely Mother is a great believer in woman's intuition. If she takes against you in the first five seconds of meeting you – then that's it. No going back, no second chances. And do you know Annie – even though I'd never admit this to her – she's often right.'

'Puts the run on all those grasping women you bring home, who have their eye on her handsome Henry, does she?' Annie teased.

'No, no, Annie. There are no … eh … how shall I put it? Well, I don't bring any women home. I'm not interested in …'

'Henry Donaldson! I never thought you were *that* way inclined. Well, well! To each his own, as my old Gran used to say.'

'Oh, Annie, no, no, I don't mean that, I love women, especially ... Oh, God. You've completely got the wrong end of the stick. I am very definitely interested in women ...' Annie was enjoying herself, enjoying Henry's discomfort. She knew he wasn't gay, but since she'd joined the practice she'd never heard him mention any girlfriend. She was curious about his dating habits. But seeing Henry's embarrassment decided to let him off the hook. That could be a conversation for another day.

'Oh, Henry. I'm really only teasing you. You're such an easy wind-up. Back to your Mum though, how is she such a fount of information?'

'That's the strange thing, Annie, for someone who never ventures far from home she has her finger on the pulse of everything that goes on in the village. And, even outside Norebridge. She amazes me sometimes, the things she knows about people. Nothing gets past her.'

'But I remember you saying she had lots of visitors?'

'Yes, but mostly elderly women like herself. Mrs. Barton-Powell is her most frequent visitor. And, of course, all the ladies from Church come to tea one afternoon each month.'

'Tea – how very civilised!'

'Old habits die hard, Annie. Mother used to be Chair of the Parish Council for over twenty years. Plus, she was on all the committees – the flower arranging committee, the Church Harvest Festival committee, and she was always invited onto any fundraising committee that raised its head. I think she misses that, now that she's not so mobile. It's wonderful that all the ladies come to see her. *And*, it doesn't always stop at tea! I've come home several times to find the good ladies of the parish more than slightly tiddly!' He smiled at the shocked expression on Annie's face. 'I've had to accompany Mrs. Barton-Powell home more than once. And that Teddy, her son, is dreadful and very rude to her. On one occasion I actually felt like giving him what for, I can tell you.'

'Oh, Henry, why didn't you! I would love to say, casually like, to friends and family, "Yeah, yeah, I work for that rabble-rousing vet, the one who was in the tabloids last week. Yeah, the very one – the one who whacked that awful Teddy Barton-Powell on the nose for being rude to his Mam!" I can see the headlines now,' she teased.

'Well, Annie, she wasn't doing anything untoward. I think most of them are quite lonely. Their *'meeting'* once a month gives focus to their lives. And Mother loves it.'

'Well, there you are then. That's where she gets all her information. Underestimate the power of the 'granny grapevine' at your peril, Henry!'

Laughing, she looped her arm through his as they sauntered back to his car. Annie was surprised at how easy he was to be with. She admired him as the professional in work, but had spent little time with him in a social capacity. What a lovely man, she thought. Will make someone a lovely husband someday – once he manages to get Mother's approval, Annie smiled to herself. Perhaps Rachel and I can rack our brains to find him someone nice, someone suitable.

They drove along in companionable silence, and a few minutes later arrived outside Annie's parents' house. Annie kissed him tenderly on the cheek as he opened the car door for her. 'You're a lovely man, Henry Donaldson. Don't waste too much time trying to please

Mother. You need to please yourself too, you know. There's a wonderful woman out there somewhere, just waiting to snatch you off the streets of Norebridge – to marry you and spend the rest of her life with you. G'night, Henry.' Annie ran laughing up the path, disappearing in her front door with a cheery wave.

'Problem is, I've met her already. She just doesn't know it,' Henry sighed into the darkness. He waited until he saw the light come on in the sitting-room, before reluctantly driving away, happy in the knowledge that his beloved was home safely.

Chapter Eleven

I'm disappointed I haven't been able to have a bath, to luxuriate in my gorgeous lavender-laced bubbles, but the effort would be too much. Hobbling up the path to the front door and into the sitting-room was enough. My ankle throbs with pain and is hot to touch. The skin feels as if it's stretched to the limits, and will burst open at any minute.

Both Henry and Annie insisted on bringing me home. Leaning on them both we made the slow journey from Henry's car into the house. And now here I am, exhausted, lying on the couch, cushions puffed up behind and on either side of me, cup of tea and choccy biscuit to hand. A large bag of frozen peas, wrapped in a tea towel, covers my ankle and this coldness causes me pain of another kind. But I'm determined to persevere in the hope that tomorrow I'll be more mobile and the swelling will have reduced.

I almost had to physically push Henry out the door,

he was so concerned about leaving me on my own, even if it's only until Jack arrives. In truth, while I know he is genuinely concerned for my wellbeing, I think he wanted to spend as long as possible in Annie's company.

But, I just want to be on my own. I'm so looking forward to seeing Jack again, and I don't want an audience. It seems like ages since he went to the States. I've had loads of time to analyse our relationship in his absence and I've made up my mind that we both need to sit down and have a good old heart-to-heart. I accept that every relationship goes through hard times. But, lately, Jack seems to be on a knife edge all the time – impatient, irritable, his mind everywhere else except in the room with us. He works hard and he's ambitious, which I understand. But we're opposites in that respect. For me it's more important that I love my job, not that there are continuous prospects available. Jack, on the other hand, doesn't even need to *like* his job, as long as it has prospects. He spends his working life striving to get to the top of the tree, even if he doesn't enjoy his work. Personally, I find that a little sad. But, hey, to each his own.

I close my eyes, remembering how we met – at the Rugby Club dance over two years ago. Annie had persuaded me to go with her soon after she'd arrived in Norebridge. The car park was full, which meant we had to park further away, and then stumble about a quarter-of-a-mile up a badly lit lane, in the pouring rain. I was pretty fed up at that stage and ready to turn back and go home. But at Annie's pleading we continued, eventually standing in the entrance of the Club House, dabbing at our mud-spattered legs with a tissue, when a voice asked 'Would this be of any help?'

I looked up and, as I reached out for the fresh tissue that Jack offered, I immediately knew I was in love. I didn't *want* to be in love. I'd sworn off men *for ever* after my last fiasco.

§

I'm sure you'll agree it's not just me, I think *all* women, who suffer the heartache of a cheating boyfriend/girlfriend, are eternally grateful to Bridget Jones. She coined the phrase that is the only possible one to describe the multitudes of lying bastards that roam the earth. But 'bastard' is such a harmless word in this 21st century, don't you think? It's almost as if it's been downgraded to the level of 'naughty man' - 'Oh, he's such a naughty man, cheating on his wife/girlfriend like that – and this is the *third* time, isn't it? *And*, she's pregnant, I hear.' So, no! The word 'bastard' just doesn't have enough gravitas any more. Now 'Fuckwit' – *á la Bridget* – now *there's* a word of full-bodied description. No mistaking that - even if it *is* Hugh Grant who comes to mind when we hear the word.

My ex-boyfriend was no Hugh Grant, but he was *there* – attentive, generous with our weekends away, candle lit dinners at fancy restaurants. And never a Christmas, birthday or Valentine's Day passed without some token of his love and affection adorning my neck or wrist. My life was one delicious romantic whirl for three years, until I had an unexpected visit at my flat one evening.

She was beautiful - a brunette bob framing an angelic face, two innocent eyes silently pleading with me to say I *didn't* know her husband. I'd absolutely no idea he was attached, in any shape or form to anyone. Hesitantly, she accepted my invitation to come in and, over several glasses of wine, we talked for ages that evening, both in a state of disbelief, after which she accepted I was telling the truth – and that was the end of another relationship.

§

So, six months later, when Annie asked if I'd go with her for a few drinks at the Rugby Club I felt I couldn't say no, even though I was still in my *Bridget Jones* mode. But, she was new to the area and trying to meet people. It seemed she'd met some chap in the frozen food aisle at the supermarket that day, who'd invited her to the Club. She didn't want to go alone and afterwards I realised she wasn't even that interested in him, but she saw it as an opportunity to meet other chaps. It certainly wasn't hard to meet anyone more scintillating than Frozen Food Freddy, who's main – no, *only* interest – was in the rugby World Cup, the semi-final of which was being played that evening. Needless to say, she didn't know a rugby ball from a football, but that didn't stop our Annie. And when I found myself looking up into those eyes as I took the tissue, all my torment and heartache seemed to fade into the past.

'Why don't you girls use the Ladies to get those spatters off while I order you both a drink?'

'Glass of white wine, please,' rattled off Annie,

totalling overriding my weak 'No, we're fine thanks ...'

He looked at me, a bemused smile on his lips and a question in his eyes. 'Oh, well, OK then. A white wine would be lovely, thanks.' We then spent a very pleasant few hours with Jack, along with his friends Doug and Ralph. They seemed like nice lads with no hidden agendas, just a genuine interest in meeting new people, especially someone as pretty and vibrant as Annie. Poor Frozen Food Freddy was dispatched within ten minutes of our meeting them.

Jack drove us both home that night, as I'd somehow managed to drink more than I'd planned. Annie was sharing my house for her first few weeks, until her family sorted themselves out with somewhere to live. Her Dad had moved to the area with his work, which was why Annie found herself looking for a job in Norebridge, and being snapped up by Henry. I was a little taken aback when I heard Annie invite Jack in for a coffee. I tried to catch her eye over his shoulder, but she was not to be deterred. I was exhausted, having had a heavy day at the clinic and we had another early start the next day. I excused myself pretty quickly, even though I really wanted to stay and chat with the gorgeous Jack. But I could see Annie's interest in him and certainly didn't feel like playing the proverbial gooseberry. Upstairs in bed, however, I found myself tossing and turning, jealously listening to them laughing and talking below.

The next day Annie was tired and grumpy, as a result of her late night. And, for some reason, she didn't seem all that enamoured with Jack anymore. When I tried to wheedle it out of her, she just brushed me off with a brusque 'Oh, he thinks he's God's gift. Not my type at all.' I was glad to hear it and, even more so when he telephoned that morning asking me out for a meal the following Friday night. And, as the Americans say, the rest is history.

Chapter Twelve

When he arrived back home after four days in Norebridge, Aidan had the distinct feeling Veronica was disappointed at his enthusiasm for the new job. Perhaps she'd hoped it wouldn't appeal to him after all, and that he would stay put, instead of moving hours away to some 'backwater near the Welsh border' was how she'd put it.

He tried to include her, telling her the details of his trip. 'Henry, the present owner of the practice, is a really lovely man. Quite shy, but he knows everything there is to know about animals. I'm looking forward to getting into large animals – in a manner of speaking!' He could see Vee didn't appreciate the joke, smiling absentmindedly as she turned back to the mirror in the hallway to touch up her lipstick. They were on the way out to have dinner with friends. He would have been quite happy to stay in for the evening, watch mindless television with a cold beer, or nice glass of wine. But, instead, a quick shower had to suffice as Vee had made the arrangement while he was away, and he didn't want to disappoint her.

'What have you been up to, while I've been away, Vee?'

'Well, the office has been absolutely manic, everyone seems to be coming down with summer 'flu. I'm sure one of my colleagues – you know Danny? – is just putting it on. I'm convinced he's headed off to the south of France for a break. Certainly throws a lot of extra work my way.'

Aidan did his best to concentrate on what Vee was saying and was pleased when, after about ten minutes, she announced that she was 'good to go.'

§

Later in the restaurant Aidan found his mind wandering back to his new work colleagues – especially the dark-haired Rachel, with her shy smile and guileless way. She had no idea how attractive she was. Reluctantly, he dragged his mind back to the present wondering, all of a sudden, why he found the conversation so boring. They'd been out with these friends many times before and, in fairness, they were nice people. Well, at least Joanie was. John, her husband, was a local solicitor, and married to Joanie for sixteen years. They had three children, one of which was about to go to 'big school' and very excited at the prospect too – this had taken up most of the last hours conversation. He used to admire John's commitment to his family – until he was let loose recently on a boys' weekend to play golf.

They'd gone with two other friends, Mike and Jerry, to a country manor house in the Cotswolds. No wives or partners allowed, John had insisted, as they'd discussed plans over dinner. At Vee's slightly belligerent 'And why not?' John said they needed no distractions as he and Aidan wanted to concentrate on thrashing the other two. Joanie laughed, saying 'Off you lot go then. I don't know about you, Veronica, but I'm looking forward to a weekend on my own – with the kids, obviously!' Aidan would have been quite happy to have the ladies accompany them, but said nothing.

§

Two pretty cabin crew from a well-known airline were checking in just as Aidan and John arrived at the luxurious hotel. Like a bee to honey, John had homed in on the petite brunette of the pair. Much to Aidan's annoyance, and just as they were walking down the stairs to the dining-room later on, John informed him he had asked the two girls to join them for dinner. Aidan was furious and, two boring hours later, had had enough. He didn't care what John thought of him, or the disgusted looks from the blonde Michelle, who seemed to assume he was her partner for the night. He excused himself, on the pretext of an important phone call, and headed up to his room and the company of the television.

Next morning John appeared very hungover at breakfast. Expecting him to be somewhat contrite, or at the very least a little sheepish after his behaviour the night before, Aidan was amazed at his lack of guilt or remorse, his wink-wink, nudge-nudge attitude and his open declaration that 'what happens on tour stays on tour.'

He tried hard not to be judgemental, deciding he had no idea of what actually went on behind the closed doors of John and Joanie's home. But he felt a cooling off in his relationship with John because of it.

He also found himself making excuses during the following months when Vee wanted to arrange another evening out with them. He knew he'd find it difficult to sit across from John and make conversation as if nothing had happened. He felt disloyal to Joanie, and very annoyed at John for putting him in such a position. But, eventually, he ran out of excuses. To his relief there was another couple with them when they first met up, and he was able to dip and dodge Joanie's questions about their golfing weekend. He put his awkward responses down to having played such lousy golf, but had to bite his tongue when John went on about how great it was to get away for a 'lads' break' and how he was looking forward to doing it again – sometime soon.

Aidan made his mind up there would be no more boys' expeditions, while having to smile indulgently muttering all the while 'Oh, well, let's see, shall we? Depends on workload and all that, right?' He was mortified to see John's lewd wink across the table, out of Joanie and Vee's line of vision. You absolute shit, he thought.

§

'Honestly, Aidan, you might as well not have been there at all. What's going on with you?'

They'd barely made it inside the hall when Vee rounded on him. Standing there, one hand on the mahogany banisters at the end of the stairs, the other grasping her slim hip, she was angry and aggressive. He didn't understand it, she was normally so cool, so disciplined. Yet here she was waiting, demanding an answer.

'What do you mean? Nothing's going on with me. I don't understand, Vee.' But in the back of his mind he knew she was right. It wasn't just John's behaviour, he knew he hadn't been fully there for Vee during dinner with their friends. He couldn't help it, his mind kept wandering back to greenish eyes and a guileless smile.

'Yes, Aidan, that's part of the problem – you don't understand. You sit there with our friends all evening, barely uttering a syllable, snorting your disapproval at John's comments every now and then – the only real proof, that I could see, that you were even in the same room with us!'

'Now, hang on, Vee. That's a little harsh. I was just a bit tired, just ...'

'And what's got you so tired? Tell me, Aidan, I'd really like to know.'

'Nothing, Vee. Honestly. I ... just have a few things to sort out in my mind. And, I had a horrendous trip back – rotten weather for driving, and traffic backed up for two miles, due to an accident on the motorway. Why don't we talk about this in the morning?' But, like a terrier with a bone, Vee wasn't letting go.

'No, Aidan. Let's talk about it now. I knew the minute I mentioned dinner with John and Joanie you weren't happy. OK, maybe it was a bad call on my part, to arrange it for the night you arrived home. But Joanie's been pushing me to have a night out. You know how she loves the break away from the kids sometimes. And, she doesn't get one very often. John seems to be working a lot.'

'Yeah, well, you're right, I wasn't happy to be going out. I was really looking forward to just relaxing in a bath, with a nice glass of wine – and, well …you,' he said, slipping his hand around her slim waist. 'Instead, we had to listen to Sally's school curriculum for the next year, subject by subject, day by day. I know, I know,' he said, holding up a hand to stem her interruption, 'it's important for Joanie. She lives for the kids. But listening to John drone on and on about it, when all the time …'

'What? All the time, what …?'

'Oh, nothing, Vee. Really, I'm just exhausted. I'm afraid I'll be asleep before my head hits the pillow tonight. Sorry, darling, it's been quite a hectic time getting used to the new practice, getting to know the staff, and the town.'

'And we haven't even had time to talk about it either. I still don't know anything about it,' she said sulkily. Aidan didn't remind her of his attempt earlier to fill her in.

'No, but on the plus side, we now know that Joanie's little Sally has geography classes with that sexy Miss Branston, who does part-time in The King's Arms two nights a week – according to John,' Aidan couldn't help tease her.

'OK, OK,' Vee laughed, 'touché.' And, grabbing a cushion from the sofa, she chucked it at Aidan, who slipped out the door into the hallway and up the stairs.

Chapter Thirteen

I hear Jack's key turn in the front door and I feel the familiar flutterings in my tummy. I'm so excited to see him and I know we can sort things out and get back on track. Perhaps he's had time too, to mull things over in his hotel room the nights he's been away. He walks into the sitting-room, throwing his briefcase and overnight bag on the hall floor as he passes through. I'm waiting for him to come over, to take me in his arms and tell me he's sorry for everything. That he's missed me beyond belief and wants us to put everything behind us and get on with the rest of our lives. I look at him expectantly.

'Hi Rachel.' His voice is flat, subdued.

'Hi, Jack,' I smile at him. But he stands there, on the other side of the room. Then it dawns on me – he's waiting for *me* to throw myself into his arms, like I normally do! Maybe he's unsure of his reception after our tiff and, of course, he doesn't know anything about my accident. He doesn't realise I *can't* physically jump up and throw myself anywhere.

'Oh, Jack,' I laugh, as I throw back the fleece blanket covering my legs and my rapidly melting cold compress. 'I had a slight accident today. Nothing serious, just a sprain, but a very painful one, I'm afraid. Can't throw myself into your arms this time,' I say, making light of my predicament.

'Oh, I see.' But he doesn't move. He stands there as if rooted to the spot. And, as usual, I'm the one who tries to make things alright. I jump verbally into the silent space, attempting to make up for the awkward silence.

'Rough flight? When did you actually get back?'

'Eh … Just a few hours ago. And, yeah, it was a pretty rough flight.'

'Are you OK, Jack?' I ask, uneasy now. 'Would you like a drink, cup of tea?' Then something clicks in and I ask myself 'why am I doing this?' Surely he's the one, looking at my predicament, who should be asking *me* if there's anything I need? While I'm thinking this the air in the room seems to change, become prickly with static. There's a huge balloon of silence and the distance across the sitting-room turns into a gaping abyss, with Jack standing on one side and me, stranded on the other.

'We need to talk, Rachel.'

Jack's voice seems to come from a long way away. Again, my stomach does strange tumblings, but this time it feels different.

§

'How long has it been going on?' I hear someone ask, then realise it's me.

'About six months,' Jack answers. He looks everywhere but at me, and is sitting in an armchair at the far side of the room. He hasn't come near me and it feels like a deliberate act of coldness. Not that it would feel any better if he'd taken me in his arms and told me he'd been having an affair with someone in the U.S. for the last six months. *Six months!* Well, that would certainly explain why things haven't been great between us. But I'm numb. His words seem to reverberate around the room, echoing off the walls as if to taunt me – *six months! Six months! Six months!*

'Who is she?' As if it makes any difference. I don't know her, never will. But illogical as it seems I have to ask. As if knowing something about her will make it any less heart-breaking.

'Rachel, does it matter? Don't do this. I didn't set out to do it, it just happened.' And I can't help thinking how funny it is, that every time someone wants to admit to being unfaithful – in a film, on TV, in a book – it never seems to have been planned. It always just seems to 'happen.'

'How? When? I need to know, Jack.'

'But it doesn't matter, does it? I needed to speak to you, to let you know that it's, eh ...'

'*Over*, I would say, wouldn't you, Jack?' Words are tumbling out of my mouth and I can't stop them.

'Rachel, I'm sorry. *Really* sorry. I know you probably don't believe me, but I didn't plan this. Actually, I went over to the States this time to end things with ... eh, her. But, well, I ... I couldn't.'

'Why not? Does she mean that much more to you? You have no problem ending things with me, though?'

'No, Rachel, it's not like that. It's ...'

'Like what, Jack? I can't believe you could do this to us. I know we've been having problems, but I was convinced it was down to work. Not for a minute would I have believed you could be such a ... liar? And a really good one at that.' I know I need to stop, as I feel the hurt and anger rising through my body, like water through an open lock gate and I feel like I'm drowning in the flood waters. But other emotions are there too – astonishment that he could bear to do the things with someone else that I thought were exclusive to us – intimate things. And as I think about our lovemaking, a sense of anger overwhelms me, followed immediately by disgust - at his total disregard for my sexual health, and I can't bear to look at Jack for a minute longer.

I struggle to get up from the sofa. Only now does Jack make some movement towards me, to help. But I don't want his help. The feeling of revulsion won't allow me to be physically near him.

'Don't touch me, Jack,' I say, shaking off his arm. I hobble towards the hallway, intending to get upstairs somehow, even if I have to do it on all fours. I just want to put as much distance between us as possible. 'I can't bear to look at you, never mind touch you. Just get out and leave me alone.'

'No, Rachel, we need to talk. I need to ...'

'I really don't care what you need, Jack. You've just bowled in here and torn asunder the last few years of our lives. What more could there possibly be to say?' I ask.

'The reason I couldn't end it ... it's not that I don't

love you, Rache. I really do. You have to believe me.'

I stare at him in disbelief. What the hell is he saying? He loves me, but has had a six-month affair with some woman in the States. Can he for one second believe that it's not going to change things? I'm so angry now. I just want him out of my sight, out of my life.

I'm *not* doing this again. No, no, no way. How can I still be so stupid? How could I not have noticed something, felt something wasn't right. To be honest all I want is to be alone now, because I know that tears are very close, and I will not give him the satisfaction of seeing me cry.

'Rachel, please,' he begs. 'It's important that I say this. I want to be honest with you.' That makes me snort with laughter, and not in a nice way.

'*Honest?* How can you even use the word, Jack? Do you even know what it means? After what you've just said? And now you want to be *honest?*'

'Please, Rachel. Just give me another minute. I don't think I can go ... without telling you.'

'Oh, there's more? Maybe you want to give me details now? Two minutes ago you didn't think it was important. What's changed?' I stand on the bottom step of the stairs on my good leg, my bad leg hanging under me, like a heron hunting in a fish pond. 'What, Jack? How much more pain do you want to inflict, because I don't think you could, even if you really tried.'

'She's pregnant, Rachel. That's why I can't end things. Please, try to understand. It was a huge mistake, but she's adamant she wants me in their lives. What else can I do?'

§

I'm cold. Freezing cold inside. My bedroom is cosy, my feather duvet warm and snuggly. Yet I'm freezing and can't warm up. Is this what it feels like when a person goes into shock? It didn't hit me like this the last time I was cheated on. Why? Sure, it was awful - but nothing as bad as this. Does this mean I love Jack more? Shouldn't I say 'loved'? Because it's over, isn't it? Jack and me. But much as I try I can't remember life before Jack. It feels like I've been with him forever. The tears start suddenly and I cry as if my heart is breaking. There's a leaden weight where I know it should be, and it feels as if all life is being pressed out of it. It's a physical pain, and I don't know if it will ever be better again.

§

Jack's left and a little later I hear my mobile phone ringing, but I ignore it. There's absolutely no-one I want to talk to. It jars on my nerves, but I persevere in my determination to ignore it and eventually it stops. But seconds later I hear the ping of the message alert. In the darkness of my room I pick it up from my bedside table, and check who it's from. Jack. I can't help myself - I need to know what he says, even though it's the last thing I want to know. I hate him, and I love him and I want to scream out loud, but don't have the strength to do so. My head tells me there can't possibly be anything Jack could say to change things. But my heart is desperate to know – and I open it.

'I love you, Rachel. I really do. Please help me. I realise I can't bear the thought of losing you. Please, can we talk?'

Chapter Fourteen

Next day Annie was run off her feet. Henry had been great, taking in his patients himself, even answering the phone on two occasions, and generally just helping out. Once or twice, though, Annie wanted to tell him she could manage, to go back into his office and she'd get on with things. But she knew he was just being kind, trying to relieve the burden of Rachel's absence. And it was this that had them both worried. Rachel hadn't telephoned, and Annie's calls to her house had gone unanswered. Neither was she responding to her texts. All Annie could think of was Jack had taken her to the hospital. Perhaps she'd done more damage to her foot yesterday than she realised.

As she bit into her egg mayonnaise sandwich, during a lull in appointments, she considered the changes which were about to take place. This morning made her realise, and she'd like to discuss it with Rachel when she was back, that if the practice was to get bigger with this new Aidan chap as second partner, then they would definitely have to get another person in to help. It could be someone part-time to start with. Then, if their client list continued to grow, someone could be taken on, on a full-time basis.

'Oh, Lord, can't I get a minute's peace?' Annie moaned to herself, as she heard the reception door open. She guessed it must be a 'walk-in' as no appointments were scheduled for the next hour. 'I'm afraid we're closed for lunch at the moment,' she called out.

'Well, aren't I the lucky one then?' she heard, looking up to see The Strop striding across the reception area towards her. 'I thought maybe Rachel and you would like to have a bite of lunch with me and I was wondering how Rachel is doing today?'

'Sorry, no can do. I have to stay here and man the phones, in case there's an emergency. Rachel didn't show in for work today, but I'm guessing she's probably had to go to the hospital for an X-ray or something. I'm sure she'll let us know,' Annie answered.

'Oh, right. Well, I hope she's OK. But who said anything about going out?' he asked, a wide grin on his handsome face, 'I wouldn't wish to be held responsible if a testosterone-fuelled bull runs amok or, God forbid, a frustrated, lovelorn hamster commits hari-kiri on his whirly wheel while we're enjoying ...this.' He lifted a wicker basket onto the counter, opening the lid to display sparkling crystal glasses, a bottle of champagne obviously straight from the fridge and dripping with condensation. Red chequered napkins were secured with leather belts to the lid, as were four plates and four sets of bone handled cutlery. A see-through glass container offered the delights of a beautifully presented mezze, with several small containers of vegetable salad, hummus, enticing smoked aubergine salad and, Annie's favourite – delicious tabbouleh. Two tiny silver salt and pepper shakers, in the shape of a man and woman interlocked in the most intimate of poses, sat cheekily suspended from the wicker lid.

'On second thoughts, it looks like you've already had lunch?' he said amused, staring at Annie.

'How do you know?' Then, following his gaze Annie reached up, locating the glob of egg mayonnaise hanging on her lower lip. Oh, bugger, she thought, embarrassed. The Strop threw back his head and a deep, rumbling laugh filled the small reception room.

'Surely you could manage a small plate, and a tiny glass of bubbly? With Rachel absent, maybe you could do with a little pick-me-up?'

'Can't, but thank you. I need to have my wits about me. Have to assist Henry with a procedure this afternoon and I can't do it inebriated on champers, can I?' Under other circumstances Annie would have jumped at the chance of downing anything alcoholic, especially if it was free.

'Oh, I see. What a pity! Well, that's more for me then.' Looking up at The Strop Annie felt he was making light of her refusal. Not upset exactly, but disappointed. She experienced a quick flash of regret, and a feeling that she'd been rude. Before she knew what she was saying, she heard the words 'Maybe some other time?' Why on earth had she said that? But he was quick on the uptake, asking 'How about this evening? I could keep it on ice? Pick you up after work?'

What's the harm, she thought, - a quick glass of champers, a bite to eat and then I can excuse myself. 'Alright then, but leave it until around six-thirty though. I'd like to stay for a while and check on one of the animals before I go.'

The Strop packed up his wares and with a wide grin, and a quick salute to Annie, made his way out to the car park.

What have I let myself in for, she thought. At the same time, she felt a tinge of excitement at the prospect of spending some time, if only a few hours, with a very handsome man. And – she'd have her free glass of champers, after all!

§

At six-thirty on the dot Annie checked her reflection in the mirror of the surgery bathroom, deciding they really needed to get better light in there. Was her lipstick a little on the dull side? And, she was a little disappointed she hadn't worn that new jazzy top she'd bought the previous weekend. Oh, who cares, she decided, she wasn't even interested in The Strop. Despite his fame, he wasn't her type – too old – must be at least forty, she thought, and at twenty-nine that's a *huge* gap. She was going for a free glass of champers and, perhaps, a nice meal? But if he had anything else in mind she'd tell him pretty sharpish.

She'd heard all the rumours about The Strop – the numerous women, outrageous behaviour, and the dubious show biz friends. But to her and Rachel's surprise they'd also heard celebrities on television, and other famous people, call him charming and sensitive.

But she'd make sure he was in no doubt that his charms – whatever they might be – would make no impression on her.

'He's not my type – at all,' she told the mirror. 'Not in the slightest.'

§

Back in Reception The Strop sat quietly on a gaudy, red plastic chair. He was a little early and assumed, when he found the place empty, that Annie was in the Ladies toilet. A door opened to his left and the red-faced man he knew to be Henry came out.

'Hello, again, how's Zebedee? It's Anton, isn't it?' Henry never had any trouble remembering an injured animal's name, he wasn't quite so hot with humans, though.

'Still having difficulty walking, but he's battling on. He's a hundred times better, though. I'm sure it won't be long before he's back to his old self again, thanks.'

'Glad to hear it. The cut was quite deep, so it'll take a while. I wouldn't worry too much. Eh … can I help you?'

'No, I'm fine, thanks. Just waiting for Annie. I think she's in the Ladies.'

Henry was surprised, and hugely disappointed. 'Oh, I didn't know you were a friend of Annie's?'

The Strop grinned in a way that thoroughly annoyed Henry. Not exactly smarmy, Henry thought, but not in any way complimentary to his Annie. He felt his hackles rise so, thrusting his chest out, he stared at the man standing before him.

'Well, Annie's a very special girl, you know. She's, well ... she's ...'

'Here,' replied Anton. 'Hi, Annie. Nice to see you again. Ready to go?' He found Henry's concern amusing and couldn't help winding him up.

'Yeah, just a minute though,' Annie said, turning to her boss. 'Henry, do you want me to come in early tomorrow morning? To check on Larry, the dachshund? I don't mind.'

'That would be great, Annie. If you're sure? You might have a late night?' Henry couldn't help himself fishing.

'Oh, believe me,' Annie said very emphatically, turning to face The Strop, 'it's not going to be a late night. How long does it take to drink a glass of champagne?'

Good girl, Annie. Henry was delighted, relieved to

know of Annie's intentions, despite whatever *his* were. But his relief was short lived as The Strop gave him a huge wink as they left the surgery.

Oh, Annie, be careful.

§

Later, when he arrived home Henry could hear the giggling as he entered the hallway. Oh, Lord! They were still here, and tonight he really wasn't in the mood. He felt incredibly down, having just seen Annie picked up from the practice by that insanely handsome mega star. He'd heard he was called The Strip, or something equally suggestive. But where was she going with him? Surely they weren't going out together, were they? And here *he* was, about to enter the sitting room, where his mother's lady friends were, by the sounds of it, still in full flow.

He'd seen the cars in the driveway, but was hoping some of them might have taken taxis home. But no, they were waiting for him, he was sure. The Good Son, who'd ferry their merry selves safely back to their respective homes. Taking a deep breath, he pushed open the door. A roaring fire was in the hearth and the room felt like a sauna.

'Good evening, ladies,' he greeted the assembled group. 'Shall I open a window, Mother? It's very hot in here.'

'No, no darling, we find it just comfortable, don't we, ladies?' A chorus of agreement was followed by muffled laughs. *Pissed as newts*, Henry thought, wondering how long would be polite before suggesting his taxi service should start.

'Be a darling boy and ask Free to bring in tea. It must be around four o'clock now, is it, Henry?' Four o'clock tea was what punctuated Mrs. Donaldson's afternoon, as did eleven o'clock coffee her mornings.

'Four o'clock? Mother, it's gone six-thirty, and Saoirse has already left for the day.'

'Who's Seersha?' asked a rotund, red-faced Mrs. Cooper, and Henry was quite sure it wasn't due to the heat from the fire. She sat twisting an empty sherry glass, gesticulating wildly with it, as if to draw attention to its emptiness. 'I thought someone called Free was your girl?'

'She is,' replied Henry. 'But Mother has trouble remembering her proper Irish name, which is *SAOIRSE*, and means 'freeedom' – hence Free,' explained Henry.

'What strange names the Irish have,' insisted Mrs.

Cooper. 'Why can't they be called civilized names like Jane, Henrietta, Emily. What's wrong with Charlotte, Edwina, Rose?'

'Well, they're typical English names,' explained Henry, somewhat exasperated. 'It's their identity, the same as those names are ours. *I* actually think Saoirse is a very beautiful name.' Henry could feel, rather than see, the look his Mother was throwing at him. So, before she could re-ignite their pet debate on the culture and vagaries of the Irish nation, Henry addressed the group.

'So, Ladies, who's for a lift home?' To which there was a collective sigh and, Henry was sure, not one of pleasure, more of resignation. The ladies were not pleased at having their afternoon cut short. Cut short - they'd been supping for four hours already! Time they were on their way, Henry decided.

Chapter Fifteen

Outside the practice, Anton held the door of his cherry-red sports car open for Annie, who slid in effortlessly, as if it was something she did every day of her life. The smell of the shiny, black leather was glorious, set off to perfection by the gleaming walnut dash. With The Strop being such a huge celebrity she'd expected a couple of telephones, even a TV perhaps? At least a sat-nav screen, but there were none of these things. The dashboard was sleek and uncluttered, if somewhat basic-looking. However, the deep growl of the engine when he started it up, left her in no doubt she was in a very powerful car. She was a little unnerved, though, by the sight of an 'Eject' button on the central console, and suddenly had a vision of being jettisoned through the sun-roof, once The Strop decided he'd tired of her. The thought made her giggle, just as he folded his long, slim self into the driver's seat.

'You alright?' he smiled.

'Absolutely,' she grinned, thinking it was just as

well she'd worn her 'pulling' cherry red thong. *Not* that she had any intention of 'doing the horizontal' with the gorgeous hunk beside her - absolutely not. But she had a vision of being cheekily colour-coordinated with his car, as she flew through the air after ejection, if it came to that. She got a fit of the giggles and had to put her head down into her lap to try and stop laughing.

'What's so funny?' he asked, looking around him as if he was missing something.

'Honestly, nothing. Really, nothing. My mind just runs away with me at times. Just ignore me, Str... eh, Anton.'

'Believe me, that's the very last thing I intend doing. Who in their right mind could possibly ignore you, Annie,' he laughed. And Annie felt herself relaxing. She didn't feel he was being smarmy. Could this rock god actually be nice? Not from what she'd heard around the village though. Tales were rife about the continuous procession of women through Mill House. In fact, she'd just heard last night, from her brother, Howie, that he'd even paired up with that Chesney Butler in the pub at the weekend. She was that busty, brassy girl from over near Forest Park. And everyone in Norebridge knew those Butlers were trouble.

Well, she was not one of his groupies, who sometimes camped outside his house just to catch a glimpse of him. She was here to get him off her back. She wondered though why he'd been so insistent at the surgery that she go for a drink with him. Anyway, – it was a quick glass of champers and some of that lovely mezze, then she could tell him 'thank you, but no thank you.'

§

He was a good driver, not a show-off at all. Contrary to expectations he wasn't in the least gung-ho, nor did he try to impress her with his skill and control of the flash car. She thought he might even try to frighten her a little, just for the hell of it. But there was none of that. He was a fast, but careful, driver and, much to Annie's amazement, courteous to other road users.

They'd been driving for about ten minutes without talking, but it was an easy silence. The sun glared through the windscreen, causing the inside of the car to feel like an oven. In the distance, a tractor stood like a child's toy in the field, the farmer making use of the hot, dry weather to rescue the last of his crop. Rising dust caused a golden haze and birds circled overhead, waiting to pounce on any furry little animals exposed in the aftermath. Inside, Annie turned to watch a bluebottle droning helplessly as it searched for a way out, crashing and banging against the pane of glass.

'Poor thing,' she murmured, more to herself than her companion, looking along the door for a handle to let the window down.

'I think I know how it feels,' she heard Anton say, as he operated the electric window, releasing the blue bottle into the air outside. Somewhat surprised, she turned and looked at the fine chiselled face, the high cheekbones.

'What do you mean?' she asked, curious as to how this person, who must surely have everything anyone could wish for – successful career, huge house, gorgeous car (actually, numerous cars, according to local gossip), women throwing themselves at his feet, and radio and TV appearances every other day – could find any comparison with a trapped bluebottle? The man must be worth a fortune, what was his problem? Did he have any idea how the other half lived? Who wouldn't give their eye-teeth to have whatever problems this joker had?

The Strop looked at Annie. There was a wistful look on his handsome features, but he suddenly shook his head and laughed. 'Oh, don't mind me. Just feeling sorry for myself, for a minute. It'll pass. It usually does.'

'What'll pass?' asked Annie, puzzled.

Anton hesitated, then laughed self-consciously. 'Nothing. No, really, forget I said that. This is getting a bit heavy, isn't it? It's supposed to be a fun picnic. Let the fun begin.' He grinned over at Annie. She got the distinct impression he regretted his comment. That he had revealed something he hadn't meant to, and was now doing his best to distract her from his slip-up.

'Absolutely,' Annie said. 'I was beginning to regret coming out with you. I only came along for the ride – in your posh car, of course,' Annie teased, giving him her best saucy pout.

'I'm in no doubt about why you came along,' Anton replied, 'no doubt at all.' And he looked at Annie with such depth, she felt he could see right through her. She reddened with embarrassment, and suddenly, didn't feel so sure of herself. Not sure at all that she had the upper hand over this man, like she normally would. She realised he knew exactly why she'd agreed to come along. And she felt thoroughly ashamed of herself.

§

Anton enjoyed their leisurely drive, as he turned down a country lane where ditches spilled over with cow parsley and wild garlic. He wasn't sure what had prompted him to invite Annie for a picnic, except that he'd felt the need for company. He was disappointed that Rachel couldn't join them, as he'd felt a connection to the girl he'd carried in his arms into the surgery. Despite the jovial atmosphere between them, he sensed a sombre, serious side to her too, almost a kindred spirit.

As he tucked the car in neatly behind a tractor laden heavily with black, plastic covered bales, he smiled at the thought of how the local people complained of 'the traffic' during the high season months of summer. They had no idea what real traffic was, like that of London, or any big city. Five minutes stuck behind a combine-harvester in the High Street of Norebridge did not, in his mind, constitute a 'traffic jam.' It certainly was no match for the two to three hours it used to take on his last commute to London. Part of the reason he'd given up his last house. Not that he'd had to drive himself. Brad, his excellent chauffeur presently on a well-deserved two-month holiday, bore the brunt of the daily grind on the motorway. Anton was usually too hungover, or catching up on his sleep in the back seat until he was woken by a gentle shake, once they'd reached wherever they were going.

Brad had been with him for ten years now, since soon after that awful event. Through the good, the bad and the *very* bad times. Nothing he did had shocked Brad back then. He seemed to understand totally what Anton was going through. Anton considered him more friend than employee, and while Brad knew everything there was to know about Anton, Anton knew very little about Brad. Just that he was fifty-eight, widowed, and had a flat in London. But he normally lived wherever Anton was, and didn't seem to mind in the least not knowing where they would be from one day to the next. Although only eighteen years older than himself Anton thought of him as a father figure in his life. Something he'd never had since his wonderful Father died.

That awful day was etched in his mind, a memory that would never leave him. The nightmare continued to haunt him nightly, and he'd wake lathered in sweat, seeing for the thousandth time the burning flames of the car in which his father died. His father, an excellent driver, had swerved rather than hit a stray dog. Anton could feel the heat from the crashed car, as he lay on the roadside. He'd been thrown clear, but had broken his legs and could only look on horrified as David Wickers-Stroppton burned to death amid the screams, which Anton heard every time he closed his eyes sober.

§

'I used to think your house was in the complete opposite direction,' Annie broke into his thoughts. 'Out towards Westbridge.'

'I *did* go and look at Westbridge House when I came here looking for a property. But there was a huge amount of renovation to be done, outside in the grounds as well as inside. Mill House suited me much better, as it had already been refurbished and I liked the style. Also, I was looking for somewhere I could move into immediately. I wanted to get out of London as quickly as possible. The other thing was, Mill House had some great outbuildings, which lent themselves very well to being turned into a recording studio – something I wanted.'

'Lucky you, eh? But, I suppose if money is not a problem it's easy find the perfect place to live. But why did you want to leave London? I can't think of anywhere more exciting to live.'

'Well, life took a few bad turns for me there. Everything, and I mean *everything*, was too accessible. Got myself into a few scrapes, so I decided I needed to get out. Find somewhere with less temptations!' he joked, thinking back to the last episode, after his father's death, when he thought his life would end, after a particularly stupid weekend of drink and a near-miss with drugs. Brad had arrived on the scene at the same time and, together, they found Mill House and moved everything down the country. 'But how about you, Annie? Where in Norebridge do you live?'

'Rachel let me share her house when I got here first, until my family found a house for themselves. We'd moved here for Dad's work. Then – big mistake! – I moved back home when they got settled. And now, I can't get away,' Annie smiled to take the edge out of her words.

'Are places hard to find around here?'

'Ones that I can afford – and that are habitable – are. There are lots of places available, but most of them are dives. And the ones that don't have leaky roofs, mouldy walls, or a colony of mice to share with, are way outside my budget. Have you ever seen that row of terraced houses on Quayside?'

'Yes,' Anton said. They look as if they were workers' cottages at some stage. Very picturesque.'

'Until you go inside. I went to see one for rent. God, I couldn't believe my eyes. Couldn't believe that they were actually offered to the public for habitation. My Dad says the landlord should be shot! And they're lived in by families with young children. He says he doesn't understand how they're not all ill.'

'But surely the landlord is responsible for keeping them up to an acceptable standard?'

'Dad says, and I've seen it in the newspaper too, that the people living there have made several complaints. They've even threatened to take the landlord to court. But he knows they can't do anything. Nobody seems to be listening. I feel very sorry for them.'

'So for the moment you'll stay put at home? But I'm sure it must have advantages, being surrounded by your family?'

'Oh, yeah! Great advantages – I queue for the bathroom every morning while my younger brother – who has just discovered girls don't really like boys who smell – spends at least twenty minutes in the shower; I get the leftover bits of toast after everyone's had theirs, and my underwear stinks of rugby pitch if I put them in the laundry basket with my brother's kit. Oh, yeah, there are *huge* advantages!'

Anton threw his head back and laughed out loud, as Annie pulled a face.

Although Mill House lay close to Norebridge there was a long, circuitous route, up the hill through the woods, to get there. A few minutes later they turned in through the wrought iron gates of Mill House where a lush expanse of well-maintained lawn spread before them, and a gravelled driveway snaked its way into the distance. Mature oak trees and shrubs broke the monotony of grass, with a copse of copper beech trees clustered in a group on a lower level to the right. Looking past this Annie could see the sun reflected on the surface of the river, where a fisherman stood mid-stream, the water thigh-high, his fishing line swishing lazily back and forth, before being flashed with practised skill into the water. Anton beeped the horn in return, as the fisherman raised his hand in greeting. Four chestnut ponies grazed comfortably, unfazed by their presence as they headed on towards Anton's home.

The house was not yet visible, hidden by a wide bend in the drive, woodland spanning acres on either side. As they approached the bend, a sleek black Labrador came racing at speed towards the car, followed behind by another, which Annie recognized as the injured Zebedee. Zebedee tried, but failed, to break into a trot behind his more able twin. His whole body trembled with excitement, as he stood on the grass staring at the approach of his master's car. Barking non-stop, Lucius bounded excitedly around the car, disappearing around the front, only to re-appear and race happily around once again.

'Heel, Lucius. Heel, Zebedee,' Anton shouted at the dogs, although it was obvious he expected neither to obey. 'They love visitors, and get overexcited when the postman, or the bakery van, bowls up. Luckily, both the guys know now and look out for them.'

'Stop, please? I'd love to give them a cuddle. Do you mind?'

'Not at all. They'll love it, they enjoy being made a fuss of. But I warn you, they won't let you go too easily! Don't say you haven't been warned,' Anton laughed.

He'd barely stopped the car before Annie was out. Lucius raced around to her side, launching himself at her full of exuberance, Zebedee trailing in his wake. Taking the full force of the dog's weight, Annie found herself knocked sideways, ending up flat on her back, arms and legs akimbo in the lush softness of the freshly mown grass. They licked and slobbered over Annie's face as she lay there, laughing at their antics. Anton joined in, grabbing their collars, while doing his best to get them to behave.

'And how are you then, Zebs? Back on your feet – or rather, paws, I see,' she laughed. 'How long have you had them?'

'Since they were pups. They came from a friend of mine in Gloucestershire. She breeds them, and rescues some, as well. I think at last count she had eight of her own. She lives and breathes Labradors, and is very highly thought of among breeders. Right, let's get back in the car and we'll give Lucius a good run up to the house. Zebedee will follow on at his own pace.'

They continued round the bend, Lucius accompanying them at full gallop, and Annie gasped as she caught her first glimpse of Mill House.

§

Through a break in the clouds marring the blue sky, a

shaft of sunlight bathed the enormous Georgian house in a pool of golden light as it sat high on a gently sloping bank. Arms of green ivy wrapped themselves around the Cotswold stone, as if in a warm embrace. Plump, purple heads of wisteria dripped over a protective canopy, under which wide, granite steps led up to imposing Palladian pillars. Gleaming sash windows stretched out on either side of a large Racing Green panelled front door. Everything seemed in perfect balance, the house sitting like some *grande dame* overseeing the surrounding landscape.

Anton brought the car to a speedy halt and gravel crunched underfoot as she followed Anton up the steps and into the hallway – a large, airy space full of light. Here the marble floor, resembling the colour of desert sand, felt hard and unforgiving under her soft, summer shoes. She couldn't help exclaiming 'Wow' as she gazed upwards to an enormous atrium, thinking its cerulean blue dome could easily be mistaken for an extension of the sky outside. In places, Persian carpets in vivid shades of red and forest green helped absorb the echoey sound, which otherwise could have sent every word reverberating around the cavernous space.

'Not exactly cosy, is it?' Annie laughed nervously,

more in awe than criticism.

'Well ... I suppose not. Not exactly cosy, but it feels like home to me. I have to admit I loved it the first minute I walked in. *And,* believe it or not, Annie, it's a lot smaller than my last place,' Anton replied. 'Let's go into the kitchen and sort our picnic out,' he pointed to his left, as Annie gazed around a little bewildered as to where the kitchen might be. She smiled to herself as she imagined what her Mum and Dad would say when she told them she'd had a meal in Mill House. Although, on second thoughts ... maybe better not tell them. It was known locally as The Shag Pad, and she might have trouble convincing them she'd only come up for a glass of free champers – no matter what else Anton might think was on offer.

Lucius bounded in, followed by a limping Zebedee, their nails *clickety-clack* on the marble floor. Lucius came to a halt by skidding at full pelt up against the bottom step of the marble stairs, while Zebedee ended up sitting on his bottom, sliding helplessly across the floor, ending with a smack against the wall panelling.

'They never learn,' Anton laughed, stroking the silky ears of the two panting animals. 'They're terrified they're missing out on something to eat. '*Down, Lucius.*

Down, Zebedee' he admonished, as they leaped about excitedly, both happily ignoring their master.

'In total control, I see,' Annie laughed. Approaching one, Annie turned her palm towards the animal and, pointing to the floor, said in a no-nonsense voice *'Sit.'* Immediately, he sat, with something approaching a whimper, looking across at Anton, as if asking for some assistance.

'Don't look at me like that, mate. I almost sat down myself,' he joked. Turning to Annie he said 'I'm impressed. They've never done that for me – ever! Maybe you could give me a few pointers about getting them to behave.'

'It's all a matter of asserting your authority. It doesn't have to be aggressive or belligerent, but definitely has to let them know who's boss. We need to be in control in the surgery, otherwise it's be absolute chaos. Can you imagine a room full of beasts that don't know how to behave?'

'Yeah, I suppose. And that's just the owners,' he joked.

Chapter Sixteen

I spent the day curled up in bed yesterday. I can't remember what I ate, if anything. My mind just whirled round and round, filled with thoughts of happy times with Jack. I called the office, late in the afternoon, using my ankle as my excuse for not going into work. I assured Annie I was fine and managed to fend off her suggestion that she came round after work. I just couldn't face anyone.

This morning, I hear the phone ring several times, but still can't bear to answer it. Surprised, I realise I've slept. Not a restful, peaceful slumber, more a fitful, broken sleep, punctuated by bouts of sudden wakefulness in which I try to remember exactly what Jack told me - was it only two nights ago? Or am I dreaming it all? Will I wake up and find him striding in through the hallway, arms outstretched with happiness at seeing me again. Then reality kicks in, and I force myself to accept that Jack is, indeed, gone.

I look at my phone. There are three more messages from him, but I don't have the heart to look at them. I can't deal with it. Anyway, I need to be at work. I look at the time and groan loudly. Oh, God – I've woefully overslept. I should've been at the surgery hours ago. What will Henry think? But instead of jumping out of bed and racing into the shower, I just turn over and curl up into a ball. And the tears come again. Sometime later, through a kind of fog, I hear the phone again. This time, I pick it up.

'Hello?; I can barely get the word out. My throat feels as if it's closed up.

'Rachel? Are you OK?' I hear the concern in Henry's voice.

'Eh …yeah. Sorry, Henry. I was just going to call you.'

'You don't sound too good. Are you sure you're OK?'

'Yes, yeah, yeah. I think I'm coming down with something. I'm sure it's nothing serious. I'll just have a quick shower and be there as quick as I can.'

'I'm sorry to disturb you, Rachel, especially if you're not well. It's just, well … I wondered if Annie stayed with you last night – she's not at home. She hasn't turned up for work, and there's quite a queue here. I'm not sure what we have on today, or in what order. People are getting a bit irate. And,' he says, lowering his voice, 'I have a feeling that Mrs. Rogers has jumped the queue with Spice, her budgerigar. She insists her appointment is for ten. But Mr. Casey is of the opinion he should be next, with Rex, his ...'

'Oh, Henry. I'm so sorry. Of all days for me to fall ill. But, as I say, it's nothing too serious. Give me a minute and I'll be there. Have you tried Annie's mobile phone?'

'Yes, no reply, I'm afraid. That's why I thought she might be with you.'

My work persona takes over, and my personal problems are forced into the background. How could I let Henry down like that? 'Henry, Mrs. Rogers is right. Her appointment is before Mr. Casey. He's probably just got the time wrong again. Remember, he suffers a bit from his memory? Tell him you've checked with me, and he'll be OK. I'll make him a cup of tea as soon as I get there. Again, Henry, I really am so sorry.'

'Don't worry, Rachel. I feel better just knowing you're on the way.' I can hear the relief in Henry's voice as he hangs up.

§

I have a two-minute shower, throw on the nearest thing, and am out the door in record time. The swelling on my ankle has gone down a great deal, although still a little painful, but at least I can limp along without too much difficulty and can, thankfully, get my foot into a shoe.

But as I drive the short distance to the surgery I can see Jack's handsome face looking at me from across the room, and before I can do anything about it, tears flow down my unmade-up face. I sob loudly as I drive, and realise I feel so empty that I could happily turn my car off the road and head at full speed into the picturesque river. The same river where I enjoyed my sun-filled afternoon only two days ago, full of joy and anticipation at seeing my lover again. It feels as if a whole lifetime has passed since then. I arrive at the car park, touch up my puffy face and hobble inside.

§

A few hours later Henry comes out of his office, having had no lull in the schedule the entire morning. His voice is full of concern, as he approaches the reception desk:

'If we weren't so busy, Rachel, I'd suggest you go

back home. But I honestly don't think I can get through the day on my own. I'm so sorry.'

'Henry, stop it. You have nothing to apologise about. I'm the one who should be sorry, letting you down this morning. But, never mind, I'm here now. Still no news from Annie?'

'No, nothing. I'm getting a little concerned at this stage. And, well ... she did go off with The Strap, or whatever he's called, yesterday. Do you think maybe ...?'

I'm a little surprised to hear of Annie and Anton Wickers-Stroppton. How did that come about? But now is now the time to be mulling over my colleague's colourful love life. 'Oh, Henry, I wouldn't worry too much, I'm sure something's just come up. In the meantime, shall we get on with things? Are you ready for Mr. Hurley?'

'Refresh my memory, Rachel?' he asks. Poor Henry, he's finding it hard to concentrate. I'm sure his mind is occupied with thoughts of Annie and her whereabouts.

'Ageing spaniel. You tried to suggest having him put down on his last visit? Mr. Hurley didn't want to know?'

'Oh, goodness me, yes. Yes.' Henry nodded. 'I think I'll have to be a bit more emphatic this time. The poor animal needs to go. He's not in pain right now, but it's not far away. And, old Mr. Hurley just wouldn't be able – physically or emotionally – to deal with finding him stiff as a board on the kitchen floor some morning. No, no, it's better if we do it humanely, and soon. Think you could have a cup of tea ready for him when he comes out?'

'Of course, Henry. Just give me the nod, poor man. Rascals is all he has left. His wife died about six years ago and the dog is the last connection he has with her. He told me they both took him from a rescue centre together, and have looked after him ever since. I think it's the link with his wife that he's probably unwilling to sever, as much as to be without Rascals. Oh, my heart goes out to him, Henry. This is the one part of the job that I absolutely hate.'

'You and me both, Rachel. Anyway, best get on with it,' he sighed. Taking the brown, manila folder which Rachel held out, he turned and called Mr. Hurley's name, inviting him to join him in his room.

'Hello, old boy,' she heard Henry say gently, knowing full well it was Rascals he spoke to, rather than his owner.

§

I dial Annie's number again, but it goes to voicemail. As far as I know she didn't have any plans to take a day off, and it's not like her to just not show up, for all her flightiness. Perhaps she's had an emergency at home. Now, I need to turn my attention back to work matters - anything to keep me from thinking about Jack.

I tackle the pile of incoming post, opening it and distributing to the relevant areas – things that require Henry's input; cheques for payment of outstanding invoices; cheques which need to be banked; then I turn my attention to incoming electronic payments, as well as the usual e-mails which need to be dealt with, after which I head into the small kitchen and fill the kettle. As I switch it on to boil I wonder how things are going inside for Henry and poor Mr. Hurley. I sympathise with the elderly man, whose loss will be devastating. I know Henry will make it as easy for him as possible. While I'm daydreaming, the surgery door opens and they emerge and I know from looking at Mr. Hurley's face that Henry has impressed on him the need for putting his pet down.

'I've just put the kettle on, Mr. Hurley. Will you have a cup of tea before you go home?'

'I ... don't know. I should get home, I need to bring Rascal's things back here, so he won't feel ... '

'Don't you worry about that, Mr. Hurley. I'll run you home afterwards, and we'll bring them back here for Rascals,' Henry says. 'Why don't you sit and have a nice cup of tea with Rachel. She's not feeling too well today, so I know she's dying for one,' he says, winking at me as he tries to cajole Mr. Hurley to join me. The old man sits down heavily, looking around as if he's lost. I know how he feels, as if the bottom has just fallen out of his world.

Chapter Seventeen

Aidan looked around the sitting room at the collection of cardboard boxes, filled to bursting with the detritus of his forty years of living. Most of it would go into storage. The rest would come with him to Norebridge in the morning. The estate agent had already found a nice couple who wanted to rent his house for a twelve-month period. He was happy with that, as he felt it gave him a year's breathing space. He'd know for sure by then if it was where he wanted to spend his life.

Looking at his watch he realised he'd be late if he didn't get a move on. He still needed to have a shower and shave. Extracting his wash bag from his overnight case, he headed to the bathroom. Fifteen minutes later he was showered, shaved and dressed for his farewell night out with Vee and friends. She'd warned him to act surprised when they went into the restaurant, as their friend, John had arranged a surprise going-away party for him. It was probably the worst kept secret ever.

Laurel, the Receptionist at the practice he was leaving, had left the office at four-thirty, telling him she'd see him later. Then, realizing what she'd said, made a very unsuccessful effort to cover up her mistake. He pretended not to have noticed.

Grabbing his keys Aidan hurried out to his car, and headed over to pick up Vee, who was looking impatiently out her sitting-room window as he parked up in front of her house. She ran out, jumped in the passenger seat, and looked at him angrily.

'Really, Aidan, I told you we needed to be there at seven-thirty. They'll all be waiting for you. We'll be late now.'

'Does it really matter, Vee? What difference will five minutes make?'

'That's not the point, Aidan. I promised to have you there at …'

'Please, Vee. Not tonight. I'd like to have a pleasant night, and not fight on our last evening together.'

'What do you mean our 'last evening together?' You make it sound like we're never going to see one another again. It's only temporary, Aidan. Remember, I'll be down to Norebridge as soon as I can.'

'I know, I know, Vee. But we agreed I'd need to do a bit of settling in first.' Why did he feel he had to battle constantly, just to get some breathing space from Vee? Couldn't she understand he was embarking on a whole new life. It might take a little time for him to find his feet. And, he wanted to do this ... 'unencumbered' was the word that came to mind. He didn't feel burdened by their relationship, but he wanted some space to explore his new world for a bit. Then, he'd be happy to welcome Veronica in. But she needed to be patient and not keep pushing for an invitation.

§

Arriving at the pub a few minutes later, Aidan leaned over the kissed Vee lightly on the cheek, before getting out of the car.

'What was that for?' she asked, slamming the car door.

'Oh, I'm just sorry for earlier. I was a bit of a heel. But I think I'm nervous about tomorrow. Now that it's actually happening it feels different. It was OK to be talking about something that was going to happen sometime in the future. But now, it's here and – I'm feeling, well ... not quite so confident.'

Unseen by Aidan, Veronica smiled triumphantly to herself. *Yes! Yes!* It would all work out for her. She'd make sure he realised what he was missing by haring off to some village in the back of beyond. To her mind he shouldn't have even thought about a move to Norebridge. Not when they were on the verge of becoming a 'committed' couple. She was sure if he'd stayed they would be engaged before long. Now – well, maybe it'd be put on hold for a while. But, not for long – she'd make sure of that. She had no intention of letting a good catch such as Aidan Millington slip through her fingers.

'Oh, don't worry, darling. It's perfectly understandable. You're heading into the unknown. You're bound to be unsettled,' she smiled at him.

'Thanks, Vee. You're always so understanding. What'll I do without you for the next few weeks,' he said.

'Oh, you'll manage, I'm sure,' she smiled. *Just don't get too used to it. I intend to be down in Norebridge before you know it.*

§

'SURPRISE!' The shout went up as they entered the crowded bar. John and Joanie came up to welcome them, with two glasses of champagne.

'Well, well, you old codger,' John slapped him good-naturedly on the back. 'Had no idea, did you? Best kept secret, eh,' he beamed.

'You rogue, John. I suppose this is all your doing. You shouldn't have – but I'm glad you did. It's a lovely idea, thanks,' Aidan fibbed – successfully, he hoped. He hated any fuss like this, and would have much preferred to have a few quiet drinks with a small group of friends. Instead, he'd have to make conversation with a group of people, most of whom he probably wouldn't see again. But he didn't want to be a killjoy, especially as, from the look on John's face, he was delighted with the turnout. 'Cheers, John,' he laughed, clinking glasses with those standing closest to him

'To old friends, eh?' John winked at him, knowing that his secret was safe and on its way to Norebridge with his friend Aidan.

§

Later that night, having left the pub, they drove over to Vee's flat. As everything, including all the bedlinen, was packed away they had agreed that Aidan would spend his last night as Vee's house guest. He'd stayed over on several occasions, but this time it felt different.

He felt a stranger in the place.

'Tea, coffee? Something stronger? Or will we just go to bed?' Vee looked expectantly at Aidan. She sidled over to him as he stood in the hallway, hanging up his coat on the wooden pegs along the wall.

'Well, I've a long drive tomorrow, love. I won't have a drink. But, a tea would be lovely.'

'Oh! OK then.' Vee sounded surprised. Aidan felt he'd disappointed her, that he was expected to jump at the opportunity to go straight up to bed. But he felt wired, his thoughts all over the place. He didn't think he could settle to making love with Vee right now - to give her the attention she deserved and craved. There were so many other emotions running though his head – excitement, uncertainty, apprehension. Yes, if he were honest with himself, he was terrified of making some huge blunder and letting himself down, *and* letting Henry down. Above all else, that was the last thing he wanted to do.

Later, Vee snuggled up to him, running her fingers over his nakedness. To his surprise he felt himself respond and, much to Vee's delight, they made slow, passionate love. He fell asleep almost immediately and in what felt like minutes he heard his phone alarm go off.

He was on his way.

Chapter Eighteen

'Where the hell have you been?' I ask Annie, a little aggressively. 'We've been worried about you.'

'Cuddling dogs, sculling champagne and generally having a great time! How about you? How's the ankle?'

'Sorry. It's just we've been very busy. I overslept, which meant Henry had to deal with things on his own until I made it in. But you should've at least called, Annie. It's not like you. What happened?'

'Well, I overslept too. How's that for a coincidence!' she grinned. I know there's something Annie's hiding, but now is not the time to enquire. We have too many patients left to be seen. Cheerfully, Annie escorted the next patient – a working Collie, recovering from being run over in the farmyard – into Henry. He beamed with pleasure at Annie's appearance, asking how her evening had gone.

'So, so,' she laughed, tapping the side of her nose as she did so. Henry was immediately chastised. 'Now,

Henry, be gentle with poor Ben. He's looking a bit down in the mouth.'

'Yes, well, that's what happens when you make a habit of trying to bite a tractor's wheels when it's still in motion. At some stage, something nasty's bound to happen'. Annie was a little taken aback at Henry's sharpness. But turning towards the door he greeted the dog's owner with his usual friendliness and courtesy. 'Hello, Mr. Aherne. I've checked the X-rays and looking at him walking now, Ben seems to be doing fine. I'm delighted to tell you no bones broken, no internal damage. But there is some damage to the tail, which may impinge on his balance. Hopefully not, but we'll just have to keep an eye on him for a while, and if you see anything untoward, don't hesitate to bring him back.'

Henry worked his way through the next three patients before having time for a break. He walked towards the staff room hoping for a reviving cup of tea. As he neared the door he could hear the girls laughing hilariously inside. Smiling, and before he knew what he was doing he'd stopped and found himself listening from outside.

'His house is amazing. I don't know where to begin to describe it – huge spaces, beautiful décor, the kitchen is so big our whole house would fit into it! And outside – horses galloping round the paddocks, and the stables so clean you could eat your dinner off the floor. Honestly, Rache, it was incredible. Oh, and he's got a chauffeur - away on holidays at the moment. *And,* he's got a housekeeper who looks after him like she's his mother, from what he said. Oh, the whole place is gorgeous. And, it's *so him!'* Outside the door, Henry had heard enough. He turned and walked back down the hall to his office, feeling very downhearted indeed.

§

'But I don't understand, Annie – when did you arrange all this?'

'Yesterday - Anton arrived with a picnic basket for us both. And to enquire how you were. You weren't here and I was too busy to have lunch, so he suggested having a drink with him later. I thought what the hell? Anyway, you know me and the offer of a free glass of champers,' she grinned cheekily. 'And, I thought we were just going to the park, or the woods. But instead we went to his house. But do you know, Rachel, what was the most surprising thing? He's actually very nice, none of that celeb nonsense you see in those magazines.

He seems, kind of ... ordinary. Despite living in such luxury, despite being such a famous person.'

'And ... staying over? How did that happen? That's a bit quick, even for you, Annie!' I tease.

'Who said I stayed over?'

'Well, Henry called your house this morning. There was no reply?'

'Why was he phoning? Surely he knows me well enough to know that something had happened, or I'd have been in work,' Annie did her best to look upset.

Despite feeling so low myself, I can't help laughing. 'Oh, my God, Annie, are you trying to change the subject?' Then pretending to look shocked, I say 'Oh, does this mean ...? You *did*, didn't you?'

'No, no, Rachel. Honestly, it wasn't like that. We just had a bit of fun. Anyway, I enjoyed my afternoon - and evening - but it was just a one-off. I have no interest in him - romantically, I mean. Sooooo – shall we go to The Spotted Peacock tonight? You can even bring Jack?'

§

That evening, as Annie and Henry stood at the bar, she leaned closer to Henry whispering 'Overslept? That's not like Rachel. And not to call in – OK, OK Henry,' she held up her hand, 'I'm sorry about this morning. I'll explain another time. But there's more to this than meets the eye, I think. Get 'em in, cowboy, and let the grilling begin, because I'm not going home tonight until I know exactly what's going on. Are you in?'

'Of course, I am, Annie. I'll do anything I can to help. I agree, there's something else going on here. I wonder has it to do with Jack?'

§

They returned to the table, drinks in hand and as Annie sat down, she couldn't help noticing how down in the dumps Rachel looked. They were in for a long evening. Henry sat down beside Rachel, and proceeded to discuss the cases that had gone through the clinic that day. After a few minutes, and with very little input from Rachel, Annie gave Henry a dirty look, which brought him to an abrupt halt. He shrugged, looking helplessly at her with a just-trying-to-help look, clearly out of his depth.

'Rache, is everything alright? You seem really out of sorts. Didn't Jack come back? Oh, no, he didn't have to cancel, did he?'

'No, Annie, he didn't cancel..'

'Well, how was his trip? Has he accomplished his mission and conquered the great US of A yet?'

'Really, Annie, do you always have to be so rotten? I don't want to hear it this evening, if you don't mind, I don't think I'm up to it. In fact, I think I'll head home, if you both don't mi ...'

'Eh, I don't think so, Rachel. You're not going to slide out of this one.'

Although talking in a light-hearted manner, Annie got the distinct impression that all was not well in the land-of-Jack. And she wasn't going to give up so easily on the chance to find out what was going on. If that bastard had upset Rachel, he'd get an earful from her. And this time, Rachel wasn't going to stop her. She'd spent her time since coming to work with her reading between the lines, every time Rachel spoke about her boyfriend having to take yet another unexpected trip to the States. Annie'd suggested several times that Rachel go with him, for a few days R & R. But the idea never seemed to find acceptance with Jack. Rachel was not a person to bad-mouth anyone, especially God's-gift-to-all-women Jack. She couldn't see the arrogance, the condescending attitude that Annie could. *And*, there was that drunken episode that Annie tried, without success, to blot completely from her mind.

§

'Right, lady. Spill.'

Henry was beginning to feel very sorry for Rachel, caught as she was in the direct line of Annie's fire. 'Perhaps Rachel would prefer to ...'

'No, Henry. She wouldn't. Now, shush,' Annie said, gesturing impatiently at Henry to be quiet. 'Rachel, you might as well know - Henry and I are committed to sitting here *all night*, if necessary. But, *you will* tell us what's happened. Anyway, we have nothing better to do, do we Henry?' she said, looking pointedly at the stricken Henry.

'Eh, no. Absolutely not,' he agreed. But at the back of his mind Henry had the strange feeling that he should, in fact, be somewhere else. Oh, well, never mind. This was more important.

Henry loved Rachel like a sister, from the first day she started working for him. He was very concerned about her and had never seen her so down before. It spoke volumes for her not to show in for work this morning, without letting him know what the problem was. He'd been completely at a loss to know how to broach the conversation with her earlier, before Annie showed up. For someone perfectly at ease getting 'up close and personal' with all sorts of beasts, he was useless when it came to people. He was terrified it might be something 'lady related,' and wouldn't for the world want to embarrass her.

§

I know Annie means every word, though I'm not sure I can talk about it. Looking at her I know I have no choice. But I don't think I have the physical or emotional energy to rehash the recent events with Jack. I take a deep breath and look at them both, knowing in my heart that these are my real friends, who genuinely care about me. That makes it a little easier, so I begin.

'Well ... Jack *did* come home. But, it wasn't quite the homecoming I was expecting. Basically, we've split up. Well, to be precise, Jack has split up with me. - there! Happy now?' Before I can stop myself, I burst into tears and if things weren't so serious I could burst out laughing at the expression of horror and helplessness I can see on poor Henry's face!

'How do you mean 'split up'? Why? Everything

was fine before he went, wasn't it?'

'Yes. Well, I thought it was, but apparently not. He's ... been having an affair with a girl in the States for the last six months. So he says, it could be longer, I don't know.' I can't bring myself to tell them about the pregnancy.

'*What!* The bastard! Oh, Rache, I'm so sorry. You poor thing,' Annie jumps up and wraps me in a great big hug. And, that is my undoing. I just cover my face with my hands, put my head down and sob as if my heart is breaking. But then, it is. It feels as if it is breaking up into little pieces, never to be whole again.

§

'Now, Annie. I don't care what you say, we're taking Rachel home – right now. No, no, don't contradict me,' Henry says, holding his hand up to Annie who already has her mouth open to disagree. His authoritative manner surprises me. He never does that in work. Even in my misery I can't help thinking '*Go, Henry, Go!*' And she does, shut up. I'm glad, because Henry's right, I'm making a total show of myself – and them – in the pub. I should howl and sob in the privacy of my own home, not here in public where all and sundry are looking over at us, mad with curiosity as to what can be causing such a spectacle. Stiff upper lip this is not.

'Thank you, Henry. That's exactly what I want to do.' I look over at my friend, 'I'd really like to go home. I just want to go to bed, and I'll see you both in work tomorrow.'

'If you're sure, Rache. Would you like me to stay with you? We could sit up and talk?'

'Thanks, Annie, but I don't have the energy. Maybe in a few days? And, trying to be as unobtrusive as we can, we stand up and leave the pub and, for the second time in two days, I'm escorted home by the two people I care most about - after Jack, of course.

Chapter Nineteen

Henry groaned as he saw the strange car parked on the driveway, tucked in neatly at the farthest end of the gravelled turning circle. Oh, bugger! How could he have forgotten something, indeed someone, as important as this. Hurriedly, he unbuckled himself from his car seat, and rushed in through the front door. He could hear voices coming from the sitting room, and was surprised to hear his mother's high tinkly laugh as he tentatively pushed down on the handle.

'Henry, there you are, dear boy. I should be furious with you. Or should I say our guest should be furious with you. How could you forget he was coming tonight? Really, what will Aidan think!'

Well, there was something he never expected to see – his ageing mother sitting as close as she could get to the handsome Aidan, patting him on his knee with one hand, while balancing a glass of sherry in the other. Aidan, good naturedly, winked at him, saying 'Well, she must be something special to make you forget my arrival.

Hope she's worth it!'

Wrong thing to say! 'No, no Aidan, heavens no, it's nothing like that, I'm sure,' Henry's mother said, quite emphatically. 'Henry doesn't have a woman in his life - except me, of course!' said with the batting of what was left of the old lady's once dark and luscious eyelashes. Oh, this was so not right. Was Mother flirting with his new practice partner? Things had just spilled over into the downright obscene.

'And why would he need anyone else, when he has you to come home to?' Aidan replied flirtatiously, patting the old lady's veined and liver-spotted hand. 'I'm sure he'd have a hard time finding someone like you, Mrs. Donaldson.'

'Oh, Charlotte, please, dear boy,' the old lady smiled coquettishly.

You've never said a truer word, thought Henry, trying to think of some way to extricate poor Aidan from the attentions of Mother – newly rouged cheeks aflame either from the sherry or the blazing fire in the great big hearth. And was that lipstick? As Henry bent to kiss her, he was overpowered by the seductive scent of *Poison*, his yearly Christmas present to Mother. For someone who normally liked to sit and be waited on, he wondered when she'd been able to hike upstairs and apply the trappings of the fairer sex.

Aidan walked over to Henry, hand outstretched. 'Don't worry in the least, Henry. I've been very well looked after in your absence. Unexpected call-out?' he asked, only too aware of how, in their chosen profession, the most important plans could be disrupted at a moment's notice.

'Well, no, actually. It was one of the girls in the practice - you remember Rachel, Practice Manager?'

Aidan remembered her very well – curly, auburn hair hugging a petite elfin face, grey/green eyes which, Aidan was sure, concealed a determined nature within. He also remembered the curvaceous body as he held her in his arms to prevent her falling, that first night as he entered the pub in Norebridge. Oh, yes! He remembered Rachel.

'Yes, I think so,' he answered vaguely, 'she came with the other girl, Annie?'

'That's the girl. Well, she was in a pretty bad state today, because of recent events and Annie and I were very concerned for her. She didn't show in for work this morning, didn't telephone in either, which is just not Rachel's normal behaviour. Seems that cad of a boyfriend broke up with her, he's been seeing another girl in the States for the last while - total shock for poor Rachel, and completely knocked her for six. So, Annie decided she needed our administrations this evening and we went to the pub. I'm so sorry, old boy. It sounds such a trivial reason to stand you up, but believe me, Rachel needed us.'

'As I said, Henry, there's really no need to upset yourself. In fact, if this is a bad time for you, I can always decamp to a hotel, or the pub, if it suits?' Aidan wasn't in the least put out, admiring Henry for his caring nature, and his availability to his friends in crisis.

'Absolutely not - I won't hear of it!' Mrs. Donaldson said from her seat by the fire. 'Henry, show Aidan up to his room. Get a move on, and hurry back down and we'll have another glass of sherry – both of you.'

And like two schoolboys being told off by the headmaster, they found themselves trotting off upstairs to do as they were told. On entering the bedroom designated to him, Aidan looked at Henry, and they both burst out laughing.

'Welcome to *chez Donaldson,*' Henry said, 'I do hope you won't regret this!'

§

Aidan was up at the crack of sparrow next morning. Unable to sleep with excitement, other than the odd drift into a short slumber, he was invigorated and full of joy to be preparing for his first day in the new practice - and a new life. It seemed ages since he'd welcomed the day like this. Perhaps it was because, without realizing, he'd just slid into a working rut, which unfortunately seemed to extend to his personal life too. He knew he was edging closer to having to grasp the nettle and make a decision where he and Vee were concerned. But – not today! He was not going to think about anything other than his new, exciting job.

Being able to stay with Henry was extremely helpful for him. It meant he could concentrate on the practice, finding his feet and where he could be of most help. He liked Henry a lot, rated him highly as a person. Even though he knew him such a short time he felt they'd get along well, and were both operating from the same platform of principles and respect.

He smiled as he remembered Henry's mother last night, and Henry's embarrassment at her flirtatiousness, which he himself found amusing. But, he could see himself growing very fond of her. A sad character, her present life seemed to have been shaped by unexpected widowhood several years ago and, like him, she'd slid into a rut – her role now that of an ageing mother, who expected her only son to look after her, and see to her every whim. As if it was now his role to make up for the awful wrongs life had thrown at her. Never mind about Henry's own life or needs, which seemed non-existent in his mother's mind. Poor Henry. But from their conversation last night Aidan knew Charlotte loved her son deeply, and was terrified she'd be left alone, if anything happened to him,

'Bread's in the toaster, old boy,' Henry greeted him as he strolled into the large, sunlit kitchen. 'Help yourself to coffee or tea.'

The kitchen was warm and welcoming, and the smell of pure filtered coffee wafted from a glass cafetière in the middle of an old, well-worn pine table sitting in the centre of the room. Looking round him, Aidan thought the kitchen was exactly as an old-fashioned kitchen should look – pale cream walls needing a paint touch-up, black slate floor, its surface dulled by time and use, and nestled into a large black hole in the wall was a four-oven Aga, a gleaming aluminium kettle gently boiling on one of its plates.

Every inch of wall space was taken up by cupboards and drawers. These too looked past their sell-by date. A well-used kitchen, and Aidan felt immediately at home there.

Seeing just two table settings Aidan asked if Henry's mum was joining them.

'Oh, no, no. I've already brought Mother her breakfast. She feels tired in the mornings, doesn't sleep at all well. She won't get up until around mid-morning. But she'll be fine until then. Saoirse will be in soon and she'll bring her another cup of tea. Then she'll be ready for the day. The Vicar will pop in later on. He's great, never misses a week and Mother loves their little chats. But how are you this morning, Aidan? Ready for your first day?'

'Absolutely, Henry, can't wait. I'm very much looking forward to it. And please, don't hesitate to show me where I can be of most help to you. After all, that's why you decided to take on someone else, isn't it? I really don't mind where you assign me.'

'Hold on, Aidan – assign you? You're an equal partner, remember. I hadn't thought in terms of 'assigning' you anywhere.'

'No, no, I didn't mean it quite like that, Henry. But

this is a great opportunity for you to offload the parts you like least. Do you know what I mean? I really am happy to take on any areas that you'd rather not do. The only thing is, I would welcome working with large animals whenever possible. If you remember that's what we spoke of at my interview?'

'Absolutely. In fact, what I thought we'd do today is take a trip round some of our clients. Especially some of the farmers, which is where you'll be involved in the large animal cases. The geography of the area is pretty straight forward once you know it, seems a bit complicated at first though. And the small animals you'll get to know as they come into the practice. Rachel and Annie are both fantastic and will give you all the help you need to familiarize yourself with the admin side of things. Don't ask *me* about it! I don't know what I'd have done without Rachel. She set up all our systems and is a genius when it comes to data and eh ... well, all that stuff.'

'Right, if I grab a quick cup of coffee and a bite of toast I'll be ready to go.' Aidan reached across the table for a mug, bearing the picture of a border collie on one side. Turning it round he saw the name 'Henry' printed on the opposite side in jaunty, black letters, matching the dark coat of the handsome dog. Smiling, he poured himself some of the rich, treacly liquid from the coffee pot.

'Mmm, this smells divine. You'll make someone a great husband someday, Henry,' he teased.

Generously buttering a nicely browned slice of toast, which he then loaded with home-made damson jam – a gift from a local farmer's wife – Aidan bit into his welcome breakfast, feeling that things were so very right in his new world.

Chapter Twenty

A change in the weather took everyone by surprise. It had been forecast, but no-one believed that the sun, which had graced the landscape of Norebridge for so long, would turn tail and run with such ferocity. I'd sat with Annie in my small handkerchief patch of garden last night for several hours in the last vestiges of the days heat. But this morning I woke up to gusting winds and misty rain.

We'd finished off two half-empty bottles of white wine while discussing the impact this new man had had on the practice.

'Well, I think it's great for Henry. He's not half as stressed as before. *And,* Aidan's not too hard on the eye either, eh?' Annie giggled, slightly merry from the wine.

'I wouldn't know about that, Annie. But I agree about Henry. It's taken a lot of the crap off his shoulders. And,' I admit a little begrudgingly, 'he really seems to know what he's doing.'

'Absolutely. That horrible Grant Bradley, from Featherstone Farm, called again yesterday. I think you were inside assisting Henry - the spaying? - well, anyway, he called and was really out of order. Accused Henry of doing God-knows-what to his bull and demanded to speak to him. When I explained I couldn't disturb him just then, he insisted he wanted to speak to "someone – but someone who's knows one end of a bull from t'other!" He was absolutely awful.'

'What happened? I didn't know any of this, Annie. Why didn't you tell me?'

'There was nothing to tell. Aidan took the phone and spoke to him, explaining who he was. I had to laugh though when I heard him say – "But I'm only new here, for the last few days. I'm not quite in the same league as Mr. Donaldson. Perhaps you'd prefer to wait until he can get up to you? I can perfectly understand if you do." Needless to say, Bradley was having none of it. He wanted someone - anyone – up there *now*. I don't know what went on, but Aidan doesn't seem to think we'll have any more problems with him! He wouldn't say anything when I asked – he was very vague. I'd love to have been a fly on the wall though.'

'Yeah, me too,' I say, a little preoccupied. Bradley

is one of our biggest customers. Slow to pay his bills, but they always get paid eventually. He's a contrary, unhappy man. But we need to keep him satisfied when it comes to his stock. I made a mental note to ask Aidan about it. Then, I realised Annie was speaking to me.

'Sorry? I was thinking of something I need to do tomorrow. What was that?'

'What are you going to do about Jack-the-lad? Have you heard from him since?'

Oh, yes. I'd heard from him. Every morning, every night there's at least one text or missed phone call on my mobile. I've never returned any of them, but I can feel them wearing me down and am afraid that I'll do something stupid. I still love Jack, still ache for him and, if he walked through the door this minute I'm not sure I'd have the willpower to turn him away. But the thought niggles at me that maybe it's habit more than need, lust more than love that makes me miss him so much. I keep reminding myself of the enormity of what he's done. He hasn't just cheated on me with someone else, he's actually formed an innocent life with her. That's not just a casual one-nighter that can be dismissed as a drunken mistake.

'What am I going to do? Well ... I don't know. I

mean, what is there to do? It's over.'

'I'm really glad to hear that, Rache. For one awful minute there I thought you were actually considering trying to fix things, to forgive him for cheating on you with that woman. But, promise me, you won't even consider it.'

'Oh, Annie, it's not that simple. There's so much to consider.' I have to remember Annie knows nothing of the pregnancy. As far as she's concerned Jack has just had an affair.

'What do you mean, so much to consider. Has he been trying to get back with you? Oh, Rachel, even Jack can't be that devious. You mean to say he goes off and has a six-month – or more – affair with someone, comes home and tells you it's over, then has second thoughts and is now trying to inveigle his way back into your life? *Please, please* Rachel, tell me I've got it wrong.'

'Eh, not exactly. No, I mean, that's about right. But, Annie, we've been together for several years - there's a lot of me invested in this relationship. I'm really happy with Jack. OK, we've had our ups and downs lately, what relationship doesn't? But normally he's kind and considerate, listens to my moans and groans, does what he can to help, and …'

'No, Rachel. Not present tense – *were* really happy with Jack; *was* kind and considerate; *used* to listen to your problems. Surely you can't think you can just continue as if nothing's happened? Get a grip, woman. He's a shit, a liar, a cheat and that definitely *IS* in the present tense. Anyway, how do you know this is the only woman he's had on the go? Wake up, Rachel. There are far better men out there than 'drop-your-pants' Jack. And you deserve much better than him.'

'I know you've never been a big fan of his, Annie. But you don't know him like I do. Really, believe me when I say he's …'

'Listen to yourself, Rachel. Did you really know him? If so, how did you not know he was at it with American Babe 2016? And possibly anyone else he thought was available?' Annie so wanted to tell Rachel about Jack's true nature, but she couldn't cause her friend any more pain.

§

Annie went home, not best pleased with me. I watched some inane television programme while drinking another glass of wine. I know I shouldn't, but it seems to dull the ache if only for a few hours, even though I know the whole sorry saga that is my life currently is back in harsh technicolour once I wake up in the morning. Just as I dozed off on the couch, the phone rang again, and *again* I ignored it, but the constant trilling began to jar on my nerves. With sudden determination, I jumped up from the couch and grabbed the hand piece.

'Jack, will you please stop this. We need ...'

'Rachel, I'm sorry. It seems you were expecting someone else. It's Aidan. If it's a bad time I can call back, but all I need is some help, if you can?

Oh, shit. I don't want to broadcast my situation to all and sundry. Certainly not someone I work with, and the new boy at that. 'Eh, no. It's OK, Aidan. Just a bit of a misunderstanding. What is it you want?'

'Well, there's a sick calf up at Fairview Farm. I was wondering if you could just give me directions. Henry's not available, and it'll mean I'll have to go into the office, as it's not showing up on my Sat-Nav. This seemed the quicker option. Again, sorry for the interruption.'

'No, sorry, Aidan, it's not a problem. Eh ... well, Fairview is a little awkward. Once you get up to the top of Brandon Hill, there's a turn off to the left, which is signposted Fairview. That's where everyone makes the mistake. It takes you on a twisted roundabout way up to Fairview Lodge on the west side of the estate. But the sheds are over on the other side. Ignore the sign and keep going straight, take the second left *after* the sign, and it will take you straight to the barns.'

'Thanks, Rachel, that sounds pretty straight forward. I'll get the lie of the land around here soon I hope. It's just so different from my last place. Anyway, I'll let you go. Thanks again. And … sorry for the interruption. Is everything OK? Anything I can do?'

'No, everything's fine, thank you.' I realise I sound abrupt, but I can't be bothered. I just want to be left alone. He only owns me from eight to five-thirty each day. I don't need him asking about my private life. I hung up, but the phone rang again immediately. *'WILL EVERYONE JUST GO AWAY,'* I scream, covering my face with my hands and the room spins around me. Next thing I know, I can feel the scratchy texture of my sitting room carpet rubbing against my cheek, as I hit the ground.

§

It's hours later when I wake up. The room is cold as the timer has turned the heating off at midnight. My hands and bare feet are icy, yet I can't motivate myself to get up off the floor. I feel as if all the joy has gone out of my life, everything that made sense, that gave me pleasure has walked out the door with Jack. I have no strength, my body feels like a leaden weight. But, worst of all, there's an empty, gaping hole which I don't think I will ever fill again.

Chapter Twenty-One

'That poor boy didn't get in until about two o'clock this morning,' Henry's mother scolded him. 'Do you think you should check on him? See if he'd like some breakfast?'

'Mother, what on earth are you doing up at this hour of the morning? Are you feeling OK?' Henry was surprised to hear someone pottering about in the kitchen as he came down the stairs. Gobsmacked would be more accurate when he realised it was his mother. A large dish of bacon and mushrooms stood on a warming plate on the table, alongside a covered plate of scrambled eggs. When was the last time Mother had made breakfast? This could only be for Aidan's benefit. No matter, Henry was delighted to see his mother with a sense of purpose again.

'I'll pop up and see if he fancies anything, Mother. I'll be right back.' Smiling to himself, Henry took the stairs two at a time, just in time to see Aidan come out of his bedroom, dressed and ready for the day.

'Good morning, Aidan. A little bird tells me you didn't get in until very late last night. Sure you're up to going in yet? I don't mind picking up the slack while you have another few hours sleep, if you'd like?'

'No, thanks Henry, I'm fine. But something smells great - I can't believe how hungry I am. I normally just grab a coffee and then I'm out the door. Have you been busy cooking? Another hidden talent, eh?'

'No, not me. *Mother*, can you believe? You're having a very strange effect on her. I can't remember the last time I saw her in the kitchen, never mind at seven o'clock in the morning. But I'm not complaining. I'm ravenous too.'

And with that, they entered the kitchen where Mrs. Donaldson was patting her hair, checking her appearance in the old-fashioned mirror on the wall. Aidan discreetly coughed, giving her enough time to compose herself and not be embarrassed being caught in such an act of vanity.

'There you both are - come sit down. No, Aidan you come here beside the Aga, it's warmer.' Henry threw an amused glance Aidan's way, letting him know he was in no way upset. He could see the funny side of his seventy-year old Mother preening herself, feeling excited by the presence of a young, handsome man in their home. *Whatever gives Mother a new lease of life is OK by me.* And he couldn't think of a nicer reason than his new friend, Aidan.

§

'How are things with Rachel?' he asked Henry, as they both tucked into their meal with gusto. Served on delicately patterned china plates, coffee in china cups and saucers, and toast, slightly burnt, in a china toast rack. A small dish of butter, complete with butter knife, was placed in the centre of the table. Beside it sat another dish with Aidan's favourite damson jam. Henry's mother had pulled out all the stops! But, Aidan suddenly realised, this was probably the way she had lived her previous life with Henry's father – surrounded by pretty things and looked after by others. His heart went out to her, and in a sudden burst of affection he stood up and went over to her, wrapping her in his arms, saying 'Oh, this is really lovely. I've never been so well cared for, Charlotte. Thank you so very much.'

'Oh, nonsense, nonsense, Aidan,' she said, and he could see she was a little flustered at his sudden show of emotion. 'Now, do sit down and have your breakfast before it gets cold.' But her cheeks were rosy with pleasure as she turned back, busying herself at the stove.

Henry looked at Aidan, mouthing a 'thank you' as they resumed their conversation. 'I'm not sure. She's not one for wearing her heart on her sleeve. Very independent type, wouldn't welcome too much intrusion into her personal life.'

'Well, I may have put my foot in it last night then. I phoned to get some directions to Fairview Farm. She'd obviously been expecting someone else on the phone – someone called Jack? When I asked if I could help, she more or less told me to mind my own business. I'd hate her to think I was prying just for the sake of prying. But she sounded genuinely upset.'

'He's her boyfriend. But I think he's treated her very shabbily. I know Annie is livid with the way he's carried on. But, Rachel seems to have trouble letting go and Annie is concerned that if he clicks his fingers she'll run back to him.'

'Well, Henry, when it comes to women I'm afraid I'm no expert. They never fail to blind me with their logic - or lack of logic - I'm not sure which! Let's hope it sorts itself out.'

'Yes, well, we were thinking of taking her out for a drink tonight. Trying to keep her mind off this Jack-the-lad, as Annie calls him. Fancy joining us?'

'Sounds good. I'd like to get to know the nice pubs and restaurants around here.'

§

I managed to make it into work this morning, despite my collapse last night. I've moved through the day like a zombie and, I hate to say, made a few errors along the way. Luckily, Annie was there to sort them out. She said nothing, but threw me a few strange looks during the day. I know it's just concern, but I'm finding the attention a little claustrophobic and really just want to be left alone. I'll work through this in my own way, and in my own time. But Annie obviously thinks I need company and has insisted we go for a quick bite at The Spotted Peacock this evening. I don't have the will to fight her.

The evening is cool, so I throw on my red, belted woollen coat. I'm cold all the time now, can't seem to warm up. I put one foot in front of the other every day, take my route to work as normal, carry out my duties as required and go home. Everything in between is like a fog, a misty screen obliterating everything that goes on in my life. Jack's done this. He's dulled my joy of life, taken away everything that seemed important - my love for him, the satisfaction I've always felt in my job, and the closeness of good friends. And the thing that makes me angrier than anything is I'm beginning to think that I have somehow – unknowingly - been complicit in this.

Should I have been more questioning? Should I have insisted on joining him on some of his trips to the States, as Annie so often suggested? Was I not paying attention? Did this let him think I wasn't interested enough? But then, if I'd pushed for that, would it have made him feel I didn't trust him? And I *did*. *I trusted him with my heart and my future.* Am I stupid? But I believe if you love someone, and they say they love you, it isn't necessary to worry about them when they're away from you. Or when you're away from them, out of sight. I believe it should be no different. Our behaviour should be the same, whether we're in the same room, or thousands of miles away from each other. Otherwise, what's the point? Stay single, and play the field if that's what you want.

Perhaps I just don't have what it takes to keep Jack interested, or any man for that matter. Four days ago, I wouldn't have said that. How things can change in such a short time. But one thing is for sure now - I won't be rushing into love again any time soon. In fact, *ever* seems much more likely.

Chapter Twenty-Two

Henry stood alone at the bar, feeling like a spare wheel, as he waited for the others to arrive. He wasn't used to spending time in public houses, certainly not alone, but every time Annie felt the need to discuss something, it always seemed to be in the local pub. She said it gave things a much more informal feel. And Henry was beginning to agree with her. He quite liked having a nice quiet drink with Annie, before returning home to Mother. And, if he were honest, he welcomed any opportunity to spend time with her. The lovely Annie, she really knew how to make his heart flutter. But Henry was nothing if not totally honest with himself. He was well aware he was no heart throb, but was hoping that eventually Annie would see his other attractive traits – he wasn't terribly sure what they were, but just hoped she'd see them – and sooner rather than later.

He saw the girls arrive into the pub - Annie with her usual cheeky smile, greeting other punters as she came towards him and Rachel, who looked as if she was there on sufferance. Henry was determined to do all he could to help her get her life back on track. And he knew he had a willing accomplice in his girl, Annie. He pulled himself up abruptly. Unfortunately, she wasn't *his* girl. How he wished she were.

§

I see Henry at the bar as we enter the warm, fuggy pub. 'Glass of wine, girls? Or, perhaps you'd like something else?' Henry offered.

'Perfect, Henry. Just what the doctor ordered. Or should I say *"just what the Vet ordered,*' Annie giggled.

'Yes, please,' I reply, doing my best to look as if I'm glad to be here. What I'd really like is to sit at home with a glass of wine, by myself, wallowing in my misery. I know I'm spending too much time wallowing, but right now nothing I do seems to raise my head above the awful cloud of hopelessness I can feel hanging over me. Thank God for my job. It's the only thing which brings me any sense of purpose – and my friends, who are sitting here with me right now, doing their best to cheer me up. What kind of a miserable person am I. So, enough self-pity I think, giving myself a good mental shake.

'Any news, Henry, on Jimmy White's greyhound? Was she badly injured?' I ask.

'I stayed on to do some X-rays – Annie was happy to assist,' he hurries to assure me, as I start to say he should have let me know and I would have gladly stayed late. 'Problem with her hind quarter. She's not at all happy to put it down, and certainly not capable of putting any weight on it. We'll have to keep a close eye on her over the next few days.'

'Poor thing,' Annie says. 'She just lay there whimpering in pain. I felt so sorry for her. And that owner of her's is cruel. I think he was more worried about whether she would be able to run again, rather than whether she was in pain or not.'

'Yes, Annie, I agree. Unfortunately, these races put such pressure on the animals, and, like in this case, when there's a pile up it can seriously injure them.'

'How did it happen?' I ask, as I've missed all the drama this afternoon.

'Well, she was well on her way to winning the 3.30 at Brides Park, when she came down the last straight and one of the other's clipped her, causing her to trip up, knocking the one behind her too. There was a pile up of animals, during which poor Gowran Girl was hurt. Externally, there are no marks or cuts. But something's not right. As I say, we'll monitor her over the next forty-eight hours and take it from there. Oh, good. Here's Aidan,' he says, looking over my shoulder to the entrance.

'I didn't know he was joining us,' Annie says, brightening up visibly at this news.

I look across at Henry's sad face and know exactly how he feels, but for a very different reason. For me, this is a step too far. With Henry and Annie, I can be myself. But with this new partner I'll have to make some effort and, again, this awful tiredness overcomes me and I just want to be snuggled up in bed.

'Evening all,' he says, pointing to our half-empty glasses. 'Another?'

'Yes, thanks Aidan,' Annie pipes up, before either Henry or I can reply. Before we know it he's already heading to the bar. Looks as if we'll be staying a while longer.

§

Aidan joins us, rubbing his hands together trying to generate some welcome warmth. 'Nasty out there now, isn't it?' he asks us.

'Very nasty night, indeed,' replies Henry. 'Nice and cosy in here though, with that enormous fire,' he says, pointing over to the cavernous black hole in the end wall of the 12th century coaching inn, which is throwing out amazing heat. The old, wide-planked wooden floor gleams in the firelight, reflected in the brass ornaments hanging on the walls, as well as numerous pieces of twinkling glass, star-shaped, tucked into the tiny windows giving the whole place a welcoming glow.

'Is Henry looking after you, Aidan?' Annie asks. 'Giving you enough to eat, a warm dry bed, brandy on tap?'

'Yes, yes and decidedly yes!' he answers, grinning widely.

'Well, actually, it's not me doing the looking after – it's Mother, believe it or not!'

'*Your* Mother, Henry?' Annie asks, astonishment showing on her pretty face. 'The woman who doesn't know there is actually morning light before eleven-thirty in the day. *Your* Mother, who feels she was put on this earth to be waited on and tended to by all and sundry? I'm amazed – what brought about this monumental change then, eh?'

'Actually, I think it's having Aidan in the house. It seems to have given Mother a new lease of life. She's up before either of us in the mornings, cooks a lavish breakfast, and is waiting for us when we get home in the evenings,' this said taking a sneaky look at his watch. 'I've never had the treatment Aidan gets. But I'm happy to bask in the glow of her fascination for him – embarrassing as it may be for you, dear boy,' he smiles apologetically at Aidan.

'Oh, I'm not complaining either. As I told her this morning, I've never been so well looked after. Long may it last, I say,' he laughs good-naturedly. 'Although,' he says, patting his washboard stomach, 'I'm beginning to feel the effects. Trousers getting a bit tight,' he whispers. Only someone who didn't have a weight problem could be so blasé about it.

'Well, I think your mother should treat you like that *all* the time, Henry. God knows you've looked after *her* for years, haven't you. Why now, just because there's a stranger in the house. I don't think it's fair to you at all.' Annie throws an angry look at Aidan, who begins to look somewhat uncomfortable.

'I hope I'm not causing any problems for you, Henry.' he says. 'I certainly wouldn't want to. You know, as I've said before, I can easily book into the pub here.'

'Absolutely not, Aidan. And do me out of those scrumptious breakfasts every morning? You most certainly will not - even if it means tying you to the bed!'

'Oh, racy, *raaacy!* Annie quips. 'Hidden depths, eh, Henry?'

'Absolutely not,' he splutters. 'I've told you ... not that there's anything wrong with ... Oh, never mind.'

I look at Henry, so disconcerted by the fact that his beloved Annie might think he's interested in men, when all the time he's hopelessly head over heels in love with the girl sitting right in front of him, teasing him so cruelly.

I look over at Aidan, sitting with an amused smile on his face, enjoying the comic scene in front of him. I believe he's already sussed out the fact that his partner thinks a lot more of our lovely Annie than just a colleague. He's already made a huge difference to Henry's work load. And, I have to admit, he seems a nice man. He's been with us just over two weeks now but, unfortunately, I'll always associate his arrival with the departure of my lover, Jack.

§

Before they'd gone to the pub Henry and Aidan had had their weekly meeting, catching up on cases completed, those unfinished and the reasons why, as well as cases pending over the next week. They'd decided to pull the plug on one particular client, who'd debated his bills too many times, and on one occasion even refused flatly to pay a penny. Henry had continued to deal with his cattle and troublesome bull, in the hope that he would settle up at some time in the future. But payment had not been forthcoming. And, he owed them now for the last two visits as well.

'I think - if you don't mind doing the dirty deed, Aidan? - that we should ask him to take his business elsewhere. In fact, the practice in West Gate is closer to him, so would actually be more convenient for him.'

'No problem, Henry. In fact, I find it a bit odd that he would come to us in the first place, if there's a veterinary practice closer to him. Do you think he might have left them under the same circumstances? Maybe they've had similar problems? If so, he'll run out of vets soon who are prepared to deal with him. Anyway, to answer your question, I've no problem asking him to move to another practice. I'll go up to see him tomorrow.

What I'll do is give him the option of settling his account. If he's not prepared to do that, then I'll make the suggestion. Next case?'

'Before we move on, Aidan, there's another matter I think we need to address. Since your arrival we've been able to take on a lot more cases, which has resulted in a much increased workload, which is great for the practice. But, it's also resulted in an increase in administration and other work for Rachel and Annie. I was thinking we may need to take on another assistant. I haven't spoken with Rachel, as Practice Manager, yet, but I will do at the earliest. What do you think?'

'I think we definitely need to get the girls' views. They'll have a better idea of how they've been affected, by the increase in workload. But do you mind if *I* speak with Rachel, instead of you?'

'No, no. That's great. I'm happy to leave that with you then,' Henry replied. They were both pleased with their new partnership, and hoped things would continue to grow steadily. Aidan was also very happy to be accepted so readily into Henry and the girls' little circle and looked forward to their get-together that evening.

§

'Not quite the success I would have liked,' Henry said to Aidan on the way home. 'I was hoping we could cheer Rachel up a lot more. She was doing her best, I could see that. But she's really been knocked for six by all this.'

'How long had she been going out with him?'

'About two, two-and-a-half years, I believe. Doesn't sound like a long time, but who am I to judge. I've never had a long-term relationship, so I wouldn't know.' Aidan heard the longing in his voice and felt a deep pity for this decent man.

'Have you ever asked her out, Henry?' he asked, purposely not looking at his friend, as he drove confidently through the darkness.

'Who?' Henry asked, puzzled.

'Henry, it's OK. Your secret is safe with me. But you can't fool me, either. It's plain to me that you think a lot of Annie. Why don't you ask her out? Have you *ever* asked her?'

'Oh, gosh no.' Henry was astounded that Aidan had rumbled him. 'She wouldn't be the slightest bit interested in me. Not her type at all, I feel pretty sure of that'. Aidan could feel Henry's discomfort and was sorry he'd even ventured into this romantic territory. 'Anyway, she's interested in that awful man who lives in Mill House – The Strip, or Strop – he's called. I shudder to think why. Ghastly man – not good enough for Annie at all. But it seems she's started seeing him lately. Met her at the surgery of all places. Probably missed my chance. And, I was just biding my time, actually. Didn't want to rush things. Wanted her to know me a bit better. How ironic is that!'

'Well, Henry. You know what they say – *Faint heart never won fair maiden* – or something similar,' he told his friend, as they entered the gates of The Old Vicarage. They both saw the sitting room light on, indicating Henry's mother was still up, awaiting the safe arrival home of the two men in her life.

Feeling like two teenagers coming home later than they should, they both looked at one another, threw their heads back and laughed heartily.

Chapter Twenty-Three

Anton Wickers-Stroppton sat up in bed, thinking about his day ahead. Marty 'Junkie' Crawley was coming down from London mid-afternoon, as he'd decided it was time to plan their next album. 'Midnight at the Grotto' had been a huge success for them, and 'Junkie' was keen to jump on its coat tails. 'Only way to keep the fans' interest,' he insisted. Anton could happily have left things as they were. They'd made an absolute fortune from 'Midnight' and Anton was more than happy with his property and investments portfolio, which had gone a long way to securing his financial future. He never needed to work again. 'Junkie' on the other hand, as his nickname implied, had not been so wise. Neither of them had ever lived frugally, but Anton, after a few dabblings in the world of drugs, had decided to steer clear of that particular pitfall - 'Junkie' unfortunately not so.

Beside the bed his mobile phone rang. Thinking it was 'Junkie,' he picked it up and hearing the voice on the other end Anton cringed, knowing it was too late to stop the conversation with someone he had hoped never to see or speak to again.

'Hey, Anton. It's Chesney,'

'Eh, ... hi, Chesney. How are you?

'Well, I've been better. Actually, we need to talk – soon.'

§

'Hey, dude, how's things?' 'Junkie' still lived in the seventies, a period when his life had made sense. A time when rude, arrogant and downright nonsensical behaviour was accepted, even expected of a heavy metal band. They'd lived their lives constantly in the spotlight and their music was the bane of most parents' lives. While never actually biting the head off a chicken on stage, Anton would be the first to admit he did things that now made him cringe with embarrassment. But at other times he could only laugh, remembering some of the wild antics all four members of The Rabid Antelopes got up to.

Dickie Medson, their drummer extraordinaire, was what they freely called a 'basket case' back then. They once had to drive to France in their clapped-out camper van - The Shag Palace - to bring him back in time for a concert they'd been booked to play. He'd somehow managed to get himself on an overnight ferry the previous night. When he telephoned early next morning he wasn't much help when Anton asked where he was. 'Not far from the ferry – in France,' was all the help he could give. Anton could hear him laugh on the other end of the phone, as if it was the most natural thing in the world to do. 'There's a castle, with a smashing bakery at the foot of it. That's where I'm phoning from.'

Anton asked to speak with the owner, who turned out to be a genuine, true-to-life British hippie, called Robert. He'd chucked in his life in the City and decamped to Brittany, to a life of growing his own wheat. He'd bought a rundown mill, did a huge refurbishment, and thoroughly enjoyed his life baking croissants and baguettes, as good as any Frenchman. He was also a huge fan of the emerging band at the time, which he happened to pick up on a pirate radio station late one night as he worked his dough in the quiet, cricket filled night in France. After all that time, he and Anton were still good friends, and he always looked forward to seeing Robert and his family whenever they visited the UK. They always managed to squeeze in a few days with him wherever he lived.

Now, looking at his fellow musician and friend, Anton was much relieved he had managed to extricate himself from the rock scene, before any lasting damage had been done. As a famous rock star, he'd had no problems tempting several happily married women into his bed. Women, whose husbands would have been only too happy to curtail the possibility of his ever fathering any offspring. But the women all seemed to love Anton, even when their fling was over. And they somehow managed, without exception, to talk their other halves out of rearranging Anton's handsome face.

Deep lines furrowed Marty's forehead, dark circles underlined both eyes, which were sunken deep into his skull and made all the more obvious by his love of charcoal eye paint. Black hair still bore the trademark inch-wide blonde stripe down the middle of his crown and two brassy earrings dangled from his right ear lobe, giving him a sexy, gypsy look. He still dressed in his own unique style, which were his trademark clothes - skinny jeans tucked into a pair of tan cowboy boots; a white shirt with long flowing sleeves and which had seen better days, worn under an olive-green, tweed waistcoat. Anton smiled, thinking only someone as flamboyant as Marty could get away with such an outfit. The press had loved Junkie during their hey days of chart toppers and wild parties, and there was no shortage of paparazzi waiting to snap them as they regularly fell out of famous night clubs, like vampires emerging reluctantly into the daylight. It was the Press who had given him the nickname 'Junkie'.

§

Anton hugged his friend, shocked to feel the skeletal frame hidden under the flashy gear. 'Come on in, Marty. Fancy a coffee?'

'Got anything stronger, mate? It's been a long drive - I'm parched.'

'Sure. Let's get inside,' and he led Marty through the hallway, into the warm kitchen, where the aroma of freshly brewed coffee lingered in the air. Opening one of the wall cupboards he picked out an unopened bottle of Bushmills, his favourite whiskey. Pouring them both a generous measure he handed one to Marty, who gulped it down in one go.

'Woah, slow down there, Marty. You're right - you have one helluva thirst on.'

'Come on, mate. Hit me,' Marty ordered, banging

his empty glass down on the pine table. Anton poured him another measure and, passing it across to him, watched as his friend took a small sip, closing his eyes, savouring the whiskey's essence.

'Right, then. You said you wanted to plan the next album. Got any ideas already? Or, do you just want to throw some ideas around and see what we come up with?'

'Yeah, yeah. Let's get something out on the table, and see what comes of it.' Marty started to tell Anton what he thought the market might be looking for now, as opposed to when they were at the pinnacle of fame. Marty had his finger on the pulse of present trends in the music world. Unlike Anton, he'd never really left that milieu, keeping in contact with those considered the oligarchs of the music world. Anton was impressed, and found himself getting interested in what Marty was proposing – a new release comprising a mix of twelve of their old songs, re-mixed and rejigged, to be followed up with radio and television appearances, culminating in a UK tour – maybe even a European tour later.

'Have you mentioned your idea to Greg? He *is* our agent, after all. Don't you think he should be involved?'

'Not at this early stage. You know old Greggers –

would want to get involved straight away, he would. No, I think we should keep this between ourselves until we have something solid to offer. Yeah?'

Anton could see the sense in what Marty was saying. As soon as Greggers could see the pound signs, he'd be hounding them for deadlines and the pressure would take all the pleasure out of the project. But, in fairness, once he was behind a project you could bet he'd give it his all. Well-known in music circles he was totally responsible, at the start of the band, for exposing them to the right people in the world of TV and radio, all of which had helped them enormously.

They talked and laughed for the next few hours, when Anton suddenly realised they'd run out of alcohol. They'd eaten nothing, so were both a bit worse for wear. And, they were ravenous.

'Let's go to The Spotted Peacock - they serve great pub grub. We can have one of their fillet steaks. You've never had anything like these, Marty – butter on the tongue. They're from the farm up the road, and are absolutely the bee's knees.'

'*Or,*' Marty slurred, sticking his finger in the air as if to emphasise a very important point, '*absolutely the bull's bollocks!*' They both found this hilarious, and roared laughing holding each other up in their drunkenness. Stumbling through the hallway, they giggled their way out to the driveway and Anton's shiny, red Ferrari.

§

The roar of the powerful engine was another form of music to Anton's ears. He loved his car. It had been his most extravagant gift to himself - other than the house. He loved the power he felt as he put his foot down, shifting the car onto the next level of speed. They roared round twisty bends in the narrow country road, the car hugging the concrete as it sped through the lessening light. Cool night air streamed past, as Anton held his face up to the sky, revelling in its inky blackness and the millions of blinking stars. 'Winking angels' his Father had called them, passing on his fascination with the skies to the then nine-year-old Anton.

It was when Marty stood on the passenger seat, ''woo wooing' across the darkening landscape, that Anton realised what they were doing was crazy - he could kill someone! Pulling in at speed to the next flat open space he unfortunately misjudged the distance needed to bring the powerful machine to a halt. He closed his eyes as he heard the cracking of tree boughs and branches, and the skidding of wheels which seemed to go on forever. And, all the time, ignoring Anton's pleas to sit down, Marty was still doing his 'Titanic,' arms outstretched, leaning against the slanted windscreen of the open-top sports car.

'Oh, shit,' was the last thing he said, as the car dropped through the darkness, landing with a heavy, abrupt thud.

Chapter Twenty-Four

Annie hid her phone surreptitiously under the reception counter, as she heard Rachel coming back down the corridor from the treatment room.

'Too late, Missy, I saw that. Who were you trying to phone? It was Anton, wasn't it?' I tease. 'What happened to playing hard to get like you normally do?'

'Well, I did. For the last twenty-four hours, but now I'm just hopping mad. He could at least have had the courtesy to phone and say he didn't want to see me again. I hate this kind of rudeness.'

I burst out laughing and look at Annie. '*You* hate rudeness – that's rich, coming from you. The woman who chucks men aside as if they were empty crisp packets.'

'I don't know what you mean,' she says, a look of total puzzlement on her face.

'Mmmm – let me see,' I say, finger on my chin as if desperately trying to find an answer. 'The latest case was poor Rodders – called you for days, and he must surely have overrun his allowance of text messages – all to no avail. You were cruel and cold-hearted. Then, before him there was Brian – from the equestrian centre, remember? He even called in here with the most gorgeous bouquet of flowers? Which *I* thoroughly enjoyed in my sitting-room for weeks afterwards, since you didn't want them anywhere near you. I think Rodders had come on the scene by then? Before Brian there was ...need I go on?' I tease.

'Oh, Rache, I don't mean to be cruel and cold-hearted. But if there's no spark, what's the point in staying together. Well, that's what *I* think, anyway.'

'A spark? How can you know if there's a spark or not if you're only with the chap for five minutes! It takes a bit longer, you know, Annie,' I say gently. 'A bit more investment - emotional I mean, rather than physical – and not just jumping into bed before you even know the chap's second name. Sorry,' I say quickly, feeling that perhaps I've overstepped the mark. 'Don't mind me, Annie. I just do things differently. But, hey, who am I to give relationship advice, eh? Two failures – two *catastrophic failures* - by anyone's standards, in the last few years. So, don't listen to me. But, I don't want to see you hurt, Annie. You're a fabulous person. Wait until you find someone who recognizes that. Someone who doesn't just want you for that gorgeous body of yours – which *I'm soooo jealous of,'* I say to lighten the mood.

With that the phone rings. 'Norebridge Veterinary Practice' Annie answers in her most professional voice. 'Yes, this is Annie Carson. Yes …? Sorry, who's calling?' I see the blood drain from Annie's face and she stares into the distance as if in a trance, so I take the phone gently from her and explain who I am. They give me the details and, having ascertained that there is no danger to life or limb, I assure them that Annie will be at the hospital as soon as possible.

'Now you know why he didn't call,' I say, hugging Annie to me, trying to rub some life into her shocked body.

'He's been injured, Rachel – in a car crash. I need to get there.'

'Of course you do. It's almost lunch time, no-one due in until three o'clock. I'll take you there, let me just tell Henry. Oh, he's out on a call. Never mind, I'll pop in and let Aidan know, then we can head off. Don't worry, Annie. They said he wasn't in any danger, he'll be fine.'

'Yeah, yeah, I know, I know. It's just ....' and to my horror my friend and colleague, who goes through men like clean tights, bursts into tears burying her face in her hands.

'I'll be right back,' I say, hurrying down to the canteen, where I know Aidan is having a break and a sandwich.

§

I catch the tail end of a conversation as I walk in. 'I know, I know, Vee. But it's a bit early. I haven't found a place of my own yet. I can't just invite you to stay with people who are doing me a tremendous favour by letting me stay in their home. Well ... yes ... hang on a sec. Yes, Rachel?'

'Annie and I usually take our lunch here in the practice, take phone calls, etc. But there's a bit of a problem. Would you mind if we both went out for an hour or so? Shouldn't be any longer?'

'Sure, of course, don't worry about it. Anything I can help with?'

'No, no, it's fine. A friend of Annie's has been taken to hospital, and they've asked if she can pop in to see them. They need some things from home, that's all. I've checked the schedule - our next appointment isn't until three o'clock. We should be well back by then. Or, at least, I'll make sure *I'm* back.'

'Yes, sure. If there's any delay, just phone.'

'Great. Thanks, Aidan. See you later.'

And I grab my coat, and Annie by the arm, as she's still wandering about as if in a trance, and head out the door to see Anton Wickers-Stroppton, who has just regained consciousness in Norebridge General Hospital.

§

'I feel so guilty, Rachel. Thinking badly of him like that, when all the time he was lying comatose in the hospital.'

'Well, you weren't to know, were you. Anyway, you're here now. Let's see what he needs and how you can help.'

'You'll stay though, Rachel, won't you? Please, don't leave me on my own. I'm not good with hospitals. And ... anyway, why is he calling me? Why not his housekeeper, or chauffeur? His buddy, his Man Friday? He does everything for him, from what I can gather.'

'Who knows, Annie. But I'm a little confused. I thought you'd be delighted to be the one he called?'

'Well, it makes things a little … intense. I don't know him that well, I don't …'

'But here's your chance to get to know him. He's at his most vulnerable right now, Annie. I'm sure he could really do with a friend. Anyway, just take things as they come, alright? If I can help, you know you only have to ask.'

§

We knock tentatively on the door of private ward 502, and hear a weak 'Come in' from inside. I push Annie ahead of me and am overpowered as we enter by the scent of lilies, emanating from a glorious display of white and green leafed blooms, taking up most of the space on a bay window at the far end of a large room. I'm also bowled over by the presence of the man lying between the starched, pristine sheets of the raised bed.

I haven't seen him since he carried me into the surgery after my ankle episode and I didn't take too much notice of his physical attributes then, as Jack was still very much on my horizon. The man in front of me looks badly shaken and an angry gash runs down his right cheek, which has been stitched, but left uncovered. A large bruise, in vivid shades of red and black, covers the right side of his forehead and his right eye is closed and badly swollen. Numerous cuts and lacerations are dotted around his arms and hands. His pallid complexion is accentuated by the blackness of his long hair, which hangs lank and a little greasy down to his shoulders. But his arms, though scarred, are strong and toned. He may be white faced and frail looking, but there is no denying the natural beauty of this man. Nor his helplessness in his present situation.

'Hi, Annie,' he smiles. 'Thanks for coming. Oh, and Rachel – lovely to see you.'

And immediately, whatever about Annie, I am a huge fan of this legend who is Anton Wickers-Stroppton.

Chapter Twenty-Five

'What on earth happened, Anton?' Annie asks. She's feeling surprisingly overwhelmed by events with Anton, and while she happily complained when she thought he wasn't bothering to call her after their afternoon picnic, it's somehow unnerved her now that he *has* called. I think she's a little uncomfortable being put in the 'next-of-kin' position, finding herself here in the hospital preparing to run errands for someone she doesn't really know, and has only spent five hours of her life with. Annie doesn't do human sickness or frailty well.

'My fault entirely, total idiocy. No excuses, I was just being stupid – and drunk! All I'm thankful for is that it's only the two of us who got injured.'

'The two of you? Who … else …?' Annie hesitates. And I realise she's afraid of the answer. She doesn't want to hear he's had another woman in the car with him.

'Anton,' I interrupt. ' How can we help? What

would you like us to do? Do you have everything you need, or is there anything we can get for you? It's no problem. We'll be happy to help, won't we Annie?' I nudge my friend, who sits at the side of the bed, totally at a loss.

'Eh ... yes, of course.'

'Well, Brad, my Assistant, is away on holidays at the moment. I really don't want to spoil his trip. He hasn't been on a proper holiday for the last two years and he needs a good rest. Anyway, he's on the other side of the world, in Barbados. So, if you wouldn't mind, I need someone to go see the dogs. They won't have starved, there's a five-day feeder there, but they'll be distraught. They won't have seen me since yesterday. They're not used to that, they'll be frightened, not knowing what's happening. And ...

'Don't distress yourself, Anton,' I say, as I can see he's working himself up into a tizzy. 'It's not a problem at all. Do you yourself need anything from the house – books, toiletries?'

'Yes, please. I wouldn't mind having a shave. Although I probably look as if I've had one already – and a very bad one at that,' he smiles, a little lobsided. 'I'm sorry, I know it's a huge imposition. It's just ... I don't know anyone in the area well enough ...'

'Consider it done. Repayment for rescuing me the other day - except you didn't have to get yourself into this state to collect! I had every intention of inviting you out to dinner some evening.'

Anton laughs, but his smile quickly turns into a grimace as the pain kicks in. He's such a sorry sight, my heart goes to him and I'm determined, no matter what Annie thinks, that I'll help him out as much as I can. And Annie can just get over it! Although, she *does* seem a little mollified when Anton asks for some toiletries for his friend, Marty, who he tells us was in the car with him. Surprisingly, he escaped with only a few minor scratches and is due to be discharged home tomorrow.

§

Annie turns the key in the front door and leads the way into a vast, marble hallway. Our steps echo through the empty house, but I can hear barking from a long way away.

'Right, let's find the dogs,' Annie suggests. I agree, thinking it won't be too hard – a safe bet being to follow the howling that's building up to a crescendo from somewhere down to our left. We open two heavy, mahogany doors which reveal a long corridor, ending in a set of enormous patio doors at the far end, through which I can see a large, stone-paved seating area. A black wrought iron table sits in the centre, surrounded by eight or ten decorative chairs. The sun bathes the whole area in light, and I can see why the borders surrounding this sun trap are bursting with multi-coloured flowers and shrubs, their tiny heads warmed against a backdrop of golden Cotswold stone. But the frenzied barking is becoming more urgent and we hurry towards a door further down.

The smell which greets us is not pleasant. Obviously, while the dogs have not starved, they have been unable to get outside to relieve themselves. Fair play to the poor animals though, they have restricted their toilet requirements to a far corner of what is obviously a study. All four walls are covered in bookshelves, groaning under the weight of hundreds of tomes. A forest green carpet spans the large room and sun streams through two enormous sash windows, framed by heavy curtains, in rich colours of claret and peacock blue. The overall impression is one of wealth, but cosiness. Not what I would have expected at all from The Strop.

'Come on, lovelies,' I coax, as the two large Labradors bound up to greet us. Slobbering over us both for a few seconds, Lucius races past us, followed by a limpy Zebedee, looking very ungainly still in his discomfort. They both sit whimpering at two enormous patio doors. 'Poor things, they're bursting.' And they're hell bent on getting outside. Who can blame them? I run and unlock the doors, throwing them wide as I'm almost knocked in the stampede of the two dogs, belting out like prisoners released from incarceration. They barely make it out, when I spy them making large deposits on the lush, green lawn. Thank God, I think, just in time!

§

Allowing the dogs time to have a snuffle and a wander Annie decides we'll have a cup of tea while we're waiting. We head off towards the kitchen, which takes my breath away when I enter. It's anyone's dream, like something out of a *House Beautiful* or *Country Living* magazine and I can imagine the pleasure of working in such a wonderful space. Luckily, Annie remembers where the floor to ceiling fridge is, cleverly camouflaged behind bespoke Shaker-style doors. I fill and set the pillar box red kettle to boil, while Annie grabs two mugs from an overhead cabinet. She removes a plastic bottle of curdled milk from the fridge, along with a few slices of home-baked ham, green around the curling edges. Between us we check the sell-by dates of yoghurts, cheeses, and mouldy pork pies. By the time we leave, the fridge is practically empty and I make a mental note to restock before Anton is discharged from the hospital.

I sit at the central table, while Annie curls up on a blue and white chequered window-seat, overlooking a well-tended, sprawling garden. She can see Lucius enjoying his romp in the freedom, followed at a more sedate pace by Zebedee, circling a giant oak, its leaves already tinged with early signs of Autumn yellow. They chase each other around the edge of a small pond, it's surface half-covered with fleshy lily pads. Rubbing themselves joyously in a mound of freshly mown grass, they come to rest in the cool shelter of an apple tree.

'We should get his things together,' I suggest, 'and a second set for his friend as well.' It'd be too easy just to sit here, but we need to drop them off at the hospital, and get back to the clinic. 'Shall we go upstairs?'

Rinsing out our cups we dry them and replace them

in the overhead cupboard, then head back to the hallway and up a wide, carpeted staircase. A large stained-glass window is on the first landing, from where the stairs divides to left and right. This beautiful multi-facetted window throws light back down the stairs, like dappled rainbows bouncing off the surface of the walls and marble floor. There are six or seven doors staggered down the corridor.

'Where's Anton's bedroom?' I ask. Annie says nothing, and I smile to myself. 'Let's start with the first one here,' I suggest. Behind Rachel, Annie stems the response which is on the tip of her tongue, following Rachel down the corridor.

Having checked the first five rooms – all beautifully decorated bedrooms, some with a definite feminine slant, others leaning more to a man's taste – without success, we find what we're looking for in room six. And I understand why what is obviously the master bedroom is located at the end of the corridor. Its situation is to the back of the house, away from the noise of arriving cars or visitors. Overlooking the charming garden, it has two doors leading out onto a balcony, large enough to house a table and four leather campaign chairs protected from the elements by a generous overhang. I unlock the doors and step outside, to see a profusion of honeysuckle has intertwined itself along the balustrade and round the end of the building, blurring and softening the sharp corners of the house.

How gorgeous, I think, looking around and feeling the peace and tranquillity of Anton's home, but quickly remind myself what we're here for. Back in the room I see what looks like a wall-to-wall wardrobe at the far end. Opening the nearest door, I find it leads into a large walk-in dressing room and my jaw drops at its contents.

'Annie, Annie,' I shout, 'you really have to see this!' Annie joins me, and together we gaze at the rows and rows of mens clothes – black, black and more black! It's like being in a clothing store for men, a slightly bizarre clothing store, as most of the trousers are leather. There are rows of waistcoats - leather, while the top of the closet is home to hanger after hanger of T-shirts – also black.

'Must be hard to decide what to wear of a day, eh?' Annie jokes. 'I wouldn't have believed it if I hadn't seen it myself.'

'I suppose this is the wardrobe of the ultimate rock star,' I quip. 'How are we going to decide what to bring him? Mmmm – it's so difficult,' I laugh.

And we can't help it – as we double over with laughter, ending up sprawled over the thickly carpeted floor of the dressing room.

§

We've selected trousers, and rummage through his vast collection of T-shirts. This takes time as we're driven to reading the slogans printed on each one. Some are downright funny, others carry a darker message, which we imagine is probably a requirement of the heavy metal music world. At last, a unanimous decision is made, and we put our booty into a leather holdall, ready for delivery to the hospital for Anton and his friend, Marty.

Then an idea hits me and I realise Anton will also need some clean underwear. This seems a step too intimate for me, groping around in a total stranger's underwear drawer - so I happily delegate this chore to Annie.

'Oh, Rache, come on, don't be so prudish. A couple of pairs of socks and jocks and we're done. It's not like he's *in* them, is it?' And so I find myself riffling through the private drawer of a man I barely know for something to clothe his nether regions as he departs the hospital.

And this is where I get another surprise. I don't know why, but I had visions of Anton as a *Boss* or *Armani* skimpy 'briefs' man – worse – possibly even a thong man – all high legs and great attention to accentuating of family assets, perhaps. But, how wrong I am! Good old Anton – a drawer full of boxers from old reliable, *Marks & Spencers!* For some reason, this makes our sexy rock star all the more endearing to me.

I grab a few pairs and stuff them in with the other clothes. Then, looking at my watch I realise we've taken a lot more time than I thought we would. Quickly we head downstairs and chase Zebedee and Lucius round the garden in a vain attempt to bring them back inside. They're having none of it. Would you? They've been inside for the last twenty-four hours and have just tasted freedom again – there's no way they're going to allow anyone to lock them inside again.

'There's nothing for it, Annie, we'll have to take them to the surgery with us. I'm sure Henry won't mind, once we explain the circumstances to him. Otherwise, we could be here for the whole afternoon.'

So, we find two dog leads hanging just inside the back door, and once secured, pile the two excited animals onto the back seat of Annie's little Renault Clio.

Not happy campers – they howl and moan all the way to the Vets, but we have no option. Hopefully they'll behave once we're inside.

But this proves to be wishful thinking on my part. Neither Zebedee nor Lucius are content to sit outside in reception, mixing with the hoi polloi of the animal world. They begin to howl – not a low, signalling of their discontent – but a loud, non-stop yowling, like the keening of a banshee warning of an imminent death. It's quite unsettling for our other canine patients, one of which decides he's not hanging around for his sterilization and forces his owner to retreat, an alternative appointment arranged for several weeks later.

Both Henry and Aidan put up with the noise as long as possible. But, eventually, they too have had enough and find it impossible to concentrate on their work with the sounds of the world coming to an end emanating from our Reception area.

'Perhaps you'd better take them home, Annie,' I tentatively suggest.

'Home? To *my home* you mean? You can't be serious, Rachel. We're already falling over each other as it is. There's absolutely no room for these two monsters.'

'What about outside, maybe in a shed?'

'No, sorry, Rache. Full of my brothers' bikes and shit. No, honestly, I really couldn't.'

'Well, what are we to do with them, Annie? They belong to *your* friend, after all.' And I know, even while I'm asking, that Annie will have no part in the solution. I'm already racking my brains trying to think about where I can let them sleep. So, it's no surprise when I hear myself say: 'Well, OK then. I'll have them, but only for a night or two. Can you contact Anton and find out when he thinks he'll be discharged?'

Chapter Twenty-Six

The events of the last twenty-four hours have, at least, taken my mind off my own heartache. I haven't responded to the hundreds (at least, it seems like hundreds) of texts and phone calls from Jack. Hopefully, he's got the hint and will leave me alone. I need the space away from him, as I don't think I'm strong enough yet to withstand the pull of emotions that could so easily see me falling back into his arms, given half a chance. I think about him from the minute I wake up in the morning, to the time I go to bed at night. Work is a wonderful respite, forcing me to blank things from my mind during the day. But as soon as I'm home, and alone, everything comes flooding back. And I miss him so much.

If Annie had come to work and told me this had happened to her I would have been incensed. I would have ordered her to chuck whoever it was, and to 'go out and find someone who deserves you.' But here I am, in exactly that situation. And the thing I'm finding hardest to do is exactly what I would expect of Annie.

But, it seems tonight will not be a night of self-pity though, as I hear the howls from the kitchen, followed by a very determined scraping and head-butting of my flimsy kitchen door.

'OK, OK. I'm coming,' I shout, leaping up from the toilet and hurry, still pulling up pants and jeans, as I head towards the rising cacophany of sound. I barely open the door before I'm leapt upon, and thrown back against the doorframe. Licked and lashed by frenetic tongues and tails, I end up sitting on the kitchen floor as we lollop and writhe around, much to the pleasure of my canine guests.

'Right, let's get you monsters something to eat.' Somehow they know what I'm talking about, and shuffle and snuffle about me, as I prepare the tinned food I've brought from Anton's this afternoon. Just as I'm placing their bowls on the kitchen floor, there's a knock at the front door.

'Stay!' I command and leave them chomping away, as I head out to see who my unexpected visitor is. Opening the door, I'm surprised to see Aidan standing under the porch, as rain lashes the street behind him.

'Aidan, what a surprise! Is everything OK? Come

in.'

'Henry told me you'd been landed with someone's dogs and I was wondering if you needed a hand taking them for a walk. They're Labradors, I believe? Not the easiest to manage, if there are two of them, and pretty strong willed, Annie says.'

'Oh, that's really good of you,' I say gratefully. 'I was quaking at the thought and had decided the only way I could do it was to bring Zebedee first, and then Lucius. But it's great if I only have to go out once. It's pretty grim tonight, isn't it?'

'Yes, it certainly is. Will we get going, before the dark sets in?'

'Absolutely. I would have liked to have taken them before they'd eaten, but hey, at least they're getting a walk.' Aidan follows me into the kitchen, where both dogs jump up and greet him like an old friend.

'Come on, you horrors. Time you two took us for a walk, eh Rachel?'

§

There's a biting wind blowing as we head off towards the park, scene of my recent unfortunate accident. It seems like a lifetime away, so much has happened since.

There's only a handful of people out around the edge of the pond, mostly dog owners, walking briskly and doing their canine duty like ourselves. All sensible people are at home, feet up, sipping a glass of wine.

'How's your ankle, Rachel? Have you fully recovered?' You don't seem to be limping as much.'

'It's much better, hardly any pain at all. Just the occasional twinge. But there was no real damage done anyway. It was just my own stupidity, trying to get somewhere too quickly.' I smile.

'Yes, back to work, from what I hear. Nice to know you're so committed,' he teases and I can hear the smile in his words. 'But I'm sure neither Henry nor myself expects you to literally throw yourself headlong into your work!'

'Yes, well, luckily Anton was around. Otherwise, I'm not sure how I would have made it back. Speaking of Anton, these are his dogs, by the way. He's been hospitalized and there's no-one at his house to look after them.' As soon as they hear their master's name, they both start barking simultaneously, whipping around as if to see where he is. 'Sorry, boys,' I say, caressing Zebedee's velvety ears. He sits down on the cold ground, and looks up at me pitifully. 'Won't be long until he's home again, I hope,' as much for their sake as mine as I'm not sure how long I can look after these two great hulking creatures. They may be good-natured, but they certainly take some looking after. Henry kindly offered to have them at the surgery kennels, but they are all full at the moment, housing a variety of recuperating animals.

We head down to the banks of the river. It's cooler now as we walk and I can feel the wet seep into my flimsy shoes. The path is narrow, forcing us into a closeness that, under other circumstances could be a little strange. But it's peaceful, and we enjoy an easy silence. Then it's broken by the *brrr brrr* of Aidan's mobile phone. Without looking at the number he answers.

'Hello? Aidan Millington,' he says covering the mouthpiece. 'Sorry, probably Henry,' he mouths in my direction. 'Oh, hi … ' he says looking a little surprised. 'Eh … can I call you back? No, no. Everything's fine …Yeah, maybe twenty or thirty minutes? OK, talk to you then,' as he hangs up.

He doesn't refer to his call as we walk further, chatting about the changes and increased workload in the practice. Aidan is keen to get my opinion on whether or not we need to take on another assistant. 'Well, there has been a significant rise in the workload since you came,' I explain, 'and it has become a little difficult for both Annie and myself to assist in surgery, *and* keep up with the additional administration. Neither of us is complaining, we're quite happy to keep things as they are, certainly for the moment. But we do have concerns that in time, if things continue to grow, we might not be able to reach on everything. And that's when things get overlooked. We've talked about it and feel it might be a good idea to take someone on, just on a part-time basis at the moment. We don't feel the practice needs another full-time person. Well and good if the business demands it, then later they could go on to full-time employment.'

Aidan nods as he listens and I continue 'This would be a good time to take someone on, as we'd still have time to train them in well. If we wait until later, when we're all snowed under, it would be a little unfair to expect them to perform to standards, if we haven't given them the proper training time in the first place. Does that make sense to you?'

'Absolutely, and I'm inclined to agree with you. From what I've seen from recent figures, from a financial point we can well afford another person - parttime, as you say. And we can see how it goes from there. Great, Rachel. I'm glad we had the chance to talk that over. Can we leave it to you to sort out the new recruit?

'Sure. Between Annie and myself we'll take care of it. And, I'd like to say Aidan, it's great having you here. It's made Henry's life much easier, he was run ragged before you came. *And,* I'd also like to say I'm sorry if I was a little apprehensive at first. I was afraid Henry would be taken advantage of. But I know now, you wouldn't do that. And, he's very happy with the way things have panned out.'

'How could anyone take advantage of Henry? He's an absolutely genuine bloke. And, it's been great for me too - it's changed my life. Or at least changed the direction of my life.' He looks into the distance as if he's talking to himself. 'Yes, changed the direction of my life. But, well, I have other things I need to do to keep that change on track.'

And, somehow, I get the impression he's referring to that phone call.

Chapter Twenty-Seven

Down south, Vee replaced the phone in its cradle, annoyed. What was going on? Why couldn't Aidan talk when she phoned? It sounded as if he was out and about and it was the second time in as many days that he'd told her he'd call her back. She was also convinced she'd heard a woman's voice in the background. She didn't want to push but, they had four years of history together, surely it wasn't out of order to want to know what was happening.

She'd been working late at the office trying to tie up some loose ends on a client's account. Deciding she'd had enough she made preparations to head home. If Aidan didn't phone later she'd give him a call before she went to bed. Grabbing her coat and bag, she switched out the light and closed the office door. Walking down the corridor to the lift, she met Grayson, her boss.

'Working late too, I see,' he smiled at Vee.

'Yes, just finishing off the Dodson Supermarket account. It's been a bit complicated, and we skimmed over a few details the last time we met with them. But, I noticed one or two things that could jump up and bite us later, if we don't sort them out now. It's not a big deal, but I'm happier now, knowing I've got them sorted. What about you?'

'Well, Veronica, I'm happy to say the reason for my late working is I've just finalised a new client for us. And this *is* rather a big deal. Do you remember the two German's who - listen, are you heading straight home? Have you time for a drink, and I can fill you in? Unless you have other plans?'

Vee was looking forward to a nice relaxing bath, scented candles lighting around the bathroom. But, who was she to refuse the Managing Director.

'Nothing I can't do later. Sure,' she said. 'I'll just nip to the Ladies and follow you to … where are you heading?'

'Why don't I meet you at The Lion's Head? It shouldn't be too busy at this time. Most of the office crowd will have left already.'

'Great. Give me ten minutes and I'll be there.'

§

She was glad she'd worn her black fitted jacket with

the narrow satin reveres, over her black pencil skirt. A lime green scoop-necked Pima t-shirt and double silver chain, gave it a casual but elegant look, high stilettos adding an air of sexiness to the outfit. But her Burberry briefcase left no-one in doubt she was a professional woman, someone to be taken seriously. In the bathroom, she looked critically at the face reflected in the oval mirror. Not bad, she thought – perhaps just the slightest bit on the thin side, but didn't someone say a woman could never be too rich or too thin? Blonde straight hair still hung thickly to her shoulders and her eyes were highlighted to perfection by cloudy grey eyeshadow. Her lips, also slightly on the thin side, were cleverly enhanced by a plumping serum, and, as always, she'd chosen her lipstick carefully – *Shocking Red*, luscious and full. To Vee's mind she looked the wrong side of forty, but to the casual observer, she could be the right side of thirty-five.

Flicking a stray clutch of hair into place, Vee grabbed her briefcase and headed out the door. Her boss was already sitting and waiting for her as she entered The Lion's Head. Contrary to what Grayson expected it was still busy with after-work drinkers, so Vee had to push her way through the crowd to join him. It didn't escape his notice how several men turned and watched Vee as she made her way over to his table. Once she was seated, Grayson headed to the bar and ordered her drink. It took some time before he returned with her white wine.

'Whew! What's going on? Didn't expect it to be so crowded.'

'I imagine it's the Food & Wine Exhibition that's on, finishes tomorrow afternoon.'

'Ah, I see. Well, if it's OK with you we'll stay here?' As Vee nodded her agreement, Grayson continued their conversation regarding the new German client, regaling her with amusing anecdotes of his trip to Munich and the many misunderstandings, due to his inability to speak, or understand, the language. 'We have our next meeting with them in two weeks. But I'm pushing for it to be here in our offices. No misunderstandings then, eh?' he laughed.

§

Later that evening Vee ran her longed-for bath, adding a few drops of her favourite relaxing lavender oils. Lying in the soothing water she thought seriously about her relationship with Aidan. Although they'd parted happily - and temporarily - Vee felt as if things were slipping away from her. Aidan seemed somewhat distracted since he'd been in Norebridge.

Up to the time he'd taken on that new job things had been on course, as Vee saw it. A course that would end naturally in their marriage and she was sure Aidan felt the same. And then ... bloody Norebridge happened. How she hated that name. She wished he'd never seen the advertisement, but he had, and now she felt things - and Aidan - needed to be brought back on track. No more waiting about, she decided. She felt better having made the decision, and slid out of the cooling water. Rubbing her skin vigorously with a thick fluffy white towel, Vee then applied her mango body mousse. She looked critically at her nakedness in the full-length mirror, appraising the still pert breasts, slim waist and long legs. Satisfied, she put on her purple silk nightdress, savouring the swoosh of softness as it fell to her ankles. Ten minutes later, holding a glass of red wine Vee dialled Aidan's mobile and felt herself relaxing as she heard his familiar voice.

'Hello, darling, how are you? Do you have time to talk, at last?' she couldn't help the slight tone of sarcasm creeping into her voice.

And it didn't go unnoticed by Aidan, who sighed heavily, although behind his hand so Vee wouldn't hear it. 'Hi, Vee. Lovely to hear your voice. How are things? Everything going well back home?' Vee was pleased to hear him refer to their place as 'home.' Perhaps things weren't as bad as she imagined.

§

They spent a good twenty minutes on the phone, at the end of which Vee was in high spirits, and Aidan had to admit that he'd missed her. He also realised he'd been unfair to her. She was still living their old life, while he'd taken on this new life, which was exciting and challenging - both professionally and socially – and he was thoroughly enjoying his new 'home' with Henry and his eccentric mother. He found himself looking forward to going home of an evening, to sit in front of a roaring fire and enjoy a nice glass of wine with Mrs. Donaldson, which had become their nightly routine. He enjoyed hearing of her life before the death of Henry's father. They'd been a devoted couple it seemed, deeply in love and, as Henry told him later, he was amazed to realise that his mother still felt the loss of her beloved Theo so acutely. He didn't know, and felt slightly ashamed that it took a total stranger to bring out the stories he heard her recount to Aidan – a willing and appreciative listener.

Aidan also took great pleasure in his new working life. The partnership with Henry suited him well, and he considered himself lucky to have him as his friend. Their client list had grown substantially, and he felt he'd settled in well and was now an asset to the practice.

There was only one unsettling thing on the horizon. He was slightly troubled by his growing attraction for Rachel, and constantly had to remind himself that they were colleagues first and last. Of course, he would never do or say anything untoward, but his heart had a funny way of racing when she was near. Either that, or his blood pressure was beginning to be troublesome, he smiled to himself. But he knew any thought of Rachel was nonsense. From what he gathered she was biding her time until her feckless lover saw the error of his ways and came running back to her.

And, there was Vee - they'd been together now for four years. He'd never been unfaithful to her and he had no intention of starting now. She deserved his loyalty, and he made up his mind that minute, she would have it. He'd also give serious thought to finding his own place. It was time, and that way he could concentrate on having

Vee come to visit which, he was sure, was the thing she really wanted. It would make her feel more secure in their relationship. The thought of leaving the comfort of Henry's home made him a little sad, but he felt it was the best for him and Vee.

Chapter Twenty-Eight

Annie checked her watch, finished putting the information into Buster's file, and replaced it in the filing cabinet. Locking the drawer, she hid the key under the mouse pad, and headed to the cloakroom. Replacing her work clothes with a short black skirt, red body-hugging sweater, black tights and flat, black leather biker boots, she grabbed her shoulder bag and headed down the corridor towards the car park.

'Rachel, I'm off. Sure you can't come with me?' she asked. 'Anton did say for both of us to come.'

'No, really, Annie. I have things I want to get done at home. Anyway, I certainly don't want to play gooseberry! This is the first time you've seen Anton since he came out of hospital. But, give me a call if you're going to be late in tomorrow' I tease.

'Actually, I hope to be in bed tonight by ten – if not, I'm going home!' she laughed. I can only smile to myself at her self-confidence. *Oh, Anton, do you really know what you're letting yourself in for.*

Then my thoughts turn to my own unexpected evening. I received a text today from Jack. He's been texting and texting and I've been ignoring and ignoring. But, today, he sent one insisting that he'd like to call round to the house, desperate to talk. Otherwise, he intimated, he'd have no option but to call into the surgery. Reluctantly, I agreed as I feel at least if we speak and get it over with, there'll be no more reason for him to pester me in the future. And, more importantly, I'm feeling a little stronger. I feel I can deal with Jack now – for the last time.

§

I just have time for a shower when the doorbell rings. Jack's early. I swipe on a covering of lipstick. Nothing to say I can't look my best, let him know what he's missing, is there? I rush down the stairs, pleased that Jack hasn't taken the liberty of using his key. But as I open the door I'm surprised to see Aidan standing there.

'Sorry to drop around unannounced, Rachel. I was wondering if we could discuss our schedule for tomorrow?' I'm so taken aback that I just move aside, which he takes as an invitation to come in. 'Checking the files before I left the office, I see there is the possibility of complications with one of the procedures, and I think it's best if we switch them round. That way, I'll have time to monitor for a few hours longer tomorrow evening.'

'Yes, of course, Aidan. If you tell me which ones, I'll get on to the owners tonight and rearrange.'

Together, we head into the sitting room and sit down, side-by-side on the sofa. Aidan takes some files from his briefcase and we scrutinize the schedule, adjusting the times allowed for each particular case, until we have what we feel is the correct order. As we are finishing our discussion I am astonished to hear the front door open and, before I can react, Jack stands in the doorway of the sitting-room. Aidan stands, and I have no option but to introduce them to each other.

'Jack, this is Aidan. New partner in the veterinary practice. Aidan, this is Jack ...'

'Rachel's ... boyfriend,' I hear Jack say.

Now is not the time for explanations. Nor is Aidan one to whom I feel the need to explain myself. So I say nothing, and let Jack's declaration of possession go unchallenged. Aidan excuses himself and heads for the door. I go with him, assuring him that I will telephone the two owners and rearrange as required. When I come back Jack is sitting on the sofa, but jumps up when I enter the room.

'Am I? Your boyfriend, I mean? I notice you didn't deny it,' he says. 'And I love you so, so much, Rachel. Please believe me.'

My heart is thumping in my chest and the tummy rumblings are back, making me feel dizzy and a little faint. I can't help myself, as I look at Jack's handsome face, his dark eyes pleading with me. Everything is wiped out in an instant – the desperate weeks of loneliness and heartache, the feeling that my life was over. Even the tiny nagging voice I hear, I dismiss without a further thought. And I go to him, into the circle of his outstretched arms, which feel so familiar, the smell of him so comforting.

His hands caress me – my back, massaging the tightness of my neck and shoulders. He slides his hands down my arms, and hugs me to him and I don't stop him when his fingers find the half-open zip on my fleecy top. I hear someone moan as his thumb finds my nipple, straining through the thin fabric of my cami top. I draw away from him, trying to gain some safe distance between us.

'Jack, I don't think …'

'Oh, Rachel, please. I can't bear to be without you. I've really messed up, I know. But, it's you I want – please believe me.'

I look at his so-familiar face. His smell assaults my senses and I close my eyes, inhaling him, delighting in his nearness. Roughly, he pulls me to him, enveloping me in his warmth, as he gently kisses my eyes, my neck, my mouth – long, lingering kisses that I've missed so much. Slowly, he takes my hand and I don't resist as we head upstairs to the bedroom. We undress each other, and it all feels so right. His fingers caress the places he knows I love, and he hasn't forgotten the things I love him to do. By the time he enters me I am tingling with anticipation and desire. It's over too soon and this time it's Jack who moans, as he shudders and then lies still over me.

'Oh, God, Rachel. I've missed you so much. *So much.*'

'I know, Jack. I've missed you too. More than I can say.'

'I'm so glad to be back. So glad you *want* me back.'

And I snuggle into the crook of Jack's arm - he's home, *we're* home. Loads of questions are forming in my mind, but I push them aside, they can wait for another time. I'm drowsy with sleep and fulfilment, and for the first time in ages sleep through the entire night, basking in this sense of being safe and secure again, and in the knowledge that the man I love has come back.

Chapter Twenty-Nine

It's only as I'm on my way into work this morning that I remember. Oh, bugger! I haven't spoken with the owners about the change in surgery times today. I completely forgot. With a bit of luck, I'll have time to do it before we start. Hopefully, they won't have left home yet. But, with a niggle of anxiety I also notice that Annie's car is *not* in the car park. Oh, hell! It looks like I'm not the only one who had a good night last night.

'Morning, Rachel. Let's get started,' Aidan meets me in the hallway. He seems a bit bad-tempered, but I don't have time to wonder about it – I need to speak with these owners. But, just as I'm trying to scoot into the office and do so, he asks the question I don't want to hear. 'Are the owners OK with the change in schedule?'

'Eh ... Aidan, actually I forgot to phone them last night. I ... eh, was just a little bit busy and it completely slipped my mind. But I'm just about to phone them now. Hopefully, they won't have left ...'

'Rachel, your personal life belongs at home, not

here in the office,' he cuts me off rudely. 'Whatever you got up to last night shouldn't impinge on your working life, if you don't mind me saying so.' Aidan has a look about him that I haven't seen before. I'm annoyed, mostly with myself for forgetting, but that's beside the point. And, because I feel guilty, I go on the attack.

'Well, actually I do mind, Aidan. I was prepared to phone those people last night – outside of my working time, for which you pay me – but in *my* personal time, for which you *do not* pay me. I am really sorry I forgot. But, if you've finished I'll go and do it now!' I turn on my heel and head into the office, slamming the door as I go.

How dare he! Both Annie and I stay on any evening our animals needs to be monitored, without wanting anything extra for it. We do it because we care about them and, one or sometimes even both of us, have been known to drop into the clinic at the most un-Godly hour, if an animal has had a particularly complicated operation or procedure. Henry lives outside town, and I've always insisted, unless the patient needs the expert knowledge of a vet, that I'm happy to drop in during the late evening, during the night or early morning. It's only a ten-minute walk for me. And, I love to do it anyway. Our animals are not just four-legged patients to us, we get to know their characters, their little foibles. Who the hell does he think he is! Also, where the hell is Annie? Ten, fifteen minutes late is one thing, but not to show at all – and for the second time? *Not this morning, Annie, please.*

The reception bell rings as I'm dialling the first owner. Dropping the phone, I head out of the office.

'Morning, Mr. Henderson. How's Timmy today?' I nod towards the wicker basket which I know holds the old man's tortoise. It's a race between them, as to who will shed his mortal coil first. And this is Mr. Henderson's biggest worry - who will look after Timmy if anything happens to him. I happen to know that Henry has decided Timmy will become a 'ward' of the practice, should this occur. And today is the day he's going to put Mr. Henderson's mind at rest. The poor man has begun to get agitated lately when he brings the matter up. 'Henry's ready for you. Would you like to come with me?' I stroll slowly down the corridor with the elderly gentleman, chatting about the changing weather, until we arrive at Consulting Room 2. Henry stands up from behind his desk, hand outstretched to Mr.

Henderson.

'Good morning, Sir,' he greets the veteran Spitfire pilot. The old man loves his visits to the surgery. It constitutes his entire social life outside his home. I'll make them a cup of tea, with some chocolate biscuits, and leave them to chat. We never schedule another appointment for an hour. This is another reason I love Henry. Sometimes Timmy gets five or six minutes attention, the rest is put aside entirely for Mr. Henderson's benefit. The practice certainly gets no financial benefit from his visits. I can't remember the last time we sent him a bill. But every time as he leaves, Mr. Henderson reminds us to let him have his bill. And each time Henry confirms that he will.

I've managed to contact the first owner and he's quite happy to switch appointments. However, the second one proves to be more problematic. I've tried his landline several times, but to no avail, and the elderly man doesn't have a mobile. Then, just when I'm becoming desperate, an idea comes to me.

§

'Hello?' a man's voice answers after the second ring.

'Hi Anton? It's Rachel here. Sorry to bother you,

but I was wondering if Annie was there? And before you think this is a little cheeky of me, I have an emergency here and need her help.'

'Sorry, Rachel. No, she's not here. But is there anything I can do?' My stomach drops. Oh, God no, not now. I really need to get this sorted with the minimum of fuss. Otherwise I won't be able to look that arrogant so-and-so in the eye. He'll think I'm more interested in my personal life. Well, my sex life, really, which when I think about it has been like a desert with no oasis in sight - until last night! And while it really is none of his business, this sort of makes it his business - I've messed up workwise. He's absolutely right – and I hate the fact that he is. But I'm desperate, so I tell Anton the situation.

'And Mr. Clooney – the second client who now needs to come in first – lives about a mile further along your road. I wanted Annie to pop along and let him know we need to change his appointment. But, don't worry, Anton. I'll keep trying his phone. Hopefully, he's just out around the yard.'

'Rachel, don't worry. I'll pop up there myself and phone you back to let you know the situation.'

Relief floods through me at his kindness. This will take me out of a hole. I could kiss him!

§

And I do, an hour and a half later as he deposits old Mr. Clooney on a plastic chair with Chubbs, his aging, and sometimes incontinent sheep dog. I hug Anton, and plant a great big kiss on his cheek, just as Arrogant Aidan steps out of his office. For the second time that day I warrant a look that would stop a clock.

'Don't let me dampen your ardour,' I hear the snide comment, as does Anton.

'Spoilsport,' I hear Anton throw back, as he gives me a wicked wink. 'Maybe we could carry on later, Rachel? Again, the mischievous wink, which only Mr. Clooney can see. He grins widely, egging Anton on.

'If you don't, young man, *I'll* try my hand with the lovely Rachel,' he laughs. I pretend to be shocked and strut back into my office. Anton comes to the door, saying quietly 'His car wouldn't start, that's what he was doing outside in the yard. I've a few things to do around town, so what time will I pick him up?'

'Anton, you're an absolute angel. You don't know the hole you're getting me out of. I owe you – big time!'

'Oh, hole extraction is just one of my many talents,' he grins. ' And, you don't owe me anything, Rachel - happy to oblige. I was coming into town anyway, to visit the pharmacy and the bank. So, if I pick Mr. Clooney up in two hours? We're going for a pint in The Maiden's Arms out near us. I don't think he's looking forward to going home to an empty house, since Chubbs is going to be kept here overnight. Anyway, see you then.' I watch as he limps towards the door. He is slightly unsteady on his feet after his car crash, which makes me all the more grateful for his help.

It's only when he's gone I realise I've forgotten to ask about Annie. And, *he* hasn't mentioned her either. How strange!

§

But thirty minutes later she arrives into the surgery. 'Hi Rache, sorry, I'm late, I got ...'

'Never mind that now, Annie. We're swamped – two procedures this morning, and three walk-ins. Can you just take over the registration? I need to get back in to assist Henry. When you're finished maybe you could go to Aidan - he'll need some help too.' I'm relieved I don't have to assist him, as I'm still very cross with him over his comment this morning. I don't get to take a break for the next two hours, at which stage I see Mr. Clooney has left to have his pint with Anton.

And, I make up my mind, it's definitely time to look for our part-timer.

Chapter Thirty

I'm trying to find something to wear that will scream Boss, Confidence and Professionalism, as I'm holding interviews today for our new part-timer, and hope to short list two or three people from today's offering. I'll then have Annie sit in with me, to have a second opinion on the final candidate. Neither Henry nor Aidan want to be involved and have left the choice to me. But I do want to have Annie's input for two reasons – firstly, I want her to feel included, and, secondly, I feel it will be easier for her to work with someone she's had a hand in choosing. Having finally chosen a fitted navy suit with a cream polka-dot blouse I head into the office.

'Well, no doubting who's in charge here today,' Annie teases as I enter the Reception. 'What time are the victims ... I mean, applicants, arriving?'

'First one at ten. Time for a cup of coffee before she arrives though, I'm dying for one. Didn't have any breakfast before I left.' I head into the kitchen and flick the kettle on, as Annie comes hot on my heels.

'We didn't get a chance to have a chat yesterday, Rache. I hear Anton was here?'

'Yes, he brought Mr. Clooney in, as his car had broken down. There was a bit of confusion about two appointments which Aidan wanted to put in reverse order. To be honest, it was my fault. I'd forgotten to phone them the night before. I was a ... bit ... distracted. But never mind me – what about you? What was going on? I thought you were at Anton's, that's why I called his house. If you weren't there, where ...?' I stop mid-sentence as Aidan comes into the kitchen.

'Everything OK for the interviews today, Rachel?' he asks. I'm still peeved with him as I really feel he overstepped the mark.

'Yes, fine thanks,' I reply, continuing to make my tea.

'What does our schedule look like this morning, Annie?' he asks. I busy myself with my task, as they discuss the order of work. After a few minutes Aidan heads back to his office.

§

Sally is a bright, articulate twenty-five-year old – pity about the heavy make-up, which looks as if it's been trowelled on, albeit by a very talented plasterer. I'd love to see her without it as I'm sure she doesn't need it. High cheekbones, accentuated by more than a smattering of blusher, draw attention to her almond shaped eyes. But eyebrows, plucked to extinction, make her long, false eyelashes look all the more ... false. She looks rather bizarre, which is a pity, as she has reasonable experience and I feel could probably respond well to training. At present, she's working at a cosmetics counter in a large store about twenty miles away and is desperate to get back to an office environment. Under other circumstances I'd love to have a heart-to-heart with Sally. She seems a decent sort.

Renee is definitely not for us. Would she have to work after five; would she have to work on Saturdays, and would it be possible for her to have a full hour of solitude for lunch as she likes to meditate – were the uppermost questions in her mind. No interest in what kind of animals we deal with, how many work in the clinic, or anything relating to the clinic itself. So, no surprise there then.

I'm finding interviewing thirsty work, so hope for a quick cup of coffee before meeting the next person. I slip off to the kitchen and make one and as I'm adding milk I hear a bit of a kerfuffle out in reception - loud, insistent barking. I'm just about to go out and see what it's all about when the barking stops, followed by silence. I presume Annie's out there restoring order, so I take my cuppa and head back to my office. As I walk down the corridor noise and turmoil break out again, when I hear a strange voice command someone to 'SIT! and it's not Annie's voice. Then the telephone rings and is answered almost immediately. Curiosity gets the better of me and I sneak back to listen at the door of Reception.

'No, I'm afraid they're both tied up at the moment,' I hear a voice say. 'But, if you'd like to give me your name and a number I'll have them telephone you back, as soon as they're free. Yes, yes, absolutely. Finley, you said? And may I ask what it's in connection with? Prissy ... Oh, poor thing. No, no, don't worry, Mrs. Finley, someone will call you back as soon as possible. You're welcome. Yes, yes, I've got it – nine-two-one-six-five-two. And the area code? Right ... Yes, thank you. Bye now.'

I look around the corner and see a very slightly overweight, middle-aged lady, stylishly dressed, with an impeccable grey bob hairstyle. She's bent over the desk, writing on the notepad. When she's finished, she looks over the top of the high reception counter at an enormous Great Dane, which sits obediently in the middle of the room, never taking its eyes off hers.

'He's never done that for me,' says the owner.

'Well, my Dad, Lord have mercy on him, was a great believer in discipline – whether for children, animals or any kind of motorized machine. We all learned to 'sit' for him. And he firmly believed all it took was one strike of the hand – in the air and facing the unruly child or animal – not anywhere else.'

'Well, I'll certainly try that from now on ' Hearing his master's voice the huge animal bounded over towards him, barking loudly again. Immediately, the owner held up his hand, palm facing his pet, and shouted 'SIT!' To his amazement, Buster came to a screeching halt, planting his heavy nether quarters on the shiny, linoleum floor. A large smile lit up the old man's face, crinkling his heavy-lidded eyes.

The Daughter of the Disciplinarian of Dogs, Children and Motorized Machines looks up and sees me.

'Are you Rachel, or Annie?' she asks, no hint of embarrassment at answering someone else's phone. 'That was a Mrs. Finley. Needs someone to give her a call as soon as possible. There's a problem with Prissy. She sounds very worried.'

'Thank you, yes, I'm Rachel. You must be Maura? Would you like a tea, coffee?'

'That'd be great. Can I give you a hand?' So I take Maura to the kitchen, and show her where things are. I think I've already made up my mind that she's the one for us – no nonsense, no hysterics, just common sense, a get-on-with-it attitude.

As we start our interview Maura apologies. 'I really hope you didn't mind me answering your phone. But the old man said you were both very busy, so I slid into proactive mode. Habit, I suppose. But I presumed that's why you advertised for extra staff?'

'Yes, we've a new partner now, which has generated more work. Annie and I've motored along for a while, but I'd rather have an extra pair of hands now, before we're overrun and things get too much. So, Maura, would you like to tell me something about yourself?'

I listen to Maura's tale, similar to that of thousands of middle-aged women. Married for thirty years, happily it seems, then shocked into the reality of sudden widowhood, eight years ago at the age of forty-four. A hit-and-run driver, who was never caught. Originally from Ireland, she met her husband while he was still in medical school. They'd run away together to England as soon as she'd found out she was pregnant. The early eighties, while a time of change in Ireland, was still not a time for a single girl to be pregnant and proud, especially in a small, rural village in the West. They'd married in a register office in London as soon as they could. Three weeks later Maura lost her baby. She tells her story without any sign of self-pity or rancour, ending with a comment about other people who have much worse to suffer in their lives.

Maura is quite open about her lack of any particular experience, or specialised knowledge. But, she insists, she's a practical person who can see what needs to be done in most situations, and does it. She's completed a computer course as a mature student, and has a knowledge of manual accounts up to profit and loss level. I have no doubt she'd be an asset to any office.

'Would you mind hanging on for a few minutes, Maura? I'd like you to meet my colleague, Annie.'

'Yes, of course, I'd be happy to.'

§

'Yeah, she seems really nice. Solid, if you know what I

mean. Motherly, but not in an old way. And, I certainly wouldn't have guessed her to be fifty-two – well-kept for her age, don't you think, Rache?' We're sitting comfortably beside a huge log fire in the pub and I'm pleased that Annie shares my view. Maura starts work on Monday.

'So, come on then, what had you so distracted this morning? We haven't had a chance to chat. And, I'm *dying* to know. Come on – spill!'

I've been dreading this, but it had to happen sooner or later. 'I know you're not going to be happy, Annie. But I need to give it a try. I mean, another try. So does he, and he's really mixed up about the ...'

'Please, Rachel,' she says, holding her hand up, 'tell me you're not talking about who I think you are. Not Jack. Please tell me he's not back?'

'Listen, Annie. He arrived at the house the night before last and we talked for hours. He's explained how things happened with ... you know. He's devastated about us. He wants us to give it another go. And ...'

'And you've just gone along with it. *Rachel,* have you gone crackers? That bastard had it off – several times, I'm sure – with some blonde bombshell in the States. Suddenly, he appears on your doorstep, apologizes, and you're all luvvy duvvy again? I don't believe you. But I *would* be interested in hearing his explanation about how he was forced – bound, battered and bruised supposedly – into infidelity. I really would. What did he say, come on, Rachel. Convince me!' Annie sits, arms folded, defiance and provocation written all over her.

'I'm not sure I need to, Annie,' I say lamely. 'It's between Jack and me. If I can accept his explanation, it doesn't matter if you don't. Anyway, he's cut ties with her and requested someone else take over the account in the States. Obviously, he'll be there for the birth, and make regular payments for ...'

'There's a *baby?* Rachel, you really haven't thought this through, have you?' Annie says, dangerously quiet, eyes flashing.

Oh, God, I could cut my tongue out! I'd forgotten Annie didn't know about the baby. I wasn't exactly lying to her. Well, I was, I suppose, but more by omission than actually lying. And I instantly recognize that I was just so ashamed. It was enough that he'd dumped me. I couldn't bring myself to lay bare every sordid detail of his affair. But I had every intention of telling Annie at some stage, I just never got around to it.

She's my best friend - I *would* have told her.

But Annie doesn't see it that way. She looks at me as if I'm a stranger, the hurt visible on her lovely face. 'This is not like you, Rachel. What about *her?* He's just going to walk away from her now? And you think that's OK? No, not you, Rachel. Look at yourself in the mirror and tell me you like what you see at this moment. I can't believe you, I thought I knew you,' she says, shaking her head in disbelief. At the same time she grabs her bag and coat and heads for the door.

I may have Jack back, but I think I've just lost my best friend.

Chapter Thirty-One

I smell the delicious aroma of chicken cooking as I let myself in and can hear Jack clattering around in the kitchen. I hesitate in the hallway, leaning my head against the wall. I'm upset about Annie, she's been a very good friend to me and, inexplicably, I feel as if I've somehow betrayed her. I hope we can talk tomorrow.

'Hi, sweetheart,' Jack calls from the kitchen. 'Dinner's nearly ready, hope you're hungry. It's your favourite – chicken, white wine and tarragon.'

'Sounds great, Jack,' I answer. 'I'll just pop up and change. Won't be a minute.'

Five minutes later I join him in the sitting room. He's on the couch, and opens his arms to me and I willingly join him. I feel safe here. Secure? – maybe not quite, not any more. But I'm sure that'll come back, with time. Things are bound to be a little rocky after all we've been through.

'I love you, Rachel, so much. I don't know how I could have been so stupid.' He holds my face in his hands, stroking my cheeks with his thumbs. Tears well up in his eyes, and he hugs me to him. 'Tell me you've forgiven me. We're OK, aren't we?'

'Yes, Jack. Of course we are. It'll take a little time, I'm sure, to get back to where we were. But if it's what we both want?' I say.

'It is, Rache, it is. You're the best thing that's ever happened to me. I can't believe I put all that in jeopardy, for a quick fling, for ...'

'Don't Jack. Not tonight, please. Shouldn't you be looking after that chicken?' I tease.

Jack jumps up and hurries into the kitchen. I can hear him yank the oven door open and it makes me smile. But my smile fades slowly, as I wonder why am I not overjoyed? The man I love has come back, has decided that he can't live without me, and is in my kitchen cooking my favourite dinner. Some women would be delirious with happiness. Perhaps the hurt runs deeper than I've acknowledged. Maybe it'll take a while longer to get my head round Jack's cheating. To be able to look at it, accept it for what it was – a one-off lapse in judgement – and move on, *together*.

We enjoy a scrumptious dinner with a delicious bottle of white wine. Jack refuses to let me even take my plate back out to the kitchen. He's insistent that tonight I'm going to put my feet up and do absolutely nothing, determined to spoil me.

Later, we settle down on the couch with the last of our wine and tune in to watch '*Great Canal Journeys of Britain*' with Prunella Scales and her fellow-thespian husband, Timothy West. I remark on how great they are together, even after being married for so many years.

'They seem to get along so well,' I say, 'rubbing along together like two people who love each other deeply.' Jack nods his agreement, and I listen, full of admiration to Prunella as she describes her illness and its effects on her day-to-day life. She says her husband picks up the slack so they still operate as a whole. How courageous! For an actor who memorised lengthy scripts without difficulty, to find herself unable to remember simple everyday words, must be incredibly frustrating. But she's still bubbly, laughing at her own shortcomings, secure in the knowledge that her husband is there for her. He's her rock.

Suddenly, I feel sadness and uncertainty, because I'm not sure that Jack would be there for me like that and immediately I'm ashamed of myself, and push the thought aside. He's come back, hasn't he? He's killing me with kindness, I think, smiling at the thought of it, as I know it won't last – he really detests cooking! But he's doing his best. And I make up my mind that I at least owe it to him to give him another chance.

§

There's a coolness between Annie and me the next day. Also, there's a coolness between Aidan and me. I begin to wonder what's happening. Never before have I been around such conflict. I get along with most people and usually, even in difficult situations, find a way of dealing with them in a civilised and polite manner. But, here I am, in an environment of unfamiliar negativity, doing whatever I can to avoid my best friend, and a man who is actually my boss.

And, the common denominator is Jack. Well, they'll just have to deal with it, I think to myself. I've never interfered with Annie's love life, so she can just back off now. This is *my* life, and I'm determined that, for once, I'm putting my own happiness first. And Annie will just have to get over herself.

And as for Mr. Aidan-busybody – I may work for him, but he doesn't own me. And my love life certainly has nothing to do with him. So *Back Off* to him too!

§

I'm sitting at the Reception desk, updating the files of those clients due in today when the door opens and a woman breezes in. She's as slim as I've always wanted to be, with perfectly coiffed blonde hair hanging straight down to her shoulders, and her make-up is flawless. Only another woman would know that she actually *is* wearing any. To a man she probably looks all natural and sunny. A lime green coat shows off her enviable figure. It falls just below her knees, displaying a pair of very well-toned legs and feet encased in black, patent stilettos. But as she approaches the desk I pick up a steeliness in her grey eyes.

'Is Aidan Millington available?' she asks, planking a black Mulberry bag on the desk. No 'Good morning' no 'Please' I notice. The steeliness extends to her voice too. Not a woman to be trifled with I imagine. Just as I'm about to phone through to his office, Aidan walks out into Reception, head down, browsing through the file of his next client.

'Rachel, did Mrs. Chapman …'

'Aidan! Lovely to see you,' the voice says. The steeliness has vanished, replaced by a softer, sexier version. Is this the same person, I wonder, looking up at the woman as she smiles at him. There's also a coyness to her manner that definitely wasn't there a minute ago.

'Vee! What are you doing here? How ...?' Aidan is surprised, to say the least. Shocked would probably better describe his reaction.

'I thought I'd pop down to surprise you. I've taken today off, so I can stay for the weekend,' she schmoozes.

'Well ... I suppose ... eh, you'd better come in,' he says, inviting her into his office. She looks over her shoulder at me as she follows him, a triumphant look in those eyes. A definite '*So there!*' look that any woman understands from another.

§

Aidan was shocked to see Vee standing in the middle of Reception. Annoyed, even, but what could he do, he thought.

'You should have let me know you were coming, Vee,' he chided, gently.

'Well, then it wouldn't have been a surprise, would it, darling?' she laughed at him. 'I missed you, and from what you said on the phone the other night, I know you've missed me too. Haven't you?' she looked at him from underneath her long lashes.

'Of course, I have. It's just ... I'm quite busy. And, in fact, I'm on call this weekend. I mean, if I'd known you intended travelling all this way, I could have made sure to have the weekend off.'

'Oh, it doesn't matter. We can enjoy the time until you get called out. The main thing is to spend time together.' She came round to his side of the desk, running her long fingers down his cheek and kissing him long and passionately. Against his wishes he felt himself responding, kissing her back. Unexpectedly, the door opened and Henry stood there, file in hand.

'Oh, dear me. I'm terribly sorry, old boy. Didn't know you had a ... visitor,' he said, starting to back out of the room.

'Eh ... no, Henry. Please, come in. Let me introduce you to Vee, my ... friend.'

'Oh, Aidan, don't be so coy,' she says, holding out her hand to Henry. 'Certainly, more than a friend. Delighted to meet you, Henry, Aidan has told me quite a lot about you. In fact, you're just the man I need to talk to,' she says sexily, drawing poor Henry back into the office.

'Me?' Henry squeaked in a rather high-pitched voice.

'Yes, you,' Vee laughed. 'Aidan tells me he's on call this weekend. But, as I've come down to see him – as a surprise, you see – I was wondering if you could possibly take over for him? I've missed him so much,' she said in a silken voice to the embarrassed Henry, who found himself agreeing, not knowing what else to do.

'No, really, Henry you don't have to. Wasn't there something you wanted to do this weekend? Hopefully, there won't be any emergencies. I can manage, honestly,' Aidan looked pleadingly at Henry, who stood like a naughty schoolboy, not knowing which way to turn or what to say.

'Well, if you're sure, Aidan. But do give me a call if you need me, yes?' Henry left, shutting the door firmly behind him.

§

Out in Reception, Henry looks at me, a puzzled expression on his chubby face. 'Have I got it wrong, Rachel, or am I not on call this weekend?'

'No, Henry, not at all. You *are* on call. You and Aidan agreed that yesterday, remember?'

'Yes, indeed I do. What on earth's going on with him? And, what about his girlfriend, eh?'

§

All hostilities are suspended the minute Annie hears about the mystery woman who's come to see Aidan.

'What's she like?' she asks. 'The sly dog. He's never mentioned anything about a girlfriend before. Has he said anything to you, Henry, over your nightly cup of cocoa?'

'Indeed he has not. I never got the impression there was anyone in his life. *Quell surprise!* Mother is going to be so disappointed,' he jokes, heading back to his office.

'*Well*, Rache? Spill!'

'She's a stunner, I have to admit, perfection to look at. Gorgeous figure, flawless make-up, very together. But, I don't think I'd like to be on the wrong side of her, if you know what I mean?' Just then, Aidan's door opens, and they both step out together. Annie turns to me, mouthing a 'wow' before turning back to Aidan and his companion.

'Eh ... Rachel, Annie, this is Vee. We're just going to pop out for a coffee. Shouldn't be too long.' And for some reason I get the impression that Aidan is doing his best to avoid my eyes.

Chapter Thirty-Two

The Plum Tree was a small coffee shop Aidan had discovered as he wandered around Norebridge soon after he arrived there. It wasn't on the high street, but tucked neatly into the corner of a narrow cobblestone side street and wasn't too far from the clinic either. He didn't want to go to Vera's on the High Street, as he felt sure he'd meet several people he knew. At any other time he would have been quite happy to sit and chat, but not today. He was quite upset that Vee had taken it upon herself to just show up. He felt it was a little too much like invasion of his privacy. *And* to walk into his place of work too! Out of order, definitely.

'Well, Vee, you've certainly given me a surprise,' Aidan said, as they sipped their coffees. 'But, as I said, it may have been for nothing. I'm not sure how much time we'll have together.'

'Well ... we'll have tonight, won't we?' she teased. 'I've really missed you, Aidan.'

He looked at her and felt slightly ashamed of

himself. She just wanted to surprise him with a nice, sexy weekend together, and here he was doing his best to sabotage it. What was the matter with him? Some chaps would give anything to be in his situation. Stop the analysing he thought, and just enjoy it. Sitting back, he smiled at his girlfriend, and said 'Well then, let's not waste a minute, eh? What's been happening since I left. Would you like a coffee? How about a sandwich, I haven't eaten lunch? I just need to call the clinic; I think it's about time I took a few hours off.'

Heading out to the car park Aidan called the office, letting Annie know to call him if required. Just taking a few hours off, he said, but was insistent they should contact him if anything cropped up.

§

They talked for several hours, after which Aidan took Vee for his favourite walk, down by the river, across the picturesque stone bridge, and back along the other side taking them up through a narrow alleyway into the High Street. Aidan noticed Vee was not lost in the beauty of her surroundings, but seemed more intent on talking all the time - about their situation, and how much she'd missed him.

They took a chance and called in to Swanns, an upmarket restaurant in the square, making a reservation for later that evening. Looking at his watch, Aidan realised they'd just have enough time to pop round to the new flat he'd been renting for the last two weeks. Time for a quick shower and they could also drop in Vee's weekend bag.

A short time later they strolled leisurely to Swanns, where they were given two menus and shown to a secluded table in a small bay window, overlooking the main street.

'How are John and Joanie? Still enjoying the golf club?'

'Yes. John is still going on his lads' weekends though, leaving her with the kids. I think she's getting pretty fed up. In fact, I *know* she is. I happened to see her at the Precinct about ten days ago, sitting in Guido's – and she wasn't alone.'

'Who was with her?'

'She was with a man, and he wasn't John. *And* they were holding hands. There's definitely something going on there. How could she? With three kids? And, John is such a nice man.'

'Actually, he's not as nice as you think, Vee. Maybe

she has good reason, who knows? Behind closed doors, and all that.'

'How can you say that, Aidan? I know he seems to spend a lot of time away, playing golf with his friends, but he could be doing a lot worse, couldn't he? He looks after her well, she doesn't want for anything. Some women would love to be in her shoes,' Vee said accusingly.

'Well, I don't think we know it all. I honestly believe there are times when things are not as straight forward as they seem to the outside world,' he said, more to himself than Vee. He couldn't help feeling that his own life at the moment was not exactly as it seemed to others looking in. Why was he not overjoyed that his girlfriend had gone to the trouble of driving for hours just to spend time with him? Why was he beginning to feel trapped by his relationship with Vee? And, why, was he upset that Rachel had been the one to witness her arrival in Norebridge?

§

'No, you're not cooking tonight – and neither am I! I've made a reservation for us, and we need to be there in thirty minutes. So, chop chop – let's go, Rache.' Jack is still in his spoil-Rachel- to-death mode, I smile to myself as I run upstairs to change.

I choose a cerise A-line skirt, with a soft white, alpaca three-quarter-length sleeved sweater. I bought them recently, having reflected on Annie's damning verdict of my birthday outfit, and I had to agree with her that, perhaps, my wardrobe did need a little 'jazzing' up. The scoop neck is dotted with tiny glass beads, and a double ribbed hem sits neatly into the waist. It's comfortable and, I like to think, looks sexy and feminine. I had my hair done today and I love it's shiny, sleek style. Jack whistles approvingly as I enter the sitting-room. He lifts my hair, kissing me longingly on my neck. 'Not now,' I say determinedly. 'Dinner first, then – who knows!'

Within ten minutes we're parked up outside the restaurant. As we stroll hand-in-hand to the front door I'm surprised to see Aidan and his partner sitting, laughing in one of the small bay windows at the front of the restaurant. *Oh, no. Not now, not tonight.*

§

A little puzzled, Henry turned to Annie as they prepared to leave the practice. 'What exactly do you want to talk about, Annie?'

'I'll tell you as soon as we get to the restaurant. Oh, did I not tell you? I've booked us a table, so let's go. Come on, Henry. When's the last time you had a nice meal out with someone other than your mother?' Henry was very pleased – an entire evening in Annie's company, and just the two of them. *And*, good food into the bargain – what was he waiting for!

Handing Annie into his Range Rover as if she were delicate porcelain, he puffed out his chest and turned the key in the ignition. The engine growled into life and, grinning like a cat with the proverbial cream, Henry turned the car in the direction of her chosen restaurant.

§

'*Rachel. Rachel!* Annie was delighted to see her friend and colleague heading for the entrance to Swanns. Grabbing Henry's arm, she propelled him towards Rachel, slowing down only when she saw it was Jack getting out of the passenger seat. 'Oh, hi' she said, somewhat subdued, more out of necessity than politeness. Jack returned her greeting in a similar vein.

'Going to Swanns, Rachel? There's a coincidence, so are we.'

'Why don't you join us?' Henry asked, another person acting more out of necessity than politeness.

'Eh ... sure, why not,' Jack replied ungraciously.

§

Aiden couldn't believe his eyes as he saw the entire staff of the clinic saunter into Swanns. He hoped, somewhat ridiculously, that they wouldn't see them and that they'd be seated at the far end of the room. But he heard Annie say excitedly 'Look who's over there. It's Aidan and his friend. Let's go and say hello.' To which the others agreed and, before he could do anything about it, he was faced with everyone circled around their table.

'Aidan! Fancy meeting you here,' Annie said. 'We're just coming to have a meal too. Why don't we join you – unless, of course, you're both having a nice romantic evening?'

'No, no – that's fine,' he replied, not knowing what else to say. But, both Rachel and Annie noticed from a quick look at his companion, it was clear it was anything but fine with her.

Chapter Thirty-Three

Somehow, they manage to seat us at a six-seater round table in the middle of the room. To the casual observer we must look like a happy group, at ease in each other's company. They couldn't be more wrong. Jack does not want to be sitting here with anyone from the surgery as he knows they don't think much of him; Aidan (from the look on his face) certainly doesn't want us sitting here with his girlfriend, with whom it's clear something's not right. The only person who seems happy to be here is Annie. And I can see she's bursting with curiosity. True to form, we're barely seated when Annie launches her first question.

'Well, Aidan, you're a dark horse,' she says jokingly. 'How long have you been together?' And one look at Vee says she's not happy to hear we're ignorant of her existence.

'Not very -'

'Long enough,' she answers, reaching across for his hand, which she takes possessively. Aidan looks uncomfortable, but smiles at her. 'We met at a mutual friend's party. He talked to me all night, wouldn't let anyone else get a word in edgeways,' she says smugly.

'Wow,' says Annie. 'Sounds so romantic. How have you managed to keep her in the dark up to now, Aidan? Afraid someone'll steal her away,' she teases. Again, Aidan's friend throws her a look of dislike.

'Well, it's obvious you don't know Aidan very well. Otherwise, you'd know he's not one to talk very much about his private life,' this is said in a low, but determined voice. And I can't help feeling if Aidan weren't present it would be handbags at dawn between Annie and her.

'Shall we order?' poor Henry asks, eager to break the tension. 'I'm famished, aren't you?' he asks of no-one in particular.

Menus are passed around and we spend time mulling over the lengthy list of enticing and varied dishes. I find it quite telling how a person goes about choosing their food. Henry chooses the first dish that appeals to him – no shilly-shallying about anything else that may, or may not be more to his taste - a man easily satisfied, I think fondly. Jack defers to me, asking what I'm having. I wonder why it matters. Surely, he should have what he fancies himself. Aidan chooses silently, not speaking until he has made his choice. Then he closes the menu and places it away from him – decision made.

Annie chooses her dish, then changes her mind to something else, then returns to her first choice, all the while giggling, with lots of 'oohing' and 'aahing'. Vee peruses the entire menu silently, and only makes her choice when Aidan informs her that the waiter is waiting. It turns out to be a chicken Caesar salad - no croutons and dressing on the side – the least fattening item on the menu. I choose my fillet steak, well done – with my favourite cauliflower cheese and grilled asparagus, *my* nod to healthy food.

It's an uneasy meal. I can feel the tension emanating from Annie across the table to Jack. He doesn't make any effort either to engage in the general conversation, or with anyone around the table. At one stage Annie asks the question 'How are things in the States these days, Jack?' To which he replies, 'I wouldn't know, I'm not going there anymore.' in as close to brusque as possible, without being downright rude.

Aidan makes several attempts to generalise the conversation, aided by a very uncomfortable Henry.

And, I get the distinct impression that Annie is deliberately trying to stir things up – with Jack and Vee in the crosshairs.

'Do you know, Vee, the first night we met Aidan, Rachel ended up in his arms, and I ended up on the floor at his feet? Does he make a habit of that?' she asked of Vee, a spiteful smile playing around her mouth. She deliberately tries to insinuate something jolly and fun. It was nothing like it - Aidan had, quite literally, bumped into us both on the first night he entered the bar. Annie had ended up sprawled over a beer barrel, and I ended up in his arms as he tried to prevent my fall to the floor. All very innocent, so why is Annie doing this?

'I'm actually feeling a bit tired, darling,' Vee says pointedly to Aidan. 'Would you mind awfully if we went home?'

'No, not at all,' he says, relief obvious in his voice. They make moves to leave, despite the fact that neither has had a look at the dessert menu. But then, I don't think Vixen Vee has been anywhere near a dessert since God was a boy!

§

'Annie, what were you up to?' I ask, as soon as they'd

left. 'It definitely sounded to me as if you were trying to provoke something there?'

'Yes, I agree with Rachel,' says Henry, 'I'm very surprised at you, Annie. That wasn't at all a nice thing to do, especially to a visitor – and Aidan's girlfriend. What's the matter? Is there something I don't know?' And I'm quite surprised that Henry would chastise Annie, whom he adores. So, it wasn't my imagination.

'I don't think she's very nice actually. And I certainly don't think she's right for Aidan. There's something not quite right. I can't put my finger on it, but there's definitely something.'

'Or, it could be you, Annie. Perhaps you're just jealous of people who can make a go of a relationship, despite the ups and downs. Who knows?' Jack says, looking pointedly at her.

'Who knows indeed, eh Jack?' she replies, her eyes never wavering from his. 'Who knows what makes some people, mostly women, feel they have to put up with whatever crap a guy feels he can dish out to them? Who knows indeed, what makes them not only forgive whatever crap they're dealt, but take the bastard back as if it was nothing – eh?'

'Well, maybe it's just as well it's not up to you, isn't

it? But then, perhaps you're not the best person to be giving advice in matters of relationships, Annie. Seeing as how you can't stay in one for longer than five minutes! You've had more "boyfriends" – he says this, making those awful quotation marks in the air – 'than hot dinners since I've known you. So, forgive me if I don't take much notice of you.'

'Now, steady on, Jack. That's no way to speak to Annie. I think an apology is in order, don't you?'

'No, Henry, I don't. Perhaps you should ask your girlfriend that question. You might not feel quite so special then.'

'Well, ... now ... Firstly, Annie's not my girlfriend. But if she were I certainly wouldn't allow you to get away with that. Not very gentlemanly of you.' Poor Henry is red in the face, and looks like he could have a heart attack at any moment. I'm stunned - what's going on here? There seems to be some undercurrent at play, of which Henry and I are the only people who are unaware.

'Don't go there, Jack,' Annie says threateningly.

At this stage, I've had enough. It's turned into a very unpleasant evening. So much for being brought out and spoiled. I'd rather have stayed at home.

'Perhaps it's best if we go home?' I suggest to Jack. He stands up abruptly, knocking over his chair. The other diners turn to see what the commotion is and I just want the ground to open up and swallow me. Having said goodnight to Annie and Henry we leave the restaurant, get in the car and I drive home in silence.

§

Back at the table Henry turned to Annie and, reaching out, covered her hand with his. 'What's the matter, Annie. That wasn't like you. What on earth's wrong?' That was Annie's undoing. She burst into tears at which time Henry was deeply disturbed to see her so upset. He came around the table and, sitting beside Annie, wrapped his sturdy arms around her. She buried her head in his shoulder. He could barely make out what she was saying.

'Oh, Henry. I'm despicable. I'm certainly no friend to Rachel. But, I can honestly say it wasn't my fault. I want to get Rachel away from that ... that ... rat! *Have* done for about six months now.'

Henry looked at her intently. 'Are you saying you've ...with Jack? Your best friend's boyfriend? Oh, Annie, Annie - I'm afraid you've rather overstepped the mark there - even for you! That's definitely not something one does, it's probably the most unforgivable -'

'Oh, Henry, shut up! No, of course I haven't. I wouldn't do that to anyone, especially not Rachel. She's always worshipped the ground he walked on. But, if only she knew. I never said anything to her - I really didn't know how to. So, I was glad to hear they'd split up. But – now, it seems she's willing to forgive and forget his affair in the States. Even, the pregnancy, when -'

'PREGNANCY! What pregnancy? Is Rachel pregnant? My God, I had no idea. Well, we'll just have to -'

'Oh, Henry, will you please just shut up! No, Rachel's not pregnant. The girl in the States is. Why he's not with her now, I don't know. When he told Rachel he said she only wanted him to be part of the baby's life. Seems he got off scot free and came running back to Rachel, who takes him back with open arms. But, he *soooo* doesn't deserve it. And, I'm afraid he'll just use Rachel again, until the next time he fancies a bit on the side!'

'But what haven't you told her, Annie? You

referred to something else before. What?'

Annie shifted uncomfortably on her seat. She'd hoped never to have to tell anyone. But perhaps it was time - and she knew she could tell Henry anything.

'I met Jack, unexpectedly, when I was out clubbing with some girlfriends about eight months ago. Rachel wasn't with him. When I asked him why, he said they'd split up. I was very surprised because Rachel hadn't said anything about breaking up. Anyway, I missed the bus that night and he offered to give me a lift home. I was delighted, I didn't know how else I would have been able to get back to Norebridge. Well, we flirted a bit - you know what I mean, Henry?' Henry wasn't quite sure exactly what she meant, but didn't want to interrupt so said nothing. 'But just as we were coming into West Gate, he turned off the road down towards the canal. I asked him where he was going and he just told me to 'wait and see'. I wasn't worried. I mean, Henry, why would I be? He was my friend's boyfriend. Well ... ex-boyfriend.'

'Annie, did he do something to you? Did he hurt you?' Henry had trouble containing his anger. He'd never felt so protective towards anyone before, but if Jack had done anything to hurt Annie ...

'Well, let's just say he certainly tried. But, luckily Henry, I've had to defend myself against my two brothers! Let's just say I'm surprised Jack has been able to father *any* children at all!'

'You mean you ...?'

'Yep, right in the goolies!' Annie couldn't help laughing at the memory of it. 'He doubled over and it gave me time to jump out. Unfortunately, it meant I had to walk home, at midnight, in a pair of stilettos, took me about fifty minutes. I was so angry with him. But I never said anything to Rachel. How do you tell a friend something like that, Henry, about someone they love? *And,* I found out later, they hadn't split up at all. He was just chancing his arm, playing away from home, you know?'

'Have you ever mentioned it to him afterwards?'

'No, I made sure I was never alone with him again. Also, we never really spent much time socialising outside work. Sure, Rachel and I would go for a glass of wine, or a meal sometimes. But never with our partners. I've been hoping that they'd break up since then. Even though I was very upset for Rachel lately, I was delighted when she told me they'd separated – for good! Yet, here we are again, the two love birds are back in the nest together. What can I do, Henry?'

'I can't help but feel, Annie, that perhaps Rachel needs to know exactly what type of person she's with. What happens if they decide to get married? You couldn't stand by and let that happen, surely?'

'Oh, Henry, I know, I know!' Annie dropped her head into her hands. 'I'd love nothing better than to give him his comeuppance. He deserves nothing better. But – how? Anyway, I don't think Rachel would believe me. She's such a lovely person, Henry, but so clueless and naive. Once she makes up her mind to do something, she gives it her all.'

'Well, it seems we'll just have to give this our undivided attention. We *cannot* allow that ... that *two-timing cad* to ruin Rachel's life. So, head's together, Annie, and we'll come up with a solution.'

'Oh, I hope you're right, you darling man!'

Henry, blushing to his hair roots, helped Annie on with her coat. Together they headed out to his car. The whole way home, all Henry could think of was that his lovely Annie had called him 'Darling.'

Chapter Thirty-Four

Vee was furious. It was obvious from the conversation at the restaurant that none of Aidan's colleagues were aware of her existence. Certainly, they were totally in the dark about the fact that he was romantically involved with anyone. Why was that the case? Had he kept their relationship a secret, and if so - why? She felt demeaned, as if it was of no importance to him, and she needed to know the reason behind it.

'Would you like a glass of wine, Vee?' Aidan asked, heading for the kitchen.

'Yes, that'd be nice.' She decided they needed to sit and have a talk.

In the kitchen, Aidan opened the cupboard, reached in for a wine glass, then stood with his back leaning against the counter top, twirling the glass in his fingers. He knew a reckoning was coming. He was sure Vee'd picked up on the fact that he hadn't said anything to his new colleagues about being in a long-term relationship. It was long-term, wasn't it? Well, he knew Vee thought of it as long-term. But did he? While he was musing over this fact Vee appeared in the doorway. 'Don't you think we should talk' she said quietly. But it was more of a statement than a question.

'Yes, Vee. I think we should,' he sighed. He took the bottle of white wine from the fridge, filled a generous amount and took the two glasses with him into the sitting-room. Vee was already there, sitting on the couch, he noticed. He had no choice, without seeming churlish, but to join her there.

'So, what's going on, Aidan. Let's cut to the chase. Why do none of those people you work with know about me?'

'I haven't had the right opportunity to discuss my love life with people I barely know, Vee. Come on, be fair. I've only been here a short time. I don't spend much time with them outside the clinic and it's not something you say over a cup of coffee in the kitchen – "Pass the sugar, please. Oh, by the way I have a girlfriend called Vee" - a bit strange, wouldn't you say?'

While Vee was pleased to hear he didn't spend his spare time in their company, she still was far from mollified to think she was so low down his list of importance. She couldn't help the feeling that Aidan was being less than truthful with her.

'Two months is long enough, I think, Aidan, to at least mention to your colleagues, in passing, that there is someone in your life. You've just taken on this flat, so you have your own place. Why didn't you invite me down before now?'

'I've been trying to find my feet, Vee,' he said, a little exasperated at the inquisition. 'It's not easy getting used to a new practice, new colleagues, new clients and a whole new way of how things are run. Up to two weeks ago I was actually living with Henry and his Mother. I couldn't just invite anyone to stay in their home too, could I. They've been very good to me.'

'But I'm not just "anyone," am I, Aidan? I'm not some one-night stand you're bringing home for the night. What's the matter? Please, talk to me.'

Aidan felt somewhat wrong-footed. He knew Vee was right – why hadn't he mentioned it? He knew in his heart that if he'd wanted to he could have found the opportunity to do so. What was stopping him?

'I ... don't know, Vee. Maybe you're right. But I'm not aware that I've *purposely* kept our relationship from anyone. Why would I do that? It's been ... a little unsettling, this change. I was very lucky to have stayed with Henry. It helped me find my feet – workwise - without having to sort myself out with somewhere to live at the same time. I would have invited you soon, Vee. But, you're here now, so let's take things as they come, eh? What do you think of the flat? It's only on a six-month lease, with the option to extend.'

Feeling somewhat mollified, Vee stood up and wandered through to the kitchen. The landlord had obviously kitted the flat out with the sole intention of rental income. The sitting-room, kitchen and small study on the ground floor were certainly functional, but couldn't be described as cosy. Neutral coloured fabric on couch and curtains gave an air of modernity, but it could have been anyone's house, or, indeed, any hotel room. It would take a lot of personal touches to make it into a personal space. *And I'm just the person to do it.*

Later that night, they made love. Not the passionate lovemaking of two people who'd been separated by time and distance. But a familiar, comfortable sharing of intense emotion, after which Aidan fell into a troubled sleep, while Vee slept soundly, all her anxiety spent along with her sexual energy.

§

Jack was furious. It was obvious from the conversation at the restaurant that Annie hadn't forgotten their little 'incident' and had come very close to letting the cat out of the bag. That would have been disastrous. Just when he was getting back into Rachel's good books. He needed to be careful, she didn't entirely trust him – yet. But he'd work at it, until she did. Time to be on his best behaviour.

§

'Why were you and Annie so nasty to each other in the restaurant tonight? I can't speak for anyone else, but it certainly made me feel very uncomfortable, Jack.' I'm very taken aback at the atmosphere between Annie and Jack and am curious to know what could possibly be behind it. I know they're not fond of each other, but tonight bordered on the downright hostile.

'Oh, Rachel, you must know by now, Annie would like nothing better than for you and me to split up – for good. I don't think she's every forgiven me for stealing away her friend. And, she doesn't think I'm good enough for you.'

'Oh, Jack, that's not true. No, I got the impression she was referring to something that only you and she knew about. I have no idea what, do you?'

'No, no, I don't,' Jack says, with a puzzled shake of his head. 'Anyway,' Jack strolls over to me, taking me in his arms. His hand caresses my cheek as he says 'Let's not spoil what's left of the evening. Why don't you head up to bed? I'll tidy up everything down here. Won't be a minute, love.'

'Well, to be honest, I am feeling a little shattered. Wouldn't mind putting my head down,' I say. But at the same time, it doesn't escape me that Jack has avoided the issue again.

§

Downstairs, Jack punched in the letters of the text with a vengeance. Re-reading it quickly, he pressed *Send,* then switched off his phone before going upstairs to join Rachel, who snored lightly as he slipped quietly in beside her.

§

Annie was just sneaking up the stairs at her Mum and Dad's when a loud *Ping* shattered the silence of the sleeping house. Damn! She didn't want to wake them up. She didn't want the inquisition which usually followed when she came home late. At least tonight they were already in bed when she arrived. Oh, what she wouldn't give to be still sharing Rachel's lovely house with her. But, no chance of that. Definitely not now – with *him* back in residence. Annie felt at a loss. She badly wanted to set Rachel straight about her beloved Jack, but she didn't know how to do it. An anonymous letter, maybe? No, that was the cowardly way. If she was going to do it, it would be face to face. But she risked losing Rachel's friendship, and that was too much to contemplate. Rachel was the best friend she'd ever had. Almost like having a sister.

Once in her room she switched on her bedside lamp. A soft glow warmed the room, as Annie changed into her jolly, red striped pyjamas. She snuggled down between the flannelette sheets, savouring the thought of her latest Katie Forde novel which was on her bedside table. Then she remembered she'd received a text. Probably Henry, with another of his hair-brained suggestions to expose that bloody Jack. They'd laughed out loud at some of their ridiculous suggestions they'd made in the car on the way home. Lovely Henry, he had such a decent heart. She felt warm just thinking about him.

Smiling, she picked up her phone and read 'Don't mess with me, or you'll regret it.' Of course, the caller's ID was withheld. But Annie was in no doubt who the sender was.

Chapter Thirty-Five

I hang my coat and bag up on the wooden pegs in the small cloakroom area. It's early and no-one else has arrived yet. I'm glad to have this space to myself, glad to be out of the house. It's feeling a little stifling at home. Much as I love Jack, I can't get rid of the feeling that all is not as it seems. I *do* trust him, as much as I can in the circumstances. But something doesn't feel right. Perhaps it's just me and my ridiculous intuition. Maybe I should admit that it's not always correct.

I make a cup of coffee and sit at the melamine table, staring at Annie's poster of the hunky figure of Aidan – Aidan Turner of *Poldark* - not *our* Aidan, and it makes me smile. I close my eyes and I'm in the middle of that golden cornfield in Cornwall, the sun's rays warming my face and bare shoulders. I can hear the rushing of the sea in the distance. In a corner of the field wild flowers grow profusely, swaying in the gentle breeze. Birds sing in a nearby copse. *Poldark* approaches, I shiver with anticipation, and can feel the warmth of his hand on my shoulder ...

'Rachel. Rachel! Are you alright?' I open my eyes, and look at the hand on my shoulder. It's Aidan – but this time it's *our* Aidan. 'Would you like another tea?'

'No, thanks, Aidan. I'm fine,' if a little guilty at being discovered day-dreaming of a half-naked man. 'What are you doing in so early? In fact, why are you in at all – Henry is on call this weekend.'

'Eh ... well, I just thought I'd pop in and see if there was anything that needed my attention. Catch up with a little paperwork. It's impossible to do it during the week.'

'But, isn't your ... friend still here? I could easily call you on your mobile if we have anything urgent. You could still enjoy some time off? '

'No, it's fine. Vee is spending the morning shopping, over in Westbridge. I'll pick her up at lunchtime. We'll be closed at one o'clock anyway. What about you, Rachel?

I look at Aidan and suddenly things become clear to me. He's hiding from her - he doesn't need to be here at all. Henry is due in any minute, as he's on call this morning. But, then I think, am I not doing exactly the same? I didn't need to be here for the last hour, sipping coffee alone in the kitchen. I could still be tucked up cosily in bed with Jack.

'Just like you, Aidan,' I reply. 'Catching up with things,' as I get up from the table and rinse my cup under the tap.

'Here, in the canteen? Catching up on what?' he asks, and I can hear the amusement in his voice.

Luckily, I don't need to reply, as Henry breezes in smiling from ear to ear. 'Good morning all,' he grins. 'Aidan, what are you doing in here this morning? Surely you should be showing Vee around, spending time with her? There's no need to be here. We can call you if we need you, right Rachel?'

'That's exactly what I've been telling him. No need at all,' I smile sweetly at him. Knowing Henry was right Aidan had no choice but to head off, with the promise that if needed we would contact him immediately.

§

'I get the distinct impression that he would much prefer to be busy here in the clinic today, than escorting his girlfriend around Norebridge. Don't you think so, Rachel?'

'Yes, I certainly do, Henry. He was absolutely

shocked when he saw her standing in Reception yesterday. And much as I don't like to say, I think she's not being entirely herself with Aidan. It's a woman thing, believe me, but I feel there's a lot more going on than she's willing to let him see'. Then I stop, realising how sinister I sound, even a little ridiculous. 'Oh, Henry, never mind me. It's just my imagination running away with me.' Or, maybe, I think to myself, it's just my own unsatisfactory situation right now.

It's a quiet morning, only three pretty routine cases come in, all dealt with quickly. Henry answers the telephone at around twelve-thirty, as I'm busy washing my hands. It's Anton who, having chatted with Henry, agrees to come in and pick up a prescription for a course of antibiotics for Zebedee, who seems to have picked up an infection. Henry seems to have overcome his feelings of dislike towards Anton, which were pretty obvious when he thought Annie and Anton were an item. We both did, until recently, over a coffee when Annie exclaimed *'What!* Me and lanky Anton? No way, he's nice – we had a picnic and a few drinks – he's really lovely, but he doesn't do it for me – no way!' Henry beamed, but was immediately deflated again when Annie went into raptures about William, some new chap she'd started seeing.

'You haven't said anything about him,' I say, surprised at the fact that she could keep something so secret. That's not like Annie.

'Well, it's early stages,' she says mysteriously. I glance across at Henry, who looks as if the world has just ended - again. You poor man, I think, why is love so cruel? Why can't we fall for the people who are right for us, with none of this awful pain and heartache?

But there's nothing I can do for Henry. My own life is fully occupied with my own love travails, and I am still totally confused and mixed up about Jack. At times I can't wait to get home, to be snuggled up in his arms, looking at TV, making love and lying together afterwards. Or going for a walk down by the river, arm-in-arm like an old married couple. At these times my world feels on an even keel. At other times though, I feel as if I'm trying to balance on a world that's tilting on its axis and I'm in danger of sliding off into the unknown.

Chapter Thirty-Six

It's Monday morning and Maura, our new Temp, has just arrived. She's all smiles and it feels as if she's brought the sunshine in with her. Henry is at Reception when she breezes in, and after formal introductions Maura asks if anyone of us would like a cuppa, complete with a slice of Irish whisky cake which she's brought in a jolly, green spotted tin. Henry looks at me, winks and says 'Good choice, Rachel,' and turning to Maura suggests she might like to take her tea with him, so they can have a chat and get to know each other. While Maura heads for the kitchen, Annie turns and says 'Hope she's not going to try and take over, Rachel.' I'm a little surprised. Annie is the last person I'd have thought would feel in any way threatened by a middle-aged woman like Maura, however attractive and well preserved.

'What's going on with you, Annie?' I ask when we're alone. 'I couldn't help but pick up on the tension between you and Jack in the restaurant on Friday night.

I know you've never been his biggest fan, but he *is* trying, you know. He's spoiling me to death,' I laugh, 'cooking things to death, too!' I look at Annie's hardened face and try again. 'I'm prepared to give him another chance, Annie. Can I just ask that you do the same?'

'He doesn't deserve one, Rache. I'm sorry, I just don't want to see you hurt – again.'

'I do appreciate your concern, but I ... well, I feel he really regrets his ... '

'Adultery? Cheating on you?' she says. 'Two-timing you with another woman and getting her pregnant? I don't know any nice way of saying it. So no, Rache, I don't agree with you. He's ... not the person you think, he is. Wise up, don't be so blind. I wish I could ...'

'What, Annie? Wish you could what?'

'Oh, never mind. Just leave it. I'm just ...'

'Just what, Annie? I'm getting a bit sick of you alluding to something, but never actually coming out and saying exactly what you mean? Is there something you know that I don't? Please, just say it. If it was the other way round wouldn't you want me to tell you, if I knew something?'

Annie stares at me, fiddling with a strand of her vibrant, red hair – a sure sign she's hiding something. She's biting her lip too – another giveaway. *'Please,* Annie,' I ask.

'Rachel, he's not the good person you think he is. Miss USA is not the only one he's tried it on with! There, I've said it.' I look at her as if she's mad. And, for a minute, I think she is. Then what she's saying slowly begins to sink in.

'You? Annie, I don't believe you. You wouldn't do that.' And I firmly believe what I'm saying. I think I know Annie enough to believe she wouldn't do that to me, her friend.

'No ... Yes ...No. I mean, he tried, but I wasn't having any of it. But, Rachel, I know if I'd given him *any* encouragement at all, he'd have been up for it. I'm sorry, I've been trying to find a way to tell you. But, it's not the easiest thing to do. Especially when you got back together.'

It feels as if someone has punched me in the stomach and the familiar sounds around me recede into the distance – the sound of Henry's voice, greeting another client; the closing of his exam room door – all a long way off. A weakness comes over me and I fall back onto a chair. My heart is racing, pounding against my chest. I'm surprised Annie can't hear it too.

'When?' is all I can whisper.

'About six months ago. The night I went to Sheila's birthday party. You didn't go, remember? Jack offered me a lift home, and I was glad of it, as I'd missed the bus.'

'What did he ...?'

'Tried to kiss me, in the car. He told me you'd split up and he got a bit too touchy feely. I promise you there was nothing else. But, I was really angry with him. You're my friend. Why would he even think I'd ...' Annie stops. 'I can't bear to be near him after that, Rachel. Can't bear to see him fawning over you. When all the time I know ...'

Suddenly, things are clearer - Annie's refusal to join us on evenings out; Jack's reluctance to include her in our outings. My mind is all over the place – thinking about incidences that I found strange at the time, but were discounted as my imagination. Now, in seconds, they flit through my mind, taking on a new meaning. And, I begin to wonder if there are more ... Annies?

I leave Annie in Reception and head to the Ladies. Suddenly, I can taste the bile in my mouth. I race inside and before I can stop it I'm retching into the toilet behind the locked cubicle door. When it feels like there's nothing left, I wipe my mouth and head out to splash some cooling water on my burning face. As I raise my head from the sink I look at my reflection in the mirror and am not sure who I'm looking at any more. The face looking back at me is tight around the jawline - the mouth is clenched, the lips pursed in ... disapproval? Resignation? There are bags under my eyes, and they look lifeless. What's happening to me? I think of what Annie's just told me, and I have no doubt that what she says is true. How can I be so sure? I don't know, but I am.

I draw my shoulders back and straighten up, realising as I do so I've been holding my body hunched over. Is this indicative of how I feel about my life – cowed? If it is, surely there's no-one to blame but myself.

Did I take Jack back too readily? Why did I take him back in the first place? If he hadn't come back to me, would I be over him now? Perhaps I'd even be happy? Because I realise now with total clarity, that happiness is not very prevalent in my life right now.

While I'm lost in my thoughts my mobile phone

rings in my pocket. I'd forgotten to switch it off. I take it out and check the caller ID. It's Jack. I'm very tempted to let it go unanswered – but I don't.

'Hello?'

'Hi, babe. How's your day going?'

'Fine.'

'I was thinking I'd cook chicken in white wine for you tonight – again! That take your fancy?'

I hesitate, but only for a second. 'Actually, Jack. I won't be home tonight,' I hear myself say, as I punch the 'OFF' button, replacing my mobile in my pocket.

I head back out to Reception, and smile at Annie. There is someone standing at the counter but I ask them to 'give us a moment, please,' and gently take Annie by the arm, leading her back into the kitchen. I need to say this, and I need to say it now. She looks at me, apprehension in her normally lively eyes.

'Annie, thank you for being honest with me. I'm so sorry you had to carry this burden with you. And please don't think you've ruined things between Jack and me …'

'Rachel, I think …'

'Please, Annie, I want to be sure you don't blame yourself for what is about to happen. I'm finished with

Jack – for good. My heart knows that everything you said is true. I have no doubt at all. It's really shaken me to the core. In fact, I can honestly say it's broken my heart. But I've been fooling myself, trying to convince myself that things with Jack could get back on track. I'm only sorry for that girl in the States. He broke things off with her to come back to me. And now I'm about to dump him. He should have stayed with her.'

'Rachel, you need to …'

'I know, Annie – I need to be sure. Believe me, I am sure. I don't think things could be any worse than they are now. But isn't it funny, *I'm* the one who feels guilty about dumping him. It's not going to be easy, but I'm determined to be strong. And, I know you'll be there for me.' And the tears start to come. Tears which I've held back for so long. Even when Jack told me about the girl in the states I was too shocked to cry. I just felt numb. Now, it's as if all my sorrow and hurt is tumbling out. Annie puts her arms around me and I sob uncontrollably, my body heaving as she soothes me and caresses me gently. Then, she pushes me gently away from her, holding me at arm's length and she looks into my eyes.

'Oh, Rachel, you really do need to be strong now.

There's someone in Reception looking for you ... and Jack. *I'll* deal with her. Why don't you stay here until she's gone. Then, I think, you should go home.' And, without Annie saying anything, I know immediately who the person is. And I make up my mind, it's the only way I can be sure.

'No, Annie. I'll do it,' I say determinedly, heading once again for the Ladies, hoping to repair my ravaged face. Then I walk towards Reception for a confrontation I know in my heart I cannot walk away from.

§

The girl is pretty, in a very American way. Dark, streaked hair is full and voluminous. Her sallow skin is flawless, her make-up perfect. Plump lips glisten with a pale pink lipstick over perfect teeth and her eyes are heavily outlined, the lids sultry with perfectly applied eyeshadow. But it's her eyes themselves which draw me in – huge, innocent eyes. Her whole demeanour is shy and gentle. There's a slight chubbiness, but it doesn't detract in any way from her loveliness.

'I believe you're looking for Jack?' I say. 'Why did you come here? He doesn't work here,' I tell her.

'No, but Rachel does,' she says in a soft American

drawl. 'Jack told me his friend, Rachel, works in a veterinary clinic. I tried the other one, they said she works here. I really need to talk to her.'

I hold my hand out to her, saying 'I'm Rachel.' She takes my hand, in a soft but strong grip.

'Where's Jack?' she asks, puzzlement written all over her lovely face. 'Has something happened to him? I haven't seen him for two weeks, since he left the States. He's not answering my calls. Hasn't replied to my texts either. Is he OK? I'm desperate to speak with him.' Then she stops, saying 'Oh, I'm sorry. My name is Jenny, by the way. I'm Jack's girlfriend.'

And I look at the woman whose relationship with my boyfriend has turned my life upside down.

§

'When Jack left the States was everything OK between you?' I ask. She doesn't seem to think there's anything strange about my question, but she's slow to answer, thinking before she replies.

'Well, not exactly. I'd just found out I'm pregnant. Jack wasn't entirely happy at first when I told him. But we talked things through, and he seemed to come round to the idea. I really want him to be part of my baby's life.

And, before he left, he agreed that's what he wanted too. He phoned me on the Sunday, the day he arrived back in the UK. Promised everything was fine. But I haven't spoken with him since and I'm really worried. Has something happened to him? Since you're his friend, I thought you might know.'

Bells ring in my head and any doubts I might have had are immediately gone. I distinctly remember Jack arriving at the house on Monday – the day I twisted my ankle – saying he'd just landed from the States. Briefly, I wonder where he spent the night – but then, to my surprise, I realise I don't care.

I look at her anxious face and I feel no anger towards her. This poor girl is totally in the dark. Jack, the bastard, has been stringing her along all the time. I realise I'm faced with two choices – I can tell her the truth and break her heart too, or I can keep quiet, give her the address of *my* house where he's holed up and hope her arrival will force him to do decent thing and come clean.

I hand her the address of the house and call her a taxi. When it arrives I walk out with her. 'Be sure to tell Jack that we've spoken, Jenny,' I say. She promises me she will. Just before she gets into the taxi, she hugs me impulsively. I'm taken aback, but then remember this lovely girl knows nothing of my recent relationship with her cheat of a boyfriend. But I'd give anything to be a fly on the wall when he sees her on the doorstep!

§

Minutes later I'm back in the Ladies and can't stem the hot, salty tears which flow down my face. I know for certain now that it's over with Jack. I cry silently, none of the strangled sobbing of before. I feel a sense of calm I haven't felt in such a long time and I think I'm crying for a past life of coupledom, rather than the person who used to be in my life. Talking with Jenny has convinced me a life with Jack would be one of uncertainty, and I really hope he'll be kinder to her than he was to me. She has a lot more to lose than I did.

But with that comes the realisation that everything from here on can only be better. I'm prepared for the loneliness which is bound to come. You can't be part of a relationship and not mourn its sudden loss. But I'd prefer the honesty of being alone, than a life in which I deceive myself every day. And I know now I *have* been deceiving myself these last few weeks. I think I took Jack back because I was afraid of being without him.

But, the future holds no fear for me now. Looking in the mirror at my dishevelled face, I force myself to smile, and promise myself there and then that this is the last time I'll cry for any man.

§

I hear murmurings out in Reception as I clean myself up, trying to make myself look normal again. Satisfied that it's the best I can do, I put on my professional face and join Annie and whoever else is with her. They're both laughing as I come out and I feel a flush of pleasure when I see it's Anton. He looks at me and a flash of concern is evident on his handsome face.

'Are you OK, Rachel?' he asks, looking quizzically at Annie, who is not quick enough to disguise her head shaking, as she smiles quickly at me.

'It's OK, Annie,' I assure her. 'I'm fine, or at least I *will* be.' And turning to Anton I ask him for an update of Zebedee's progress. He's not doing too well, it seems and, having spoken with Henry by phone, Anton has called in for another prescription for antibiotics as Zebedee seems unable to shake off his infection. As we're sorting this out the door to Henry's office opens and Henry comes out, with Maura.

'We're finished for the day, girls,' Henry says. 'We're off to have a bite to eat. See you all in the morning,' he beams. He has a quick word of reassurance with Anton about Zebedee, then he helps Maura on with her coat and they both head out to his car.

'*See!* What did I tell you, Rachel?' Annie says crossly, watching them through the door as they cross the car park to Henry's car. 'She's only here five minutes and she's already snaffled the boss! Men - they're so gullible. If it's not Jack, it's Henry. And I thought he ...'

'What, Annie? What did you think about Henry?' I say, a little aggressively, knowing it sounds a little sharp but I can't help myself. I know full well even if Annie's not interested in someone, she's most upset to think that *they* might not be interested in *her*. But I won't let her treat Henry like that and at the moment I feel just a little impatient with her.

'Oh, never mind. But Rachel, are you sure you're OK? You've had quite a shock today. Would you like me to come home with you?'

'Eh ... no, no, thanks Annie.' I can't think straight, everything seems a little fuzzy but I'm clear about one thing. 'Actually, I'm not going home tonight. Jack is there ...'

'Well then, you'll come home with me. I'll just give Mum and Dad a quick call and let them know we're coming. You can share my room, eh?'

'No, you'll come home with me,' Anton offers, without knowing the reason why, or any other details. 'I insist – no buts,' he says as he sees me open my mouth to refuse. 'You can help me monitor Zebedee tonight. I'd feel better if you were there. Would you mind?' he looks at me pleadingly. And before I know it, I've agreed. We'll stop at the shops on the way, so I get a few things. I really don't want to have to call at my house with Jenny and Jack there. But I'm sure they'll be gone tomorrow.

§

Later, after everyone else had gone, Annie checked the patients before turning out the lights. Knowing some of the sick and vulnerable animals could be frightened when separated from the familiarity of their home and owners, Annie made sure the soft glow of the night light came on, before closing the door gently and returning to her desk. She looked around the empty space and suddenly, for the first time in her life felt totally alone.

Who was *her* night light? She thought of her boss – kind, gentle Henry – and ... Maura? No, surely not! And, for some unknown reason which she couldn't quite fathom, young vivacious Annie felt bereft, and incredibly sad.

Chapter Thirty-Seven

We enter Mill House to a loud chorus of frenzied barking. Lucius bounds joyously up to Anton, but there's no sign of Zebedee. As we enter the kitchen I see him, lying on a pile of blankets in front of the cream AGA. Forgetting my own misery for a minute I go over and take a quick look at him, stroking his velvety coat. I can see how the lovely animal tries his best to get up, but can't. Anton looks worriedly at me.

'Don't be concerned,' I tell him confidently, 'it's perfectly normal. There was a possibility of infection. But let's get the antibiotics into him, and he's due in to the practice again in two days. He'll be fine, he really will. Henry wouldn't have discharged him if he had any misgivings whatsoever.'

'I know, but it's just so hard to watch an animal suffer, isn't it? It makes you feel so helpless.'

'Look at him, Anton. If he could he'd be jumping all over you,' I tell him. 'Just give it a few weeks, and he'll be back to his boisterous self. In the meantime, he may need a hand to take a trip outside, to relieve himself. It could cause him further distress if he can't keep to his toilet habits. Keep an eye on him, he'll let you know when he needs to go.' Anton is leaning back against the counter. He's the picture of misery, and my heart goes out to him.

Then he turns to me anxiously. 'Never mind about us though, Rachel, I'm supposed to be looking after you, remember? Would you like a nice cup of tea? Or something stronger?' he smiles cheekily. I love the fact that he hasn't asked me anything – I don't think I want, or could, rehash things right now.

§

Having made tea, he rummages around in the enormous fridge and, over his shoulder I see two tomatoes, some cheese and pot of fresh-looking chives. 'Those chives are the freshest things in your fridge,' I tease.

'I know, I adore them. I eat them on everything – sandwiches, omelettes, salads. A chunk of good Wensleydale with chives – what more could a man want?' And picking up a small wheel of cheese, wrapped in bright red wax, he asks 'Hey, have you tried this Snowdonia cheese? It's amazing, especially this one – Red Dragon – it's a cheeky little number! I brought some back when I went to Wales a few weeks ago and I've set up a regular delivery since then – can't live without it! It's absolutely gorgeous – try some.'

'Was it a business trip, or a holiday?' I ask, as he puts together the makings of a cheese board and crackers.

'Just a quick few days - I wanted some time alone. I needed to think about ... something.' I notice his hesitancy, but let it pass. 'I took the most amazing cottage in Snowdonia. The weather was absolute crap, but the landscape was stunning. It really is a very special place, Rachel. Good for peace of mind and it brings tranquillity to the soul, and the dogs loved it too.'

'Did it give you the answers you needed?' I ask this strange man. Before I got to know him, he would have been the last person I'd have thought would be happy in a tiny cottage in a wild, unpredictable landscape. But now it seems not strange at all. I think nothing about this caring man would surprise me anymore.

'Well, I wasn't exactly hit by a lightning bolt of clarity. But I certainly sorted out a few things in my mind. More, I suppose, the things I know now I *don't* want. And that is an answer too, don't you think?'

'Yes,' I murmur, more to myself than to Anton, 'it certainly is an answer,' and my thoughts begin to wander momentarily, until I hear Anton speaking again.

'But enough about me,' he says. 'When I came to the surgery today you didn't look particularly happy. Is everything OK? I'm not prying and we don't have to talk at all. But, just so you know, if it helps I'm happy to.'

'Well, as we speak my ex-boyfriend is at *my* house, about to meet his pregnant girlfriend who he dumped a few weeks ago, and who he thought was still safely tucked away in the States. *She*'s worried sick thinking something's happened to him, because he hasn't had the courtesy to tell her that he'd left *her*, and come back to me. He doesn't even know she's in the country, let alone in Norebridge, so I think this is the closest he'll ever come to having a heart attack' - and I look at my watch – 'just about now!'

'Oh, wow! How did you meet her? How did you find out?' he asks, astonished. Then, pushing our mugs aside he takes me by the arm, saying 'This calls for something much stronger than tea. Let's go to the sitting-room and get comfortable? Have a chat, if you like?'

And that sounds like the nicest invitation I've ever had. But first we take Zebedee gently, lifting him together through the French doors out onto the lawn, where he very slowly finds a comfortable position - half standing, half sitting – and relieves himself. The poor thing can barely stand for long and starts to tremble, so we wrap him up gently and carry him with us into the sitting-room, laying him gently before the fireplace. Anton searches for the makings of a fire. He looks a little helpless, so I join in the search. Everything is close to hand, but hidden discreetly behind a beautiful handmade fretwork door – logs, some coal, papers and firelighters. Soon, a warm glow emanates from the black marble fireplace, and Zebedee leans back, savouring the heat while finding a comfortable position for his poor aching body.

I take a seat on a squishy, forest green sofa, which is big enough for three or four people. It's strewn with large, flowery patterned cushions in autumn hues of russet and yellow. As I lean back, the sofa wraps itself around me, like arms in a comforting embrace and, slipping off my shoes, I tuck my feet up under me. Anton heads over to a butler's trolley in the corner of the room.

'Wine, gin, vodka?' he asks mischievously. And I decide to throw caution to the wind and choose a welcome glass of white wine. Instead of having to head to the kitchen fridge, Anton magically opens up a trapdoor in the floor. He pops down two or three steps of a circular staircase. I head over to see where he's disappearing and, to my astonishment, see a tiny cellar below the floor. Rough stone walls are banked on three sides by shelves of wine bottles and I can feel the cool air float up into the room. Anton selects a perfectly chilled *Sancerre* and returns with two clinking glasses, which he sets down on the coffee table in front of me.

'This house is full of surprises,' I laugh. 'Do you never feel lonely here on your own, in such a large house?'

'No, not at all. And, I'm not really alone. There's Brad, who lives with me. Well, in an apartment around the back. But we often eat and watch TV together. He's a decent chap, and great company.'

'Where is he tonight?'

'Remember, I told you at the hospital, he's on a well-deserved holiday. He'll be back in a week,' he says. And I can tell he's looking forward to his return. 'He's been a good friend to me. Especially, during my crazy days!' he smiles.

'Crazy days?' I say, as if it's the most unheard of thing in the world. 'You? Surely, not,' I laugh.

'Oh, I'm afraid so. You wouldn't have liked me in my crazy days, Rachel. Thank God, I've 'seen the light' as Brad says. It certainly makes *his* life a lot easier. Not to mention, probably adding a few years onto mine. He got me out of several scrapes. And, at times, gave me a very deserved mouthful when I went off the rails completely.'

'Oh, I can't imagine that, Anton,' I tease. 'And I'm sure I would have still liked you, even in your 'crazy days.'

'Believe me, Rachel, you wouldn't – no-one would. But Brad stuck with me. I owe him a lot. He's like a brother to me. But never mind me. We still haven't sorted out your problem, have we?'

What can I say, what *is* there to say? But I find myself telling Anton how I met Jack. How I thought my life was at last on track and I was happy. After two disastrous relationships I felt I'd found the decent, caring man I could spend the rest of my life with.

'What changed?'

'I'm not sure, but there was definitely a change in the relationship. And now, thinking about it, I can probably pinpoint it to the time when Jack started going away on business trips – to the States. I just put it down to the stress of work. He'd often talked about how difficult the Stateside client was.' Then I can't help but laugh.

'What?'

'The Stateside client – yes, very difficult. Especially when she goes and gets pregnant on you! I've just realised his stress was of a very different kind, Anton,' and I giggle. It must be the wine. 'He used to come home and wouldn't even speak for hours. I'd do everything I could to make him feel at home. But, all the time he must have been so resentful of having to come back to me,' I say. And this time I don't giggle. It hits home to me that for the last six months at least, I have been very much second-best in Jack's world. That makes me incredibly sad, and I can feel my eyes well up. Oh, no, please, not now. Anton excuses himself to go to the kitchen. Quickly, I dry my eyes with my sleeve, and have a couple of sniffs. *Hold it together, girl.*

Anton returns, and moves from his comfy armchair to the other end of my couch. 'Rachel, I don't think you should do yourself down like that. You're a gorgeous woman – not just physically, you've a kind heart, and you're a great friend, according to Annie. If Jack has cheated on you then he's a fool. I'm sure he already regrets it. If he doesn't, then he's even *more* of a fool.'

'May I have another glass of wine, please?' I hold out my empty glass to Anton, who takes it, looking at me with raised eyebrows.

§

It's some time later, I'm not sure how long. We've laughed a lot, and I know I've hugged Anton a lot and it felt good – not in a sexual way, just warm and comforting. He's a really good hugger too. We've eaten the remainder of the cheese – with chives - and I've had several more glasses of wine. Life looks decidedly rosy, Jack and his treachery are fading into the distance. But then so is everything else …

§

I feel something warm on my face. Opening my eyes, I'm blinded by a ray of sunlight forcing its way through a narrow gap in the curtains. I attempt to sit up, but am knocked back by a vicious stabbing pain in my temples.

Oh, God, I hear myself moan. Just then the door opens and Anton peeks around it. Seeing I'm awake, he checks if it's OK to come in.

'Of course,' I say, holding my forehead, as I sit up gingerly. He enters the room with a cup of tea, which he hands to me carefully. It tastes delicious – sweet and strong. I'm sure there must be at least two or three spoons of sugar in it, but I'm not complaining.

'Thanks,' I try to smile, but even that hurts. Then I look down, and realise I'm undressed. Well, down to my bra and pants, anyway. And, even in my misery, I experience a little frisson of gratitude that they match – midnight blue, with scraps of lace on the legs and across the boobs. Thank God I didn't wear my usual *Bridget Jones'* once-white-now-grey number.

I look at the other side of the bed. It's very crumpled and looks as if it's also been slept in too. Oh God - I'll never criticise Annie again! How *could* I? How could *he*? As these thoughts flash through my thumping brain, I see Anton smile at me. That gorgeous full-mouthed smile, which invades his liquid eyes and he reaches out and strokes my arm.

'*No,* Rachel, we didn't, I wouldn't take advantage of you like that. Why don't you just relax, and have a lie-in.

There's no reason why you should rush off, is there? I've called the surgery, Henry says it's all quiet. And they've Maura there too, so no panic.'

'Right, well, if you're sure you're OK with that, it sounds like a rare pleasure. But how is Zebedee? Have you checked on him yet?'

'Definitely, twice during the night, and first thing this morning. And the reason I slept in here last night – fully dressed, I might add! - was to make sure you were OK during the night. You'd had quite a bit to drink last night,' he grins. 'I didn't want you getting sick. Nice underwear, by the way!' he says cheekily. All I can do is laugh. I lie back and the last thing I remember is hearing the click of the bedroom door.

§

The next time I wake I look at my watch and am astonished to realise it's already eleven o'clock. I can't remember the last time I had such a long lie-in. But don't push it, Rachel, there's a thin line between a lie-in and downright laziness I think, turning over once more in what must be thousand-thread sheets, which feel like silk on my skin. As I luxuriate in bed, I look around the beautiful room. Good old-fashioned Farrow & Ball -

Chapell Green, I imagine, because I know it well and it's my favourite colour - brings the outside in to this restful room, with matt white accentuating window frames, shutters and door frames. Curtains and bed linen are in gentle pastel colours of cream and terracotta stripes, picked up by the upholstery on a delicate looking chaise longue dominating the curve of the bay window.

I slip out of bed, a deep luxurious carpet underfoot, and head towards what I think must be an en-suite bathroom. Again, no expense has been spared here. Black slate tiles form the floor of a wet room, with large shiny black-brown floor to ceiling tiles set on their ends, cleverly increasing the visual impression of a very high-ceilinged room. In the corner, I dip my toe into a plunge bath, amply filled with freezing cold water. There is also a small seating area (heated, I discover!) by the side of the plunge pool, more like a large step to ease one's descent into the icy water. The overall impression is of a large, private Roman bath. Huge, white fluffy towels are laid out in two neatly folded stacks, one at either end, convenient for both the waterfall shower and the plunge pool.

I switch on the shower at the far end and step inside.

As the door glides closed, the lights dim, and tiny pin-head lights glow in the ceiling, like thousands of stars in the distant night sky. I lift my face to the water, which gently caresses me. No harsh skin-lashing jets of water here. Instead, it feels like I'm bathing in a secluded pool under gentle drops of rain in the Amazon jungle. I expect to hear the 'cawk cawk' of jungle parrots, and the tick-tick-tick of unseen cicadas.

After what seems like an age I reluctantly close off the gentle rain and step out of the shower. The lights immediately come back to normal, a little harsh after the soft lights before. I wrap my damp, lime smelling, tingling skin in one of the thick, chunky towels. It's enormous, and covers me from my boobs right down to my ankles. Feeling relaxed - and no more hangover - I pad my way back out to the bedroom, almost dropping my towel as I see Anton relaxing on the chaise longue.

His eyes are closed and he doesn't hear me, so I have time to study his face and body. He could be in one of those sensual adverts for a man's deodorant. I can see the caption – *'The strong man's choice.'* It would be a black background, only his strong, chiselled features staring at the camera – he'd be clad head to toe in black, a skinny black polo neck to emphasize his handsome face. Today he's wearing black jeans and, surprisingly, a grey shirt with the sleeves rolled up to the elbow. Where did that come from, I wonder? His feet are bare, and I notice they're long and lean, the nails white and square cut. I'm beside him before he realises, starting a little when he does.

'Oh, Rachel. Feeling OK now?'

'Yes, much better thanks. I ... I feel I should apologize for last night – for *whatever* I said ... or did?'

'Oh, please don't, you made me feel really special, and the things you did, well ...I've never seen anyone do *anything* like that before. Certainly not to me, and wearing only a smile – even one as gorgeous as yours - definitely a night to remember!'

I'm shocked into silence, before I remember what he said earlier. I cuff him on his arm, and we both laugh.

'Seriously, Rachel. Neither one of us did anything we need to be ashamed of, or be embarrassed about'.

'Apart from drinking more in one night than I normally would in a month! Oh, I had such a headache this morning, Anton. Thank you for my lovely lie-in, it really helped. And, to say 'thank you,' how about I cook you a nice breakfast?'

'As long as you stay and join me, yes please,' We

head downstairs to the kitchen, where Anton hands me an apron, with the slogan '*May you be in Heaven five minutes before the devil knows you're dead*! 'on the front. I look at him with raised eyebrows. 'A friend brought it back from Ireland to me,' he laughs. I fill the kettle while Anton heads into the village for the makings of a full English breakfast. It's surprising, but I'm absolutely ravenous. I make a cup of tea and head into the sitting-room, heading straight for the French doors, leading outside.

A short while later, as I'm sitting comfortably on the flagstone steps, which form a wide, semi-circular patio, I hear my mobile phone ringing in my bag in the kitchen. For some reason, I imagine it's Anton checking our breakfast requirements and, smiling, I run in and answer it.

'Well, you sound very happy with yourself!' I hear Jack say. My heart skips a beat and I nearly drop the phone.

'What do you want, Jack?' I hear myself ask. But I feel suddenly very subdued. 'Why are you calling me?'

'Why do you think, Rachel. What the hell did you send Jenny here for last night? I nearly died of fright when I saw her at the door. I didn't know what to say!

What *were* you thinking?'

'Well, how do you think I felt when she arrived in my place of work, Jack?'

'I don't even know how she found you. Said it was something I told her about you working in a vet's. Anyway, we need to talk. When can we meet?'

I can't believe what I'm hearing. As I'm digesting this I hear the crunch of gravel in the distance. But I'm too preoccupied with Jack's demands to talk to register what it means. Do I want to talk to him? My heart is still thumping in my chest. To my disgust I realise that part of me *does* want to meet him.

'Rachel, I thought you loved me. You said you did, enough times. How can you just walk away and not even see me, let me explain.'

'I don't know what there is to explain, Jack. Jenny came over to find you. She didn't know anything about me and you. She seemed to think you were with her. That you're an …'

'Who are you going to believe, Rachel? I was trying to let her down gently? And, I don't know how she got that idea. It was a fling, Rachel, nothing more. I've told you, over and over.'

My mind is a jumble of confusion. Am I mixed up

here? Or is Jack trying to gloss over the truth? You hear of girls trying to hold on to men by claiming to be pregnant, don't you? But, at the back of my mind, I also hear a voice telling me there are men – and women - who cheat, and think it's OK, as long as it's only a one-night-stand. That's not actually 'cheating' in their minds.

I hear a noise behind me and I turn to see Anton standing in the doorway, a cardboard box of organic eggs, bacon and mushrooms in his arms. His face is unreadable. He walks over to the granite counter top and deposits his bounty gently, before turning and leaving the kitchen. I can't explain it, but I feel as if, this time, I *have* done something very wrong.

Chapter Thirty-Eight

I find Anton in the boot room, sitting beside Zebedee on the heated flagstone floor to where we've moved him. Anton strokes him calmly from head to toe and he's loving it. I look at the long, sinewy hands and find myself wishing they were stroking me, down the length of my slightly-chubbier-than-I'd-like body. Then I stop myself. What's the matter with me? Am I so desperate for a man that I'm fantasizing about the first man who shows me kindness. *Get a grip, Rachel.*

Neither of us speaks. Zebedee acknowledges my presence by raising and lowering his head and whining pitifully. I kneel and stroke his lovely head and I get licked and slobbered over for my pains. He places a paw on my knee as is to say 'I'm doing OK. How about you?'

'He looks a little livelier, doesn't he?' I say.

'Yes, he does,' Anton answers. The stroking continues in silence.

'That was Jack on the phone,' I explain needlessly.

'I thought as much. Unless you express profound love for everyone who happens to call you.' I know it's an attempt at lightening the atmosphere, but I also feel that there's a slightly sarcastic undertone.

'I didn't express profound love,' I say, a little miffed with him.

'Not in so many words, no. But I think it's fairly obvious from your tone with him. You still care for him, Rachel, don't you? After all he's done? The way he's treated you?'

'I don't ... You have to understand, Anton. We've been together for over two years. We ... '

'You don't have to explain anything to me, Rachel. But I do think you owe yourself more than this. Have you really thought about your situation? Have you decided what it is you want? More importantly, what it is you need? No, no, even *more* importantly – what it is you deserve, Rachel?'

'No, I .... I'm not sure, anymore. I wish I could ...' And suddenly, it's all too much. Why is Anton so angry with me? And the whole sorry situation with Jack – I've loved him with all my heart and soul. He said he loved me too. Then he cheats, regrets it, asks me to take him back. I do - then it turns out he hasn't really left the other woman at all. If a stranger was looking at the situation from the outside I'm sure they would tell me to wake up. That's certainly what I would tell Annie, if she found herself in my predicament.

But, the thing I find the hardest to do is to stop loving Jack. And, to be able to tell if he does still truly love me. Because, ridiculous as it may sound, I don't want to turn Jack away if I am really the love of his life. That would be tragic, I think. Everyone deserves to be allowed to love, and to be loved, despite their faults and failings. But everything is buzzing around in my head, like flies around a light shade on a sultry summer evening. I'm beginning to feel overloaded. I can't think straight. I see Jack standing in front of me, then Annie with a look of disgust on her face as she turns away from me, then Anton, who seems to be calling out my name …

'Rachel, are you OK? Don't move. You'll be fine, just stay where you are, don't try to get up.'

§

I'm lying on the floor, the flagstones warm against my back. I can't get up. I look up at the ceiling, lovely old wooden rafters form a pattern and I start to count them. So I know I'm OK, I haven't gone mad, but why can't I get up? I can hear Anton's voice in the background, but can't quite make out what he's saying. Then a huge shadow looms over me and I cry out, shielding my face. But, it's Zebedee and I feel a hot, rough tongue scrape across my cheek as a paw is placed heavily on my chest. I realise he's trying to comfort me, to let me know he's there for me. He's quivering as he stands over me, but he doesn't leave. I raise my hand and stroke him, along his flank, where Anton's hands have been.

§

I open my eyes and realise I'm back in bed in the lovely forest green bedroom. I feel warm and secure and no longer afraid. I hear Anton's voice, and another voice, one I don't recognize. They seem to be miles away, but I can make out what they're saying.

'She'll be fine. Needs plenty of rest. I would say it's total exhaustion, brought on by stress, possibly? Has she been under a lot of stress lately?'

'More than most, I would say. And, she's been working full time in the local Vet's, as well as trying to deal with a very personal problem.'

'Perhaps that's been her way of coping. You'd be amazed, Anton, at how many people take refuge in their work when dealing with problems. They do the very opposite of what they need to do, and work themselves into the ground. Sometimes,' the man says, taking hold of Anton's arm, 'all they really need to do is find somewhere quiet, to sit and think over their problem, and decide on a solution. But then, you don't need me to tell you that, do you?' He talks to Anton in a fatherly fashion and I get the impression that they know each other very well. 'Just keep an eye on her. And, if you can, persuade her to take a little time off. To do nothing, or to do something just for herself. No looking after other people, no looking after animals – she needs time out.'

They leave the room and a little later I try to open my eyes, but the lids are heavy. I hear dogs barking way off in the distance. The world is warm and cosy here, no problems in this lovely cocoon, no Jack to battle with ...

§

The next time I wake I can see it's dark outside and I have no idea what time it is. There's a soft glow from a lamp in the corner of the room, casting shadows in the far corners. Suddenly, I start, as a form lurking there moves, and a figure rises from the shadows.

'It's alright, Rachel, it's only me,' I hear Anton's voice. 'I'm just sitting here, making sure you're alright. Do you think you could manage a cup of tea? A little toast, maybe?' And, I think, nothing has ever sounded so good.

Chapter Thirty-Nine

It was Monday morning and Annie was in the surgery at the crack of sparrow. Henry called around to see her on Sunday night. He'd had a phone call from Anton, telling him that Rachel had had some sort of collapse, needing complete bed rest for a while. She phoned Anton straight away, who assured her everything was fine, but he sounded very concerned and Annie promised to call round after work. In the meantime, she didn't look forward to spending the day in the surgery with Ms. Bossy Boots. She'd certainly tell her where to get off if she started throwing her weight about. Only five minutes in the place and already she was having it off with the boss - Annie was livid. Henry was *her* friend, *her* pal, *her* confidant. She told him everything, even stuff she hadn't told Rachel – especially about that rat of a boyfriend of hers. *Now* who was she going to tell her troubles to?

She heard the front door open, and could hear Henry and Maura laughing and joking as they came in.

RIGHT - bring it on, you friend nicker! Just one wrong word ... Annie straightened her short black skirt, smoothed down her tight yellow sweater, and ran a hand briefly through her hair, giving it a quick, careless flick. She'd show her.

'Morning, Annie. How are you today? Have you spoken with Anton?' Henry asked.

'Sure. Rachel's fine, slept right through and had some toast for breakfast this morning. I said I'd call round this evening after work. Maybe you'd like to come with me?'

'Oh, I wish I could, Annie. But I'm going to pop up at lunch time, as I'm a little busy this evening.' Annie didn't miss the sly look he threw in that old biddy's direction! *And,* she had the gall to smirk back at him.

'That's fine, then,' she replied brusquely. 'Wouldn't want you to forget the person who's been your right hand – up to now, that is.' Annie couldn't help herself - how dare he! 'Wouldn't want to think "Out of sight, out of mind" was your thing, Henry, would we!' And with that, she grabbed the stack of files on the desk and slammed them onto the counter in Henry's direction. Immediately, she regretted her action, feeling horrible but not able to stop herself. She turned away from them both and headed into the kitchen to make her first coffee of the day. She couldn't, though, find it in her heart to offer to make one for either of *them.* That was just stretching her generosity of spirit a mite too far, in Annie's mind.

Returning from the kitchen Annie busied herself on the phone. She spoke with Mr. Hilton, ensuring that he hadn't forgotten his appointment at three o'clock that afternoon. He was in good health for his 82 years, but the same could not be said for his ageing moggie, Bells. Lately though Mr. Hilton was beginning to experience sporadic episodes of memory loss, and had missed appointments on several occasions. Rachel and Annie had agreed to call and remind him before each scheduled appointment, and it was working well.

Maura approached the counter, but Annie pretended to be too preoccupied to talk. She kept her head down, buried in files. Maura, however, was made of sterner stuff, and came to stand in front of Annie.

'Annie, I know I'm new here, but whatever you need me to do to help, just tell me and I'll get on with it. I know you're worried about her, but I'm sure Rachel will be fine. In the meantime, let me help in whatever way I can, OK?'

Despite herself Annie was touched. Even if she *did* have the hots for Henry, it was good of Maura to jump in to help. She looked at her - the kind, slightly wrinkled face with the grey eyes crinkled up in a smile - and said 'Well, how good are you at making tea, Maura?' The older woman smiled to herself as she headed down the hall towards the kitchen.

They both heard the tinkle of the front bell. Their day had just begun.

§

Henry came back after lunch with the news that Rachel was up, sitting at the table in Anton's kitchen, and had just polished off some eggs, bacon and fried tomatoes. But she seemed emotionally fragile, and both Henry and Anton were a little concerned. Anton had got Rachel's agreement that it would be best to stay at his house to recuperate, rather than head back to her place, as there would be no-one there to look after her. Henry noted that Anton seemed quite happy to take on the role. But he kept his thoughts to himself.

They worked through a very busy afternoon, and at five-thirty Henry came out from his office. Leaning on the front desk, looking at Annie he smiled, saying

'Thank you, Annie. You kept everything running very smoothly today. It can't have been easy; we were rather busy.'

'Well, in fairness Henry, Maura has been a great help. The main thing is, Rachel doesn't worry about us here. We know what she's like, she'll be feeling guilty about not being here.'

'I assured her at lunchtime she wasn't to feel like that. I told her we'd cope, but were looking forward to seeing her back. We don't want her to think we can manage without her for too long, either!'

'Oh, don't worry Henry, I'll make sure she gets her bum back here at the earliest! But only after she takes some time off. This whole episode with Jack has really taken it out of her. Any news of where Jack-the-lad and Miss America have gone?'

'I didn't ask, Annie. But I wonder what the situation really is. *Has* he left with the American woman? If so, where have they gone?

Chapter Forty

Jack sat on the side of the bed in the small, city centre hotel room. Jenny slept quietly on the other side. The reality of his situation had come crashing home yesterday, as he'd packed his belongings and left Rachel's house – but he hoped *not* for the last time.

He hadn't been able to meet with her, she'd gone off to stay with some friend. But he wasn't too worried. He was certain he could sort things out with her. She loved him, he had no doubt about that. And, he had at last realised that Rachel was the person he wanted to spend the rest of his life with.

But, first, he had to sort things out with Jenny. While her appearance at Rachel's house two nights ago had shocked him, he also had a grudging respect for her determination to find out what was going on. He realised her actions had been motivated by concern, and he'd been stupid to just cut off communications with her like that. He should have just slowed things down gradually, then he could have disappeared without too much bother. But it was certainly ludicrous of him to think she'd just 'go away,' simply because she hadn't heard from him. She was pregnant with his child after all and he wouldn't shirk away from that responsibility. But that was as far as he was prepared to go. For a very brief period he'd almost given up everything with Rachel to go back to Jenny. But, once he'd come home and tried to break things off with her, he realised what a huge mistake that would be. Though he and Jenny needed to sort things out, once and for all, if only for the baby's sake, and that was what he intended to do – today.

§

Jenny heard Jack in the shower. He'd been up for a while, sitting on his side of the narrow bed - thinking, most likely. She had decided to give him time, to come to some conclusions for himself, so she'd pretended to be asleep.

She thought back to the night she'd met Jack at her office drinks party in the States. It was to welcome the members of the UK team, who had come over to take on the company she worked for, Terra Logistics, as a new client. Jack was the more senior of the two, and in Jenny's mind, the more handsome also. He was friendly when introduced by her boss and owner of the company, Ted Rawlinson, and singled her out later that evening for special attention.

Jack had been deep in conversation for most of the evening with Ted, and his second-in-command, a young twenty-seven-year old, called Seb, who thought he knew it all. He was arrogant and full of himself. Jenny's friend, Tara, had warned her that she was the target of Seb's attention. They both burst out laughing, as they sat in the Ladies, having a quiet five minutes, discussing the pros and cons of being the object of his affection. The cons seemed to far outweigh the pros.

'Can you just imagine going to the movies on a date with Seb?' Tara asked. 'You'd only be there five minutes before he'd think it was OK to have his tongue down your throat. That's probably his idea of foreplay!' They rocked around laughing, until Lizzie French, their Supervisor walked in.

'Just on your way back out, girls?' They both knew it was not a question and scurried out through the door. She could hear the squealing laughter as they ran down the corridor to the open-plan office and the drinks party, which was now in full swing. They were OK really, she smiled – dependable, thorough, and never minded working a little late if required. But, heavens, they could be silly around young men. Especially that Tara – no sense, whatsoever. Ms. French, as she was referred to in the office, was sure there wasn't a single young man left in the office with whom the brash Tara hadn't at some stage 'been familiar' as her elderly mother, back in rural Montana, would have put it. Jenny, now she was another story. For all her young girly 'goings-on' with Tara, Ms. French would have bet a month's salary she was still 'a respectable girl.'

As they returned to the gathering they were stopped by the handsome man from the UK, who broke off his conversation with Seb when he saw Jenny come back down the corridor. 'So, what exactly do *you* do, Jenny?' he'd asked, totally ignoring Tara.

'Oh, Jenny's the b...' Tara gave Jenny a reproachful look after she'd elbowed her, none too gently in the ribs, at Jack's question.

'I've just moved from being Receptionist up to Accounts Training. I intend to become an Accountant. I've also done stints in Human Resources, Purchasing Department and Logistics. As Mr. Rawlinson says, it's best to start at the bottom and work your way up. That way you're familiar with all aspects of the business later on.'

'Really? That used to be the way in the UK before – on the job training, it was called. Now most young people come into a company with a Degree, and more or less concentrate on the area that they're interested in. But, I suppose, there's some sense in doing it his way?'

'Well, he is the Boss so he can do things anyway he wants,' Tara jumped in again. 'And this is really a great company to work for. I know I'll be promoted to the next level in six months, if I keep my head down and do well. Another twelve months after that I can climb up to Level 3, so I can plan my life financially. I want to buy a downtown apartment and I know I'll be in a position to afford it in about two years. Not everyone my age can say that.'

'And what about you, Jenny?' he asked, again turning all his attention on Jenny. 'Will you be buying your own apartment too, or do you live with your parents?'

'No, I already have my own apartment. I guess I was lucky, I bought when everyone said it was the right time to do so.'

'Yeah, and it also helps having a ...' Tara stopped short again as Jenny looked daggers at her. This time she decided it was time to leave her friend with the English guy, who obviously had the hots for her. *And*, it was time to move on before she let the cat out of the bag. Sometimes, she couldn't understand why Jenny insisted on keeping her secret. But, Tara was really pleased that she was the one Jenny had confided in. It made her feel special, and it also confirmed her 'best friend' status in her eyes. But, boy, was it hard sometimes to keep it zipped!

§

Jack visited the States on a fairly regular basis after that. Jenny was always pleased to see him, and after a very short time knew she was falling in love with him. He was always one hundred percent attentive to her. Unlike some men, who seemed driven to answer phone calls even during dinner, breaking off a conversation to take a call, Jack seemed happy to leave his mobile phone switched off when they were together. As if he couldn't bear for them to be interrupted when he was with her.

When she found out she was pregnant it came as a huge shock. At first, she hadn't said anything to Jack, wanting to get used to the idea herself. Also, she wanted to decide for herself what she was going to do. She'd made her decision by the time Jack had visited two weeks ago. But she wasn't prepared for his reaction to what she considered her very happy news.

'You're *what!'* He seemed stunned, and not at all happy. She was a little confused.

'You heard, Jack. Pregnant. But ... why are you so shocked? It *does* happen, you know. Especially when people are in a relationship,' she smiled as she said this. Of course he'd be shocked, she reasoned. What did she expect? They didn't know each other *that* long.

'How the hell could that happen, Jenny? I thought you'd be ... taking something... using something ... you know?' Jenny laughed outright at his embarrassment. 'Jack, it's OK, these things happen,' she smiled at her lover.

'Yeah, but this wasn't supposed ...I mean, it's such a shock.' Jack was totally at a loss for words. *Shit! Shit! Shit!* This was *not* what he wanted at all. It was supposed to be a bit of fun. He thought Jenny knew that. The contract with Terra Logistics was due to be signed soon anyway, and then he'd intended to cut out the trips to the States. Rachel was becoming a little unhappy about his trips, so he'd known he'd have to knock them on the head soon. But he'd enjoyed his times with Jenny.

She was lovely. But *this* – no, this didn't fit in with his agenda at all.

§

They'd gone out for dinner that evening, and Jenny was aware that Jack was very subdued. Soon after that, his phone calls became less frequent. Then his trips to the States stopped completely. All her efforts to reach him – voicemail, messages, texts – had gone unanswered. Even her attempts to contact him through his office had met with 'Mr. Montgomery's not available at the moment/He's in a meeting/He's away from the office.' Her Dad had even threatened to fly over to the UK and 'sort him out.' But she'd dissuaded him from this course of action, insisting there was something wrong which prevented Jack from contacting her. And, she decided, she'd rather sort it out herself.

Jenny's 'cute girl' appearance belied a very practical and decisive mind. And last week she'd made the decision she wanted to know the worst – whatever that might be. Maybe he'd been in a car wreck and was lying somewhere in hospital. But she also had an uneasy feeling that Jack wasn't being entirely truthful. And, having flown to the UK, and met Jack's friend

Rachel, Jenny knew for sure things were not as Jack had told her. But, she loved him – really loved him. She was having his child. She was determined that she would not give him up just like that. But she said none of this to her Dad. She promised him if she needed his help she'd call him straight away.

'Good, honey. And you know I'll be on the next plane to the UK,' Ted Rawlinson said, smiling at his only child, who would one day take over his very substantial logistics empire.

Chapter Forty-One

Anton opened the door to Annie and she followed him into the kitchen where she could smell the delicious aroma of freshly brewed coffee. As she sat at the large kitchen table, Anton poured her a mug of the dark, treacly liquid, adding two spoons of sugar, and a quick splash of almond milk.

'You remembered,' Annie smiled her wide, freckly smile.

'As if I could forget,' he grinned. 'That was one great night, Annie, thank you. I really enjoyed it, as I hope you did.'

'Oh, yes! One to tell the grandchildren, eh Anton?' she giggled.

They heard a noise and, looking over, saw Rachel standing in the doorway. Anton moved to the door and, taking Rachel gently by the arm, lead her to a seat at the table. She was wearing a man's dressing gown, grey with brown stripes, which swamped her girly figure making her seem fragile and vulnerable. Her feet were bare, but the legs of black, cotton pyjamas were visible underneath. Annie was shocked at her appearance and threw a quick look in Anton's direction. He shook his head slightly, unseen by Rachel.

'Hey, Rache. How are you feeling? Better than you look in those pyjamas, I hope!' Annie teased. Rachel smiled, and stretching across the table, took Annie's hand in hers.

'Thanks for coming, Annie. I'm fine really. Just feeling a bit weak. I don't know what happened, just seemed to lose it. Imagine – *me,* the queen of cool, falling in a faint! Poor Anton didn't know what hit him.'

'Oh, don't listen to her, Anton. I've known her throw herself at mens' feet before – loads of times!' They laughed and Anton moved to pour Rachel a cup of coffee.

'So, what now, Rachel? What's happening with Jack and Miss USA?' Anton winced slightly at Annie's bluntness. 'Have they left?' Just then Annie noticed Anton's look of horror. 'It's OK, Anton. Rachel and I know each other well. She knows I don't pussyfoot around, right Rache? Call a rake a rake, that's my motto.'

'Oh, no-one could accuse you of ever pussyfooting around, Annie,' Rachel laughed out loud. Turning to Anton she said 'It really is alright, Anton, she's only asking the questions everyone else wants to ask. And the answer, Annie, is I don't actually know. He was anxious to talk, but I'm not sure there's anything to talk about. It's become apparent what he's been up to. And I don't think I could ever trust him again.'

'I certainly hope not. That bastard's been playing …'

'I think Rachel is aware of that, Annie,' Anton interjected, afraid rehashing things would put Rachel under too much pressure again. 'We thought Rachel could pick up some things from her house today, then come back here and take things easy for a few days. Unless you've changed your mind, Rachel?' Annie could see the look of tenderness he gave Rachel, and almost shouted *'YES, YES!'* She was so delighted for this lovely man to have found someone *real,* someone as nice as Rachel. The danger was that Rachel was too damaged, at the moment, to realise it.

§

As she drove home Annie pondered Anton's attraction to

Rachel. She was so pleased for them both – or would be when Rachel came to realise it and, hopefully, feel the same. She and Anton had had one very drunken night together after their picnic. They'd rolled home to Anton's after a lovely day by the river in a *very, very* inebriated state, having polished off two bottles of champagne and a bottle of white wine under the warm afternoon sun. Neither one of them remembered getting back to Mill House. Until next day when a local taxi driver arrived for his money. And to bring Anton back for his car, which he'd sensibly left parked at The Spotted Peacock the previous day. Anton had paid him, but declined to collect his car that morning, feeling sure he was still well above the acceptable limit to drive.

Having sorted the driver out he'd returned to the bedroom where Annie was waiting for him. Hopping onto the luxurious satin sheets he threw his arm around Annie, saying 'Where were we then?'

Tracing a line along his handsome face Annie said, putting on a huge pout, 'Well, Anton Wickers-Stroppton, I should be feeling very *dejected* right now. What with being *rejected* last night, by you - the sex god of the rock world an' all,' she teased, in a high-pitched girly voice. 'But, I suppose I rejected you too, didn't I?'

Anton pretended a huge pout on his lower lip, giving him a pitiable, hang-dog expression. Laughing out loud, Annie sat up, and leaning over hugged him warmly. 'Seriously, though Anton. I'm glad we found out we didn't fancy one another – in *that* way, before ... you know ...'

'Yeah, me too, Annie. I'm not saying you're not desirable, sexy and gorgeous – just not *my* desirable, sexy and gorgeous!' God knows he'd fallen into bed with Annie, fully intending, and indeed very much looking forward, to making passionate love to this bubbly, gregarious girl. But when it came to it, he found he couldn't. As they lay together on his bed that night, still fully dressed, but writhing with anticipated passion, he'd looked into Annie's somewhat blood-shot eyes, brimming with mischief - and rolled back on the bed. Putting his arm over his eyes, he said 'Oh, God, Annie, I'm really sorry. I can't. I've just realised ... ' He kept seeing someone else's face before him. Someone he'd only come to realise he cared for deeply. The thing was, he hadn't really spent any time with her. But he'd never been so attracted to anyone on such a deep level before. And it shocked him to the core.

'You fancy someone else? Oh, Anton, thank God.

You too? No offence, but I was trying to force myself to go through with it. I mean ... you're dead gorgeous, but ... I don't know ... I think I fancy someone else too!' And for the first time in her life Annie had never been so sure of anything. *She was in love – yay!* But she was also very surprised. And they laughed together, then going downstairs they made coffee to sober themselves up, before eventually falling asleep in each other's arms. It was the nicest evening Annie had had in a very long time of pretend orgasms, pretend affections, and pretend everything with guys she tried to convince herself she cared about. Or, harder still, tried to convince herself they cared about her!

Next morning, she left his house knowing she'd made a friend for life. She loved Anton – as another brother. But for some reason she hadn't told Rachel about their night of unbridled un-sex! That would remain *their* secret. But from then on there were no meaningless dates for Annie. She surprised herself at the simple pleasure she felt just spending evenings at home with her family. Sure, they still drove her crazy and she could have killed her brothers at least once – every night! But for the first time in her young life Annie realised how important depth and meaning were in a relationship. Of course, she didn't confess this lightbulb moment to Rachel. After that, when questioned about whom she might have been with the previous night, Annie would become very mysterious, throwing a name – Justin, Geoffrey or William – over her shoulder as she busied herself with something. Eventually, Rachel stopped asking, assuming she'd tell her when she was ready.

§

After Annie had left, Anton took Rachel over to collect some clothes and toiletries from her house. She opened the front door and entered the quiet hallway. Anton followed behind, with a leather holdall he'd brought for Rachel's things. She entered the kitchen and was surprised to see it neat and tidy. No unwashed cups in the sink, and it was obvious the floor had been swept and the counter top wiped down. A cleaning cloth had been rinsed out and was placed over the dish rack to dry. No guessing who'd done that. Jack wouldn't have known where to find one! Rachel couldn't help but feel grateful to Jenny. She'd dreaded finding the detritus of Jack's life strewn around her home.

Tentatively she went upstairs. But here again

everything had been tidied up. In her bedroom, the curtains were drawn back and the bed stripped, sheets and other bedlinen stuffed together into one of the pillowcases. Rachel was very grateful for Jenny's sensitivity. The shower too showed signs of someone having given it a good clean - no long hairs clogged up the shower hole, and the sink had been Mr. Muscled and dried off, leaving porcelain and taps clean and sparkling. The house looked as if it had been made ready for new tenants. And Rachel decided right then that's exactly what she would do – rent it out and move away.

She opened her wardrobe and selected a few items of comfortable clothing. She folded them neatly and stacked them, ready to be put into the holdall. Anton watched her from the doorway, noticing how she moved as if on automatic pilot. He was very concerned. Rachel had been deeply hurt, and he was worried the hurt had broken her. Damn that man - if he could just spend ten minutes in a room with him ... Anton was shocked at the strength of his loathing for the man that, he now realised, Rachel had so truly loved.

Chapter Forty-Two

Annie was desperately worried having returned home from her visit to Anton's. She'd never seen Rachel so vulnerable, and was furious with Jack for causing her friend such heartache. Much as she'd wanted her to leave Jack she had no idea that she would be so traumatised by the break-up. She'd drunk a large glass of white wine before going to bed hoping it would help her sleep. But, instead, she'd had a very restless night, and kept having the same recurring dream every time she dozed off.

She was lying on the bank of the river, enjoying the sunshine, when she heard a dog barking. She looked around, but couldn't see where the sound was coming from. Lying back down, she tried to drift off, but was disturbed again by the persistent barking. Listening more intently this time she identified it as a frantic type of bark, not just the normal barking-for-attention sound. Getting up she walked slowly down to the river bank.

After about a hundred yards or so, she could see something bobbing up out of the water, just at the turn in the river. Immediately she knew something was wrong. This animal wasn't doggy paddling back to some owner – it was in difficulty. Without thinking of her own safety, she shouted 'HELP' as loud as she could, diving headlong into the fast-flowing river.

It wasn't easy getting across the current, it seemed to take forever. But Annie did her strong over-arm of which Mr. Davies, her teenage swimming coach, would have been proud. She counted her rhythm in her head, all the time pounding through the water. As she arrived beside the stricken animal it disappeared again under the water. No, no, please, don't let me be too late, she prayed. Diving below the surface it became clear what the problem was. One of the animal's hind legs had become entangled in a long section of discarded string, which itself was caught up in an old rusty wheel, anchoring the distressed animal securely.

As she became aware of this, she heard what sounded like a distant splash. But there wasn't a minute to lose, the poor thing was becoming frantic with fear. Annie wondered how long it had been struggling like that and felt sure it's strength must be giving out. She spoke a few words of comfort to the stricken animal, in a calm and reassuring voice. Diving below the water again she managed, with a great deal of effort, to snap the piece of string, releasing the frantic animal. Then, hoping it wouldn't bite her out of terror, she grabbed the dog in one arm, trying desperately to swim towards the shore with her free arm. Unbalanced, and with the weight of the wet dog dragging her down, it was hard going. The river bank looked very far away.

Suddenly, the animal struggled, and she couldn't hold it any longer. She had to make a decision – and quickly. Against all her natural instincts she released it, and watched in amazement as it paddled happily to safety. She knew now she'd spent all her energy trying to save the stricken dog, only to find that she had none left to get herself to the bank. Strangely, all she felt was a surge of happiness as she saw the little thing jump around, and wag i's tail joyously as it watched her sink slowly beneath the murky waters.

She was aware of a great whooshing sound, but other than that there was a peaceful silence as she slid gently into her underwater world. She saw bits of trees, their branches reaching out eerily as if to grab the unsuspecting passer-by, there was an old bicycle, a *shopping trolley and a large old-fashioned television set, the big fat kind used to play long defunct VHS tapes. As her mind registered this cemetery of discarded detritus she was suddenly swept up by a pair of strong arms, flipped over and grabbed somewhat roughly under the chin. She felt the water separate and could see the sky again. Suddenly, she was being pulled effortlessly through the water, backwards. She could hear a voice too.*

'Annie, Annie, my darling, hold on. Not far to go, my love.'

And then she was dragged unceremoniously up the rough bank, where she and her unknown rescuer were greeted joyously by the little dog. She was aware of a shadow looming over her and she suddenly felt cold. She heard the voice again – 'Annie, Annie, can you hear me? Please don't go, don't leave me,' and, opening her eyes, looked up into the kind eyes of Henry, who was gently caressing her cheek. He picked her up as if she was light as a feather and ... Annoyingly, she kept waking up at this point.

§

It was just gone seven o'clock when Annie arrived at the

clinic. She couldn't lie there in bed any longer, so she'd showered and dressed and headed into work, surprised to find the front door already open. Oh, yeah - who else could it be but Ms. Country Life 1962, trying to impress the Boss, no doubt. And sure enough, there she was already engrossed in a stack of files on the counter in front of her.

'What are you doing in here this early?' she asked Maura, a little rudely.

'Well, I noticed before I left yesterday we had a very crowded list for today. I thought if I got the files out, ready for you, it might help,' Maura answered. Annie felt a slight wave of shame, but only for about two seconds, as the older woman continued with a cheeky look at Annie, 'anyway, no-one to keep me snuggled up in bed on a rotten morning like this, unfortunately. But, who knows, that might be about to change, with a bit of luck, eh?'

The cheek of the woman - setting her sights on Henry! Annie felt a rush of dislike towards her, and knew she had to protect Henry from her at all costs. *Right, bring it on.* Henry arrived an hour later, whistling as he came into the building. Annie saw him wink suggestively at her rival, and could have happily slapped both their ruddy little faces.

"Morning, Annie, Maura. How are you both this awful morning?' And without waiting for a reply breezed into his office, asking Maura for a coffee – 'you know how I like it, Maura'. And, that was the exact moment when Annie decided. So Henry was a little surprised five minutes later when Annie came in, carrying his coffee and a chocolate digestive. 'Annie? I didn't expect you to do that. Where's Maura?'

'Busy. Doing what she should be doing, Henry. Anyway, I wanted to talk to you, and I won't take no for an answer. I want to have a chat with you and I want us to go for a drink this evening after work. Don't make any other plans.' All said with a very determined and authoritative air. With that, she turned on her heel and left his office, leaving behind an open-mouthed Henry sitting in amazement – and delight. Two minutes later Annie would have been very surprised to see a rather smug Henry pass the reception desk, wordlessly high-fiving a grinning Maura as he went.

Chapter Forty-Three

Annie headed straight over to a small table beside the roaring log fire. The pub was busy for a Wednesday night, not exactly the milieu she wanted for her heart-to-heart with Henry. But, no matter, it needed to be done, and it needed to be done *now*. She was prepared to look foolish if it didn't work. But she'd prefer that than not having tried at all.

'A large glass of white wine, Annie?' Henry said, setting it carefully in front of an ever-increasingly nervous Annie. 'Are you warm enough?' he asked solicitously.

'Yes, Henry. I'm fine,' she answered as he took the seat opposite her on the other side of the table. 'Are you?'

'Indeed. Now, what was it you wanted to talk to me about?' he asked innocently. 'Don't tell me you're leaving? Emigrating to the other side of the world, or anything drastic like that?' he chuckled.

'Would you be upset if I was?' She couldn't believe

her luck. He'd given her the exact entree she wanted by broaching the subject of leaving.

'Well,' Henry said slowly, 'I suppose it would be very selfish of me to try to stop you, or to stand in your way, don't you think?'

Annie felt her heart do something strange, like it missed a beat or something. She couldn't believe her ears. He wouldn't even try to stop her if she *did* decide to leave Norebridge. Oh, she'd got it all wrong. She'd left it too late! So she did the thing she always did when she was upset or disappointed – went on the attack.

'Oh, I suppose you wouldn't even miss me. Now that you've got Ms. Maura. Seems you two are very cosy lately. She lost no time getting her claws into you, Henry,' she said petulantly. She was livid with him. Typical man! Couldn't see past his ...

'I'm sure the practice would miss you sorely, Annie. You've been an amazing employee over the last two years. But for a young, vibrant person like you we must seem very boring indeed. I can understand you wanting to see further horizons, experience a more exciting life than what I ... I mean, *we* ... can offer you here.'

'*Employee?* Did you just say employee, Henry?' Annie was raging. How dare he! 'Is that all I've been to you?' She'd been more than just an employee, she'd given her all to his stupid practice. She'd given extra time without hesitation, stayed on some nights to make sure the sick animals were alright. She'd always cooperated with him and Rachel on whatever needed to be done. And all without question. *Employee!* She thought she was more than that. She felt that she and Henry were ... special? That they had a 'special relationship' as some American president had once said about the UK. So she hadn't always acted towards him as if he was special, but he *was*. Surely, he must know that. No, she thought to herself, I haven't ever said as much, but did I need to? And suddenly, it was all too much – she knew she was going to burst into tears. Her head was spinning and her heart ached.

'Excuse me, Henry,' she said, rushing away from the table towards the Ladies, which she hoped was empty. It was. Annie tumbled into the first empty cubicle and, flinging the toilet lid down, slumped onto it putting her head into her hands. She couldn't stop herself, as the tears flowed hot and fast down her pretty face. She sobbed out loud, knowing no-one could hear her. Oh, Henry, Henry. He *didn't* care about her. OK, he liked her as an *employee*, but nothing more. How unemotional that sounded – his employee. Someone he could replace within a week.

A loud, snotty sob escaped, and she grabbed at the toilet tissue to wipe her nose. Unfortunately, she pulled too hard and had to watch helplessly as it hopped off the holder, bounced off the side wall and rolled out under the door. At the same time, she heard the outer door open as someone entered the toilets, but she was past caring.

'*Shit, shit, SHIT,*' she sobbed loudly. Then, to her surprise, a hand appeared under the door, offering her the rogue roll.

'Is this what you need, Annie?' she heard Henry ask. 'Or is there anything else I can offer you?'

'Like what?' she asked ungraciously.

'Like my heart, you silly girl. Or have I been totally on the wrong track all this time?'

Annie tore open the toilet cubicle door, slamming it loudly off the wall, as she tried to get out to Henry. He stood there in his gentleman's country attire – looking more confident than she'd ever seen him. But there was also an air of uncertainty in his eyes.

'Oh, Henry, you great big lummox! No, you're not wrong. It took me too long to realise, but I do now. Oh,

Henry – I love you! Love you, love you, love you,' she squealed, standing on her toes as she threw her arms around his neck, kissing him repeatedly. He stopped her by taking her face in his hands and drew his lips gently down on hers. Her lips were sweet and soft; his kiss gentle at first, becoming more urgent and fierce until he could resist no longer, pulling her to him and folding her in his strong arms.

The door opened and a little white-haired, stern-looking lady came in. She stopped in her tracks as she saw them wrapped in each other's arms. They turned to her, both smiling with happiness, as she said, 'Humph, this certainly wouldn't have happened in *my* day – more's the pity!' She chuckled to herself as she entered a cubicle. Annie and Henry laughed out loud as they made their way back out to the bar.

§

Seated once again by the fire Annie looked happily at Henry. 'What will Ms. Maura say about this then. I don't think she'll be very happy that I've snatched you away from under her nose!'

'Annie, you silly girl. Maura's been in cahoots with me for the last while. She realised within minutes of starting work with us that I was head-over-heels in love with you. She said as much to me. Caught me on the hop, I can tell you. But it really made me stop and think. About how I really felt about you. And I knew she was right.'

'Clever old Ms. Maura, eh? I feel really bad about her now.' Annie said.

'She advised me not to go ploughing headlong in. Told me to play a waiting game, make you jealous. But it's been unbearable, my darling – so, so difficult. But she'd picked up on the fact that you were going out on dates with … eh... how shall I say it -'

'Lots of different chaps, Henry?'

'Eh... well, yes. They weren't all … you know? I mean, did you … with them all? No, Annie, I'm so sorry. Forget I ever said that,' he said gently, stroking her cheek. 'That was very ungentlemanly of me. What you did before is none of -'

'No, you silly man – not *ALL* of them!' And Annie smiled sweetly at Henry, because that was as far as she was prepared to go. A girl had to have her secrets, didn't she?

Chapter Forty-Four

It had been a week since Vee came back from her unsatisfactory visit to Aidan in Norebridge. She sat at her dressing table scrutinising her reflection in the oval mirror. Had she made a mistake – a really bad error of judgement? Perhaps she *should* have waited to visit until he was ready, like he'd suggested. Given him time to settle in a bit more, before arriving unannounced on his doorstep. Because no matter how she liked to dress it up in her mind, she had to admit that he had been anything but pleased to see her. Why?

She'd missed him so much when he left and assumed he missed her too. Not just assumed, he told her several times during their phone calls. What it came down to in the end though, was she loved him – really loved him and wanted to spend the rest of her life with him. After so many years of the proverbial frog-kissing she'd met Aidan – by chance, at a dinner party given by someone she wouldn't have described exactly as a 'friend'. She found out later that another couple had cancelled and, desperate to make up the numbers Diane had phoned her at very short notice. She accepted, not wanting to be rude. Aidan told her later that he had almost refused, as the hostess wasn't exactly a friend of his either. When a few weeks later they started their 'official relationship' both admitted they were very glad they'd gone to the party.

But when had things started to cool down? *Had* it started to cool off, or was she worrying unnecessarily? They'd had a nice few days together, after his initial shock at her arrival in the surgery. But they'd made love only once during her three-day stay. Surely he would have missed her more than that? Or was that a fair yardstick to use – if you're apart for six weeks, you make love three times in three days; apart for eight weeks, you should make love five times in three days! She knew she was being ridiculous. Aidan probably wasn't even worried about their situation like she was. Didn't every magazine say women always over-analysed everything?

§

But Vee was wrong. Aidan, sitting at his desk in the surgery in Norebridge *was* doing a lot of analysing. He *hadn't* been pleased to see her. In fact, he'd been furious that she'd taken it upon herself to just arrive in what he considered his 'new space, his new life.'

When he took on the job in Norebridge he looked on it as a chance to re-start his life, which he felt had become mundane and, if he were honest, very boring. When he looked ahead ten or twenty years he could see himself doing the same job, with exactly the same woman accompanying him to the same Friday night restaurants, meeting exactly the same people. And it scared the hell out of him. Finding that advertisement for a vet, in a practice in an unknown village, seemed an omen to Aidan at the time. It was as if the world was saying 'Here's your chance!'

And from the moment he'd arrived in Norebridge he'd loved it. He felt, not so much as if *it* suited him, more that *he* suited *it*. He loved the slow pace of life, people greeting him in the street – even old Foley, who insisted on greeting him with 'Hiya Doc!' He loved the High Street, with its eclectic mix of individual shops, some of which had been in families for hundreds of years. Powell's Chemist Shop was a good example, and was now in the hands of Malachy, a very switched on – if somewhat bizarre, Goth-type – young man, who swore his grandfather would turn in his grave if he saw him manning his life's work. They'd become friends in the pub, and met up every few weeks for a pint in The Spotted Peacock.

Aidan loved to walk through the park, down to the banks of the river and, much to his surprise, found himself thinking of taking up fishing again. He'd had a few conversations with two fishermen who sat happily on their fold-up stools by the bank each evening. They discussed flies and lures and how they'd happened upon this very lucrative pool, of fat, fleshy trout. He was welcome to join them if he wished, they said.

He loved his clients, even the contrary farmer, Joe FitzSimmons who lived on an isolated sheep farm high up in the surrounding hills. Gruff and sometimes obnoxious, Aidan had come to understand the man and formed an unlikely bond with him. Now, when FitzSimmons phoned the surgery he always asked for 'the blow-in'. Aidan took no offence as that was exactly what he was – a newcomer to Norebridge. He happily accepted he'd probably be 'the blow-in' for the next twenty years!

He loved his partner, Henry. He'd been very good to him from the day he arrived. Aidan had enjoyed the time spent as Henry's guest, living with him in his home until he'd found the comfortable two-bedroom flat he now occupied. Both he and his mother had been extremely kind to him and he knew he had a good friend in Henry.

And then there was Rachel. Aidan admitted to himself this was the crux of the problem. He'd felt a ground shift the moment he'd shaken hands with her that evening in the pub. Henry had arranged it as a way for him to meet Rachel and Annie, in an informal setting. He literally bumped into them both as they entered the pub. Rachel took his breath away. Not exceptionally beautiful, but there was something innocent in the way she looked at people. Her manner was gentle and kind, and Annie, the feckless Annie, thought she was the best friend a girl could have. Aidan always felt there was a vulnerability about Rachel, which he wanted to safeguard. To keep her from hurt. But, to his disappointment, he found out from the beginning she was very much committed to her boyfriend, Jack.

§

But arriving like that, Vee had forced him to take a good, hard look at their relationship. If he was honest, Aidan had looked on his break with his former life as a possible break with Vee. But he hadn't said anything to her at the time. His intention was to move to Norebridge, be on his own for a few months as he settled in, by which time he felt he'd know what he wanted from his new life. *And,* if he wanted Vee to be part of that life.

After a while he found he'd started to enjoy his freedom. He liked not having to think of anyone else when he made plans. He liked not having to explain why he had to work late, and he very much enjoyed popping in to the local pub whenever the fancy took him. He could savour a quiet pint while chatting to the locals. And, he could stay on for another if, by chance, Malachy dropped in. All in all, to Aidan his life had started again – and on *his* terms. But, now, Vee had pushed him into taking a longer look at his new life - and making a decision. He knew it wasn't fair to keep her dangling. He was in no doubt that Vee's next box to be ticked was 'Marriage.' And she'd made it quite clear on several occasions that she'd like it to be with him. But was it what *he* wanted?

Chapter Forty-Five

I hear a gentle tap on the bedroom door, and sit up when it opens slightly. 'It's OK, Anton. I'm awake,' I smile, touched that he's so thoughtful about not waking me. 'What time is it?'

'Ten o'clock, just gone. I thought I'd better bring you breakfast. Remember your appointment at the doctor's is eleven-thirty.'

'Oh, my God, Anton, I'd forgotten completely about it. I'll get up and shower now,'

'No, you won't,' he insisted, as he places a tray across my lap, shaking out a pristine white napkin. 'Chin up for Daddy,' he laughs, pretending to tuck the point into my pyjamas. Playfully, I slap his hand away, pulling the sheet modestly up over my chest.

'Too late for that, I'm afraid,' he teases. 'I've already seen your loo basey underwear – I mean, your *blue lacy* underwear – see, you've got me stumbling over my words just thinking about it!' I can't help laughing out loud.

'Anton, you've been absolutely wonderful. I don't know what I'd have done without you, or this calm and peaceful haven you've given me here to rest and get my strength back. I've loved it, and I want to thank you so much. You're a terrific person.'

'Now, now, enough of that. You know what us celebs are like. I'll get a big head from all this praise and adoration.'

'Hang on, hang on! Who said anything about adoration?' I joke. 'I'm just saying thanks for being a mate - definitely no 'adoration' on offer here. Now OUT, while I get ready for this appointment'. And, smiling, Anton leaves the room heading back down to the kitchen.

Taking a sip of the deliciously aromatic coffee, I look at the breakfast in front of me. A white tray cloth, tiny roses embroidered in the corners, covers a wooden tray. On top of which Anton has thoughtfully placed a tiny red rosebud, straining to burst into bloom, in a small silver bud vase. A breakfast plate contains two herby sausages, two slices of perfectly cooked bacon, some mushrooms in melted butter, and a huge portion of scrambled eggs topped with a sprinkling of chopped chives. A silver toast rack contains four pieces of toasted home-made bread, complete with a small dish of soft, yellowy butter and another with what looks like cherry jam. The perfect start to a day - for any fifteen-stone rugby player! But I'm so touched. Anton has made it his mission to fatten me up while I've been staying with him. And, I have to admit, I feel so much better. My strength has almost fully returned, and I'm now sleeping through the night, albeit with the help of a mild sleeping tablet prescribed by the doctor.

I do my best with the mountain of food, not wanting to offend Anton, and within an hour am showered and changed, ready to head off. Anton offers to drive me there and I gratefully accept. Driving is the one area I still feel a little shaky about.

'I'll drop you at the doctor's and you can give me a call when you're ready, Rachel. How does that suit you?' And that was what we did.

§

'That's perfectly normal, Rachel,' the doctor assures me. 'I wouldn't worry at all about it. Some areas of our lives take longer than others to get back on track. Remember, you've had an emotional trauma, which manifests itself differently with everyone.'

'I just feel as if I've been knocked for six, Doctor Morton. Every day I get up intent on doing this, that or the other. But by the end of the day I realise I've achieved nothing. I don't seem to have either the physical or emotional energy to get stuck into anything. I need to look for a place to live, I need to get back to work – so many things I *need* to do. But…'

'Just take your time, Rachel. Remember, with physical damage we're all quite happy to give it the time it needs to recover. But with emotional or psychological damage, just because we can't actually see it, we're not prepared to give it its own time to heal. And some people – like yourself – feel a sense of guilt at doing nothing, as if you're 'lazing about.' Nothing could be further from the truth, Rachel. *Especially* in your case. You're no shirker - I know your boss, Henry, very well and I've often heard him high in your praises. Believe me, we really can't rush these things. You owe it to yourself to give it time.'

§

Armed with a repeat prescription for a sleep aid, which I've assured him I'll take, I leave Dr. Morton's office. Anton and I are going for a walk in the park, as I feel like a breath of fresh air to blow some cobwebs away. The air is crisp and the sky a delicious, clear blue. Outside the clinic door I take a deep breath, enjoying the sharp coldness as it enters my lungs. I raise my head and release it back into the air, blowing it out in rings like a young child, pretending to smoke a cigarette.

'Remembering stolen moments at the back of the bicycle shed?' I hear an amused voice. I hadn't noticed Anton sitting on the low wall by the side of the building.

'I wish. Unfortunately, I was a 'good girl' at school. Never got up to some of the things my friends got up to. Missed all those vital experimental things kids find out behind the sheds. I was still very naïve going into young adulthood.'

'Nothing wrong with that. You were entitled *not* to want to do those things, if that's how you were,' Anton says in my defence.

'Oh, no. I really did want to join in. But I was just too afraid of being caught,' I explain, as we make our way towards the park. 'Honestly, it really *was* a case of *Murphy's Law* where I was concerned. If *anyone* was going to be caught doing *anything*, it was me, even when I wasn't actually involved.

'Once, I was left standing looking after everyone

else as they made their escape, and *I* was blamed, even though I'd just been an onlooker. I was made to stand up in front of the entire school and made an example of. Supposedly, I epitomised "the makings of a very bad girl" someone on the slippery slope to a possible life of crime even. *Me!'* Anton laughed out loud at that, shaking his head in disbelief.

We park up and walk along the banks of the river for about half an hour, Anton's arm companionably linked through mine, holding my hand. It feels so nice, relaxed and easy. Suddenly, I feel Anton stiffen beside me and I look at him. His face looks stricken, as if frightened of whatever he sees ahead of him. I follow his gaze and see a pretty girl, in a sort of blowsy way, looking straight at us. She starts to head in our direction as Anton takes my arm from his, hands me his car keys and says 'Rachel, would you mind going back to the car without me? I'll catch you up. Won't be long, OK?' He looks troubled, so I tell him not to worry and head off on my own.

Looking back, I see them both deep in conversation, and it doesn't look like it's a very happy one. Anton is trying to say something to this girl, but she's having none of it, interrupting him and gesticulating wildly every time he starts to talk. Who is she, to have such an effect on my friend, I wonder?

§

'Chesney ... Chesney ... no, I wasn't avoiding you. No, I haven't been away, I've ...' But it was useless, she wouldn't give him a chance to speak. She bulldozed ahead with her accusations, so he just clammed up, gritted his teeth and waited until the onslaught came to its natural conclusion.

'... and we need to get this sorted. You can't just go around using people like me, and then walking away as if nothing's happened. You could at least have called.'

'You're quite right, eh ... Chesney. But I have no intention of just walking away. I *did* ask you to contact me, when you knew for sure. But I haven't heard from you, so I assumed you'd been mistaken.'

'No mistake, Anton. You and I are going to be parents. How great is that?' she said, smiling smugly at him, full lips pouting in a manner which he'd probably found very sexy on that drink-fuelled evening – although he still had absolutely no recollection of it. Now looking at this unfortunate girl who, through his abominable behaviour, was left expecting his first child, he hated himself. And, suddenly he felt the brightness drain out of what had been, up to then, a lovely, hope-filled day.

§

We're sitting in Anton's sitting room, sipping coffee. He's been very subdued since meeting that girl in the park. I haven't asked anything about her, as I feel he'll tell me if he wants to.

I'm surprised at how comfortable I feel here in Anton's house. Like I've always been here and it has a strange feeling of 'home' to me. Anton has been fantastic over the last few days. He has looked after me with a care and tenderness I wouldn't have given him credit for before. I feel cherished and stronger with each day and I think I can even return to work very soon.

'Rachel, can I discuss something with you?'

'Course, Anton. Is there anything I can do to help? You sound troubled?'

'No, there's nothing anyone can do. I need to sort it out myself. But I *need* to tell you about it. To explain, so you understand properly.'

'Gosh, Anton, that sounds ominous,' I tease, trying to lighten the mood. But that familiar feeling of unease returns, just like that time with Jack. Anton doesn't smile. He sits back on the squishy couch and covers his face with his hand. Suddenly, I think I know what he's going to say. How could I not have realised it myself? Stupid, stupid girl. Of course! He's trying to find a nice way to suggest that perhaps I'm well enough to cope alone now. He wants his space back! Oh, God, I've been so stupid and I've taken advantage of his good nature. But I didn't mean to. I can only try to make it easier for him, save him the embarrassment of having to ask me to leave.

'Anton, it's good we have this time to chat. I was just thinking, it's been days now since I moved in with you. I'm feeling a lot better each day. I think it's time I stood ...'

'No, Rachel, wait. Let me get on with this, please? It's nothing to do with you being here. In fact, that's been the nicest thing that's happened to me in a long time. It's been fantastic having you here with me. Waking up, knowing you're in the next room. I love ... knowing that you're getting stronger, and that I'm able to help you get back on your feet. But, there's something you need to know.' Concerned, I look at this kind, gentle man and wonder what can be so troubling for him.

Chapter Forty-Six

I'm stunned. Anton is only three sentences into his revelations and already I want to run away.

'It's the result of our 'wild boy' lifestyle, Rachel. The way, for whatever reason, we all felt we should behave. All part of keeping in the limelight, keeping ourselves in the fans' minds. Like everyone in the world of show business, we needed to keep a high media profile – the "badder" the better – I know, I know,' he says, rubbing his hand over his handsome face, up through his raven hair. A long, deep sigh accompanies the anguished look in his eyes. 'Now, it seems so *stupid*, the whole thing. It was this episode recently that made me realise I had to stop the outrageous behaviour. But I had no idea it would result in this.'

I don't know what to say. I feel as if I'm being bombarded with words I don't want to hear, but I can do nothing to fend them off. They keep coming, like unrelenting arrows that pierce my heart. 'But how could you not know, Anton? When ...?' There are so many questions I want to ask, but at the same time I don't want to hear the answers.

'It was after our last concert in London. Jamie, one of the lads from the band, asked if he could come up here with me to get away from London for a few days. Of course, I said yes. They're not just fellow musicians, they're my friends, even if they do behave outrageously. They're really good guys and we've been good mates ever since we formed the band.' He sits on the edge of the sofa, elbows on his knees, hands clasped in front. But he gesticulates wildly as he speaks, his frustration showing with every word. Suddenly, he stands and asks if I'd like a coffee. It's the last thing I want, but agree.

As Anton heads to the kitchen I sit back in my armchair trying to make sense of what I'm hearing. This can't be the behaviour of the Anton I've come to know and ... and ... what, I wonder? Know and *love*? No, I assure myself. If I love Anton it's purely as a sister loves a brother. He's kind, generous, caring and has proved himself a wonderful friend to me in my time of need. The rattling of cups on saucers indicates Anton is coming back. He places the tray gently on the footstool and hands me my coffee, complete with chocolate digestive on the side.

'I'd like to tell you the whole thing, Rachel, if you'd care to listen? I promise you, it's not just a case of me whoreing around. Although, if you believe everything you read in the newspapers it would seem I do nothing else.'

'Well, Anton, it does seem as if you've had your fair share of women. Every picture I've seen of you there's some other beauty on your arm. Believe me, I'm not judging you by any means. I've always been amused to read of your exploits. *And,* you've certainly done your bit in putting Norebridge on the tourist map!' I say, doing my best to smile the hurt out of my words. But, to my surprise I do feel hurt by my own words. As if I've somehow been let down by Anton's actions. But, I reason, that doesn't make sense. Anton's actions have no bearing on my life.

'Can you just listen, Rachel? I really want to tell you how it happened. I ...'

'I think we both know how it happened, Anton,' I say light heartedly. 'It usually happens the same way for everyone. Even being famous, like you are, doesn't impact on the natural biological process of procreation!' I try to be funny, but as soon as the words are out I realise it just sounds smart-aleccy.

Anton does too, as he stands up abruptly, saying 'Rachel, can you just listen, please. Without the smart comments too, if you don't mind.' Again, the hand sweeps through his hair, as he sits down again. 'Sorry, Rachel. I didn't mean to snap. It's just ... I want to explain ... to let you know ... I don't want any barriers between us ... any secrets ...'

And in that moment, I know I don't want to hear anymore. I don't *want* to know whatever sordid little explanation Anton feels he needs to give to me. It's *his* sordid little secret, and I don't want to be party to it. I can't even bear to hear him verbalise it. As if by not hearing it hasn't happened, it's not real. I stand up.

'Anton, really, I don't need to know. No, no, *really*,' I insist, holding up my hand to stem his words. 'It's nothing to do with me – or anyone else. It's *your* life, and you can choose to live it however you want, with whoever you want, too.'

'Do you really feel that way, Rachel? As if my life has nothing to do with you?'

'Of course I do,' I reply, a little puzzled at his question. I've only known Anton a few weeks, although it seems as if I've known him forever. But that's normal, isn't it? People get to know one another on a much deeper level during times of trauma or crisis. 'I have no right to question or criticise your actions or lifestyle. No more,' I say with unfamiliar confidence, 'than you have to dictate lifestyle to me. Or *with whom* I spend my life.'

Anton looks at me intently. And, to my surprise, I think I see sadness in his dark eyes. 'Does that mean what I think, Rachel? Are you going back to Jack?'

I look at Anton and the only thing I know is that I have to get out of here – out of his house, out of his presence, out of his dark, piercing gaze. And it's suddenly clear what I have to do. 'Who knows, Anton? But I certainly intend contacting him. I need to see him, talk to him …' And without hesitating I turn and leave the room.

§

Anton sat down heavily, all strength gone from his body. For the first time, since his father's death, he cried. Great heaving sobs, as he saw his wonderful new world come to an abrupt end. He was still sitting there, hours later, in the darkness, when Brad found him. Concerned for his friend, he approached him, touching him gently on the shoulder.

'Hello, Boss. Just got back,' the chauffeur said

jovially. 'What's been happening in my absence?'

Chapter Forty-Seven

Up ahead the road disappears into the mist, the mountains long gone from sight as I make my way up through Snowdonia and the spectacular Aberglaslyn gorge, leading to the village of Beddgelert. I've decided I need some time away from everything to do with my life right now and have rented a cottage for a week in the heart of North Wales. It's been an eventful journey since leaving Norebridge several hours ago. The wettest December since records began it seems, according to the car radio, as well as the mildest for one hundred years and it hasn't stopped raining for the last two hours of my journey, turning some of the roads into small rivulets and causing traffic chaos. I've been listening to the news and weather forecasts and it looks as if I couldn't have picked a worse time for a trip to Wales. I've never been here before and I desperately wanted to be somewhere different, away from all that's familiar. Everything that reminds me of the black hole that is my life at present.

I had no trouble picking up a holiday let, a few miles outside the village of Beddgelert, in Snowdonia National Park. The owner was glad to take me, as most of her bookings have been cancelled due to this atrocious weather. In fairness, she did warn me that the weather was dire before she took my booking, and very likely to get worse. But the weather is the least of my worries. I've told no-one where I'm headed. No-one, that is, except Jack.

The mist lifts briefly and I catch a glimpse of a dark, foreboding lake, mirroring a steep, conifer-covered mountain to one side, while the other sweeps majestically up to the summit of Snowdon. It's a tantalizing view, as if Mother Nature is saying 'Look how beautiful I can really be, when I wish.' But not today, as the rain pounds my windscreen and I strain to see the ribbon of road ahead.

At last, just as darkness envelops the landscape, I find my destination – a small, Welsh cottage, half a mile up a one-car track. Grass grows in the centre and numerous pot holes make for an eye-wateringly slow and bone rattling trip to the low, wooden front door. The owner, a local farmer's widow, has very kindly left a lamp on in the hallway to light my way from the car to the house. Unfortunately, it's not enough to help me avoid the potholes in the yard and I arrive in the hallway with my feet freezing and soaked up to the ankles - my own fault for wearing such inappropriate footwear - tomorrow the wellies come out! For the moment, though, they'll have to stay in the boot of my car, as I'm not venturing back out in those conditions.

Dropping my luggage in the hallway, I carry the groceries which I've bought in the village to the back of the house, where I imagine the kitchen should be. I click on the old-fashioned brass, toggle switch and look at a room which time forgot. The floor, made up of large blue-black slate, is uneven in places. Lime-washed white walls are rough and pitted with stone edges. A small, four-panelled window is hewn out of the massively thick wall and a miner's brass lamp, sitting decoratively in the hollow, is lighting and sends out a soft, mellow glow.

There's nothing so modern as a fitted kitchen here, instead, a free-standing oak Welsh dresser sits proud of the wall, displaying an array of colourful china. On the other wall, a dark wooden table is snug against the only nod to modernity - a large *Smeg* fridge/freezer, complete with ice maker. On the third wall is the back door, beside which is an old butler's sink and slate draining board, deep ridges directing excess water back into the sink. Two cupboards are housed beneath the extended slate counter top, and that comprises the entire kitchen. Even in my present state I can't help but love its simplicity.

I put away my meagre supplies and fill the kettle. I'm gasping for a cup of tea, as I chose not to stop on the last leg of my journey, just wanting to get to the cottage and relax. As it boils I head upstairs for a look at the bedrooms. There is just enough headroom for me on the narrow, wooden stairs, its risers high and irregular. Four doors lead off the small landing at the top – one to the main, double bedroom with a second, smaller double next door; one to a single guest bedroom and the last to a tiny bathroom. Here, the walls are panelled in a soft, ferny green, distressed in places by wear and tear I imagine, rather than any attempt at fashionable décor. A pristine Victorian wash basin with a tall, brass goose-necked spout, sits atop the white, china pedestal. Cream, ceramic indicators show HOT and COLD in old-fashioned, black lettering on the taps. A large wicker basket holds a stack of neatly folded green and white fluffy towels, and high quality gels and soaps are stacked on the slate window ledge, along with a large Church candle in what looks like a hand carved wooden holder. The large, claw-footed bath at the far end looks very inviting after my long trip. I know where I'll be shortly – once I've opened my bottle of red!

As I head downstairs I hear the small *Velux* window on the landing rattle with the increasing wind outside. It's beginning to sound wild and ferocious and I experience a small flutter of anxiety at being here, in this strange environment, alone. But I chide myself for being silly. This is what I wanted - to run away from everything and everyone I know, to have time and space to myself, to get my head straight. 'So, get on with it then, Rachel and stop being so self-pitying,' I say out loud, hearing my voice echo off the centuries-old walls.

I make my cup of tea and head into the small sitting room, delighting in the room before me. A cast iron wood burning stove sits in the middle of an enormous inglenook, one side of which is stacked high with chopped wood. I can't resist, and finding some firelighters and a large box of matches beside the stove, I light the already prepared paper and wood. Immediately, a warm glow emanates from the stove, sending welcome heat into the small, chilly sitting room.

Looking around I see a large three-seater couch along one wall, with a smaller, matching two-seater pulled in close to one side of the inglenook. A well-travelled wooden trunk, numerous old shipping decals decorating its surface, serves as a coffee table on which stands a vase of beautiful flowers. Then I notice an envelope with my name on it propped up against the vase. A bottle of red wine nestles against the other side. Inside, Megan, the considerate owner has written me a welcome note, giving details of emergency numbers I might need during my stay. It seems a flood warning's been issued, which shouldn't affect the cottage I'm in. She tried my mobile several times to let me know, in case I changed my mind, but I'd already been on my way and couldn't be reached. Also, I'd purposely turned my mobile off, as I don't want to be bothered with any calls, from *anyone* over the next few days.

In the light of this news I make up my mind to just hunker down for a few days in this delightful place and ... think. Megan also gives me her own number and issues an invitation to pop over for 'a panad' which she explains is a cup of tea! How kind of her. But I don't feel up to chatting right now.

Nursing my warm tea, I snuggle onto the comfy

couch with a fleecy blanket I find hanging over the back. Staring into the flames I'm soon lost in my jumbled thoughts. After a while I feel drowsy and place my empty cup safely on the wooden trunk. I slip down under the blanket, a great weariness coming over me. I must have nodded off, because the next thing I know is hearing a repeated loud knocking on the front door. Stumbling from the couch I head down the narrow hall, opening the swollen door with a jerk. I step back, astonished, at the person standing in the darkness outside.

'Jack? What on earth are you doing here?'

Chapter Forty-Eight

I set the kettle to boil for a second time since my arrival and busy myself finding a mug for my visitor. What is Jack doing here? He's the only one I told where I was going, but we agreed he would come up on Saturday, two days from now. I'm not ready for him, I want some time to myself. I *need* some time to myself. Why does he always do this – do things when it suits *him*, rather than when I need him to. Suddenly, he's behind me and I start at the sound of his voice.

'Sorry, Rache. I just couldn't wait. I left almost immediately after you phoned. Boy, you certainly picked the back of beyond for your road trip though, eh?' he teases.

'Yeah, well, I took the first rental I could find. I wasn't too interested where it was. But I think I'm lucky to have found this.'

'*Really?* You can't be serious, Rachel. Why on earth would you want to spend time *here*? I'm sure I could find a much nicer place to run away to?'

'I'm sure you could too, Jack,' I say, looking intently at my ex-boyfriend. This is part of our problem, I've always gone along with whatever Jack wanted. But this is something for me, not him. Supposed to be on my terms only. 'Something five-star would be more up your street, wouldn't it?' I say.

'Absolutely. You know me,' he says. 'Like my little luxuries, and not ashamed to say it,' he smiles that wonderful smile and I feel myself drawn in. 'Remember that time we went to Thailand – that was more than five-star, wasn't it? We had such a brilliant time.'

'Yes, yeah ... I suppose it was,' I say slowly.

'What do you mean, "suppose"? If I remember correctly you enjoyed everything about it. At least you said you did,' Jack says, taking on a slightly petulant look. 'You can't say that hotel wasn't amazing - right there on the beach, drinks on tap, incredible food served to us on our loungers without us even having to move. And, at the end of the day a massage right there on the warm sand, with the sun going down over the water.'

§

Yes, I think, as my mind wanders back to what really would be anyone's idea of a dream holiday. But, again, I think, this has always been part of our problem. Why didn't I speak out when we were there – about how I felt I was constantly taking advantage of the local Thai people, paying them a pittance for a massage I would have had to pay twenty times that amount for back home; about the awful tourists who spoke rudely to the friendly waiters and waitresses who served everyone with a smile and a graciousness we've long lost at home.

Remembering one particular occasion, I can still feel absolutely appalled at the behaviour of a hotel guest to a cleaner in the lobby. He spoke to him in a manner I know he would never have used in his own place of work. But did I intervene? Did I jump to the man's defence? No, not at all. I moved on – reluctantly, I admit – but nonetheless, moved on at Jack's insistence that we 'shouldn't get involved.' To my shame, eyes down I did as he suggested, heading off for another carefree day on the sun-kissed beach.

My cowardice that day has always rankled. What was I afraid of? Standing up to Jack? Or just making a show of myself? And, if I *had* stood up to Jack what did I think he was going to do – leave? Did I keep silent, just to keep him? How far am I prepared to go to keep him, I wonder?

Suddenly, I realise Jack's talking to me. 'Sorry, Jack. I was miles away,' I say. 'Why don't we head into the sitting-room? I'm sure it's nice and warm by now,' and I lead the way into the cosy room, which has heated up nicely, taking my place on the couch closest to the stove. Red flickering flames show through the glass panelled doors, and I'm surprised, despite my present predicament, to feel that I could happily stay here in this wonderful cottage, for a very long time.

§

'I was really glad you called, Rachel,' Jack says. 'I thought I'd never hear from you again.'

Looking across at him I feel the familiar yearnings well up in me, and I'm surprised. After all that he's done, how can I still have feelings for him? When does the heart take a step back? When does it say 'Enough!' before gathering a protective shield around it to ward off further hurt? When does the heart help us to hate, rather than love? Maybe it doesn't. Perhaps it's only capable of love?

I drag my thoughts back to this room, where I have decided to finally make decisions about my life, on my own terms, and with no input from anyone else. Least of all the man sitting expectantly in front of me. But, in the meantime, before we can move on, I have questions.

'Why, Jack?' That's all I say. And, this time, I wait.

'Oh, Rache, do we have to do this?' he says impatiently. But I say nothing. This time I don't break into the silence like I normally would. It stretches between us like a deep valley, and I know Jack's just waiting for me to jump into the void. When I don't, he continues 'I came up here for *you*. Saturday was just too far away. I needed to get here as soon as possible, to see you again.'

'You haven't answered my question, Jack. Why? Why did you ruin our relationship? What I thought, by the way, was a *good* relationship. What was so wrong that you had to go and get involved with that girl in the States?'

'Oh, God, Rachel, I don't know. It ...'

'Don't even think of saying *"It just happened"* Jack.' And I say this with such force that, for once, Jack looks at me. *Really* looks at me, as if seeing me for the first time.

'Well, if we're going to get into this do you think I could have something stronger than tea?'

I head back into the kitchen, returning with two

large glasses of red wine, which seriously depletes my supply and chances of a hot bath and a glass of red. I find I'm annoyed at Jack for that.

§

'So? You were saying?' I encourage Jack, handing him his wine. It doesn't escape my notice that he has switched seats, and is now sitting beside me on the couch.

'You're really not giving up on this, are you?' he asks. I can see uncertainty in his eyes, an unfamiliar emotion for Jack.

'No, I'm not. And if you'd rather not discuss it, then we have nothing to say to each other. I mean, we were together for over two years – don't you think I deserve some sort of an explanation? That was part of my reason for asking you up here.'

'And the other part?' he asks seductively, reaching over to caress my face. Oh, that touch. So familiar, and I find myself leaning into it, but only for a second. I remind myself this is Jack's way of avoiding issues – we've always ended up in bed. It's hard to resurrect a thorny subject when you're basking in the happy afterglow of passion, so I move ever so slightly away from Jack, but enough that he notices.

'OK, Rachel. You want to know why I played away?' I wince at his casual use of the phrase. It's as if he's asking my reason for wanting to know why he chose a blue shirt as opposed to a green one. Does he think it's that trivial?

'I want to know why you cheated – sexually, as well as emotionally. I want to know why you made a conscious decision to deceive me – and this other person – not just on a one-off basis, but over and over. You lied with such ease, Jack, that I'm …'

'It wasn't like that. I never went to the States with cheating in mind. It really did seem to just happen. I know, I know …,' he says, holding up his hand to stem my objections.

'But there was that first moment when you spoke to her, and decided to ask her out? *That's the moment to my mind, Jack, when you chose to cheat.* You could have just gone on your way? Why do men - and women - think it's OK to do things when they're away that they wouldn't do at home? For me, the rules are the same – at home or away.'

'Yeah, yeah, for you maybe, Rache. But you're making a moral judgement about a situation you've never found yourself in. I don't think you can do that. You're not ...'

'I've never found myself in that situation, Jack, because I've never *put* myself in that situation and I think it's a little arrogant of you to imagine that *I've* never been tempted too. But I've made up my mind to say *'NO.'*

'Really?' he laughs a little derisively, as if it's beyond the realms of possibility that I should ever be tempted to cheat on him. Has he always felt so sure of himself, I wonder. Have *I* always made him feel so sure of himself? 'Look, Rachel, I was sent to the States from work, you know that. I had to socialise with a lot of people over there, Jenny included. We had to spend a lot of time in each other's company, so ... I suppose ... well, ...' he looks at me, with an air of indifference. In that moment I feel a coldness towards him, towards his shrugging off of his decision that changed both our lives forever.

'So, what now, Jack?' Again, I sit back and wait. I can see now that my silences are very disconcerting for him.

'Well, Rachel, that totally depends on you. I genuinely don't know what madness took hold of me, but I've never stopped loving you. I'm hoping you can see your way through all this. I know you haven't stopped loving me, either. We can ...'

'How do you know, Jack? After everything you've done? I don't think ...'

'No, Rachel, I *know* you. You can't switch off just like that. It was all a mistake and I realise that now and it's OK if you want to make me suffer – but, just a little,' he smiles. 'You're one of nature's truly genuine people, I've always known that. Sometimes, maybe, you're a little too enabling, you know what I mean? A little too accepting of everything, a little too trusting.'

I sit beside my one-time lover as he reels off my virtues, faults and failings. I want to be angry with him. Instead, to my surprise, I feel as if something monumental is happening within me. Slowly, like water finding its way down an unfamiliar incline until it finds its level, or like the proverbial onion, the layers of which are being peeled away, one by one, to reveal the very core inside. And, slowly too, I decide I like that core. For the first time in my life I'm entirely satisfied with the person he's just described – me!

'What are you going to do about Jenny?' I ask, more out of curiosity than interest.

'Don't worry about her, Rachel. She'll be OK, she's going back to the States on Saturday.'

'What about the baby, Jack? Surely, you're not just abandoning the baby?' I say, shocked at his casual dismissal of his child's mother.

'Oh, no, no. I'll certainly visit every now and then. And, of course, I'll provide financially for them both. But, well ... that's as far as I want to be involved, I know that now.'

Chapter Forty-Nine

Annie grabbed Henrys hand as he drove up the short driveway. 'I'm so nervous, Henry,' she said. 'What if she hates me?' Henry laughed, squeezing her hand reassuringly.

'There's no way she'll hate you,' he laughed. 'Anyway, even if she does it'll make no difference to me. I love you dearly, Annie, my darling. I'm sure she'll love you too, seeing how happy you make me.'

Annie wasn't so sure. She'd been so happy over the last few days - Henry loved her! Despite the lovely warmth of the day, she shivered a little thinking of how close she'd come to ruining it all. But he wanted her, despite her silly (and numerous!) encounters with all the Rodders and Williams since coming to Norebridge. Henry was the least judgemental man she'd ever met. It was part of the reason why she was madly in love with her chubby, rosy-cheeked man. Well, she'd just have to make Henry's mother see how much she adored him –

'Bring it on!' she said quietly to herself. And, too soon for Annie's liking, they were pulling up outside the door of The Vicarage.

They were barely inside the front door when a slightly shrill voice called out from one of the rooms down the dimly lit hallway. 'Henry, darling, is that you? I'm in the drawing-room.' Who else would it be? Annie thought.

'Evening, Mother,' Henry replied happily as Annie followed him down the hall. Stepping aside, he gently coaxed Annie in front of him through the door. Her first thought was 'What a lovely room.' Softly lit by several lamps, and the glowing embers of an open fire, the room was warm and inviting. A neutral creamy-white colour scheme on carpets and sofas was broken up by floral curtains and wallpaper like splashes from Kew Gardens. Annie felt like she was walking into a Spring garden.

Mrs. Donaldson sat on one side of the enormous fireplace, ensconced in an overstuffed armchair. Wearing a bright orange bag-like dress, stretched over a very ample bosom, she was the only thing which clashed in the otherwise pleasant surroundings. In her white wavy hair, which looked rock hard with hairspray, sat a sparkly diamond slide, holding it firmly on one side. A little too girly, Annie thought. Bright red lipstick which, under other circumstances, would have appealed to Annie, stained thin lips, drawn back in a straight line of disapproval. *I knew it, she hates me already.*

'And, who have we here?' the woman asked in a silky, smooth voice. Annie threw a puzzled look at Henry, who shook his head ever so slightly. He'd told her his mother was expecting them both for tea. He'd also told her all about Annie.

'Mother, this is Annie,' Henry smiled, his arm around her waist, squeezing her reassuringly. 'Sorry we're a little late,' he said, reddening at the thought of what exactly had kept them late. Annie was such an unpredictable little minx!

'Hello, Mrs. Donaldson. Very pleased to meet you, I've heard so much about you,' Annie smiled.

'While I know practically nothing about you, my dear,' the overweight woman replied, holding Annie's hand limply.

The eyes of both women locked on and in the slowly ticking seconds, each one punctuated loudly by the grandfather clock in the corner, Annie knew she was fighting for her future survival in this household. *'Start as you mean to go on'* her father had always said.

Hearing his voice in her head, Annie drew herself up slightly, 'Oh, *really?* I'm surprised, Mrs. Donaldson. Henry assures me he's told you all about me. Perhaps you've just forgotten.' Annie said firmly, the implication clear to both women and the battle lines drawn.

Hesitantly, the older woman spoke. 'Oh, yes, yes ... of course. How forgetful of me. You're the Receptionist in Henry's practice, I believe?' the woman said silkily.

'Receptionist and Assistant, actually,' Annie replied, equally smoothly, smiling all the while.

Totally oblivious to the tension in the air, Henry basked in the joy of having the two women he loved most together at last. 'Shall I make some tea, Mother?' he suggested. Annie jumped up to help. 'No, no, darling, you stay with Mother – get to know each other a little better,' he beamed, almost skipping out of the room.

§

Silence followed, in which Annie looked everywhere except at the person she now knew to be her rival for Henry's affections. Well, there was no way she was going to be put off. Henry was the most precious thing that had ever happened to her.

The older woman waited until the door closed behind Henry. 'As it happens, I do remember what Henry told me about you. You live over on the Westcott Estate, I believe. Quite a large family, am I right? What does your father do? And your mother, does she work too?' Henry's mother looked straight at Annie, a slight sneer on her crimson lips.

'Yes, she does indeed, Mrs. Donaldson. Very hard, as it happens. Not only is she a housewife and mother, but she works full time doing respite for parents with autistic children. She's a marvellous woman and I'm very proud of her. As for my father – he had his own construction business. Unfortunately, he went bust, eh ... bankrupt, though not through any fault of his own, more because some of his wealthier clients didn't pay up when they should. But he paid off his debts, which not everyone does, and that left him bankrupt. He sold our house so no-one would be left out of pocket, as a result of which we had to move here. Now he's the Manager in the local C & Q – nothing to be ashamed of, is there?' Annie stood, hands on her hips, looking defiantly at the older woman. To her surprise the older woman's cheeks reddened slightly, and not from the heat of the fire, Annie was sure.

'Oh, I see,' she said slowly, turning to look into the embers of the now dying fire. Deep in thought, she said nothing for a few minutes. Annie was beginning to feel uncomfortable when the woman spoke, more to herself it seemed, than to the young freckly, red haired girl standing uneasily before her.

'I'm so sorry, my dear,' she said quietly. 'I've just realised my own dear father would be heartily ashamed of me at this minute. *He* was the son of a very skilled carpenter, who built up a very successful furniture business. He bought a small premises and operated from there until, much later, he moved to a larger shop. He was lucky there was a huge demand for his wares back then. By the time he died, he owned four large joinery businesses and he was one of the first people in our area to specialise in bespoke kitchens. He later amalgamated things, and it was this huge company which Henry's father, my husband, took over when my father died. Father had no male heirs, you see, and Theo, my husband, worked for years with my father, who saw his potential – both as his heir and as a husband for me. A female running a business back then wasn't very common, I'm afraid.' The old woman stretched out her hand to Annie. 'Forgive me, my dear, for being such a frightful snob. Your pride in your parents is to be admired.'

Annie took the woman's hand, giving it a gentle squeeze. 'Mrs. Donaldson, please don't worry. I absolutely adore Henry. Have no fear, we're both on the same wavelength there. He's wonderful and I ... I mean ... ' she suddenly felt incredibly shy in front of Henry's mother and couldn't bring herself to say it. But the old lady wasn't about to save her any blushes.

'Yes? You what?' she teased, smiling up at a flustered Annie. Looking into the old lady's eyes Annie saw tears welling up and rushed to reassure her.

'Oh, gosh Mrs. Donaldson, I love him to bits, what else can I say,' she said and suddenly found herself in tears, too. Before she knew what she was doing she leaned over, throwing her arms around Henry's mother. In return, she felt herself being hugged warmly.

'Just keep him on his toes, my girl,' the old lady laughed. 'That's how I kept his father for forty-six years!'

Henry returned to the sitting room to see both women laughing heartily, Annie sitting companionably on the arm of his mother's chair. He was in absolute heaven!

Chapter Fifty

After a very fitful and sleepless night I head down to the cottage kitchen, gasping for a cup of strong coffee. The wind kept me awake for most of the night and at one stage I seriously thought the roof was being stripped away. I'm sure on further inspection outside I'll see some damage, if not to the cottage itself than to some of the outbuildings forming the small courtyard to the back.

Locating a glass cafetiere and two cups I make a full pot, relishing the rich aroma wafting around me. As I pour myself a cup I hear Jack's sleepy voice, and see him lounging against the kitchen door. My heart skips a beat as I see his familiar bare torso which I've caressed so often; his dishevelled, tousled hair and have to restrain myself from reaching out and running my fingers through it.

'I hope you slept better than I did,' he grumbles. 'That guest room leaves a lot to be desired. I was freezing all night, that duvet is paper thin. I wasn't expecting such primitive conditions, Rache.'

'Didn't you look in the bottom of the wardrobe? There are several blankets in there – gorgeous pure Welsh wool ones - you would have been nice and toasty,' I hear myself goad him. What does he expect? 'Anyway, Jack, if you're so cold shouldn't you put something on?' He has the grace to be a little embarrassed and I know immediately what he's hoping for. While I may have been awake half the night, it has served a purpose and given me plenty of time to think things over. Our talk last night has also thrown some light on things for me – most importantly, about what I *don't* want in my life. Jack's turning up unexpectedly has helped me in that decision. 'Perhaps, Jack, when you're dressed we could continue our discussion of last night.' He throws his eyes up to heaven, and sighs loudly.

'Honestly, Rachel. I don't know what else you want me to do. I've ...'

'Let me light the fire, Jack, so we can at least sit in comfort. But it'll take a while to warm the place up. In the meantime, I just want to pop outside and check if any roof tiles have come down in the night, so I can let the owner know.'

'Why should you be bothered about that? It's not your property. He can check things for himself, if he's concerned,' he says petulantly. 'It's howling a bloody gale out there!'

'*She*, actually. The owner is a lady called Megan, and she's been very kind to me Jack, letting me have the cottage on such short notice. So, it's just something I want to do. Perhaps I can save her some problems, if she knows about any damage early enough. Do you want to come with me?'

'No, you're alright. I'll stay here, thanks. Any more coffee?'

'Sure, help yourself,' I say, heading towards the rattling front door. Pulling on my coat and a woolly hat I open the door which is practically torn off its hinges by the wildly gusting wind. Head down, and bent almost double, I grab my wellies from the boot of the car, then make my way with great difficulty to a nearby fence, from which I imagine I'll be able to get a clear view of the roof. Sure enough, I can see where two or three slate tiles have been ripped off, leaving a gaping hole where rain now has free access. I imagine, from the geography of the house, that the hole is approximately above the lovely bathroom. I'd hate anything to happen to it –

especially before I've had that warm bath and glass of red!

To the far end of the building I also see a steady stream of water, gushing down the hillside, hitting directly against the gable end. To my mind it seems a bit too much to be a normal occurrence. This looks like something's burst higher up and water has found its own way down the shortest route to the lower lying stream. I'm very concerned and grab my mobile phone from my jacket pocket. No signal! Then I remember Megan telling me she lives in a 'mobile black spot.' It was actually the deciding factor for me in getting away from everyone and everything. But now it's working against me. I'll have to go over to Megan's house myself. Running back into the cottage I tell Jack, who insists we should get back to our 'chat,' as he calls it. I can hear the inverted commas in his voice. 'We need to sort things out, Rachel.'

'I'll be back as soon as I can,' I promise.

Outside, the wind whips my hat away, sending it skidding along the wet, muddy ground. I head towards my car and reverse out of the yard. I've only gone a few hundred yards when it becomes obvious I'm not going to get any further by car. Shallow water has submerged what was the road, and two large trees have come down, one blocking the road entirely while the other has crashed through an old drystone wall bordering the neighbouring field. Only one thing for it, so I head off towards Megan's house on foot, slithering and sliding my way down the hill through mud and water. Before long, some water has slopped into my wellies and I'm regretting my urge to rush to Megan's rescue. But I know it's not far and can see her house through an avenue of trees, swaying helplessly in the vicious wind. I push my way towards it, and as I get closer I can see what I think is a shallow stream, flowing fast in front of the house, and realise the bottom floor of her house is under water.

'Megan,' I shout at the top of my voice, but am sure the wind's just whipped my voice away. The noise around me is deafening, my ears feel as if they're being assaulted. I shout again and again, and am at last reassured to see a woman's head leaning out of one of the upper floor windows of the two-storey farmhouse.

'Are you OK?' I shout. I can't hear her reply. She's gesticulating wildly and pointing to something. Looking around, I can't make out what she means, but see a grassy mound a little closer to the house and decide I'll head there, in the hope of hearing what Megan needs. It's obvious now there's no-way she can get out. The torrential rain in the night has completely cut her off from the road where I am. Tentatively, I try to pick my way towards the mound. It's hard going, and a little scary.

Suddenly, without warning, the submerged ground beneath my feet disappears and, too late I realise this was no shallow stream. I've stumbled over what must be the edge of a narrow river. Before I can do anything, my feet are swept from under me, and I'm in freezing, murky water, being tumbled over and over, like clothes in a washing machine. I can't get any purchase underfoot and my water-filled wellies are leaden on my feet. Somehow, I manage to rid myself of them, terrified they'll drag me further under the fast-flowing water. But I'm being swept along like a paper boat and there's nothing I can do.

I glimpse snatches of the sky, threatening in its greyness. Rain beats mercilessly against my face, and my ears fill with the thundering sound of flooding water. With great effort, I raise my head and spy a narrow farm gate up ahead, realising the floodwater will take me through it. The water is foaming into white-tipped eddies, as it's forced through the narrow gap, and as I pass through I reach out, trying desperately to grab hold of the gatepost. But I scream in agony as my wrist is almost wrenched from my arm. But at least it slows my progress, if only for a moment. Then, in a flash, I'm flipped around, and my head hits the stone wall with tremendous force. After that, there's only blackness.

Chapter Fifty-One

I hear voices, but they seem to come from very far away and I don't have the energy to open my eyes. The voices are angry, someone tells them to be quiet - something about the patient needing peace and quiet.

'Who the hell are you, anyway?' I hear someone ask.

'I'm a friend of Rachel's – a good friend. I came up as soon as I heard about her accident. You're Jack, aren't you? What are you doing here?'

'Not that it's any of your business, but Rachel invited me here. Asked me to join her here. I'm her boyfriend, actually.'

'*Ex-boyfriend*, I think you mean.' This voice I know, but I can't place it precisely.

'Not any more, Miss Smarty-pants! In fact, that's what Rachel asked me up here to discuss - getting back together.'

'In your dreams, Jack! Did Rachel actually tell you that?' the girl's voice asks. Something in me wants to shout out, but I'm not sure what it is I want to tell them.

Then I hear the other man's voice again – soft and gentle.

'Let's just wait until Rachel wakes up. She's very ill and I think the nurse is right. We should leave her to rest. I've found the number of the owner of the cottage Rachel was staying in and I've spoken with her. Although due to flooding we'll have to take a long way round to get there, she's happy for us to bunk down there, while we wait for Rachel to wake up. Let's head over, have a bite to eat and come back here later this evening. Is that OK with you, Annie?'

Annie, Annie – yes, of course. My best friend, Annie. I'm really pleased she's here. I want to see her, speak to her. But I can't, I have no voice. No words come out, although they're racing around in my head. And my eyes are too heavy, they won't open. I raise my hand to stop them leaving, but I hear a door close and then there's silence.

§

At the cottage, Anton stoked the dying embers of the fire which Megan had very thoughtfully lit, trying to encourage them back into life. Yesterday's newspaper lay on the couch, so scrunching it up, he chucked it into the stove, and found some firelighters and matches close to hand. Within minutes a bright, warm glow cheered the room. Annie came in from the kitchen with two steaming mugs of coffee, handing one to Anton while ignoring a surly Jack, sitting alone in the corner.

'Won't be a mo, just popping to the loo,' she said to no-one in particular, placing her mug carefully on the coffee table.

Anton and Jack sat in silence, broken only by the crackling of dry wood in the stove. Jack resented Anton's presence, while Anton's thoughts were only for Rachel. *Please let her be alright,* he begged. He wasn't sure to whom he was praying, but at that moment he would've sold his soul to the highest bidder to know Rachel was OK. She'd looked so small, so vulnerable, lying in her hospital bed and he'd been frightened looking at her lifeless form. His heart felt tight in his chest and he knew if he'd been alone he'd have broken down and wept for her. His thoughts were interrupted by Annie, who skipped into the room, smiling broadly.

'Oh, Jack, I'm so sorry. I made a mistake looking for the loo. I'm afraid I wandered into *your* room, – *the spare room*, I mean.' There was no mistaking the look of satisfaction on Annie's face as she turned to Anton, winking cheekily. Neither was there any mistaking Anton's great sigh of relief. Jack glowered at them both from his corner.

§

Several hours later a very silent trio made their way slowly back to the hospital in Anton's car. No good news awaited them – there was no change in Rachel's condition. The doctor looking after her was concerned, having expected some response, however small, by now. The following twenty-four hours would be crucial.

They were joined later by Megan, who'd been helped from the house by a neighbouring farmer. He'd pulled Rachel to safety, and called the rescue services, who arranged for Rachel to be flown by air ambulance to the hospital. On hearing of her condition, Megan had insisted on Jack calling Rachel's family or friends. Knowing she had no family, Jack reluctantly called the surgery, informing Annie of the circumstances of Rachel's accident. Much to his annoyance, Annie had lost no time jumping into her car with that Anton for company, haring her way up to Rachel's bedside. As far as he was concerned, they weren't needed at all.

Megan sorted out something to eat for them all,

while Annie slipped away to telephone Henry. He was horrified to hear of the seriousness of Rachel's condition and suggested he come straight up to North Wales. Annie assured him there was nothing he could do, but promised to call him back once they'd received an update from the doctor.

Returning to Rachel's room, Annie settled down in a hard, plastic chair along with Anton and Jack. She and Jack had dozed off when they were interrupted by a nurse coming to check on her friend. Shaking her head regretfully she indicated there was still no improvement. Anton, seated closest to Rachel, took her hand gently in his, speaking softly to the sleeping girl. 'Hi Rachel, it's Anton. We're here with you and really want you to wake up. Please try. I'm sure it's very difficult. But we're not going anywhere until you tell us to,' he smiled, stroking her hand slowly. 'We're going to sit here for however long it takes. The only way you'll get rid of us is to wake up. Annie and Jack are here too.' Annie was moved to tears by his tenderness towards her friend.

'Yeah, Rache, come on. I've absolutely *loads* to tell you. You'll never guess what's happened with Henry, since you've been away. Not in a million years, I promise you,' she said to Rachel.

'Hi, Rachel, it's Jack. Come on now, you need to wake up. We still have a lot to discuss, remember? We're just about to get things back on track. Don't give up now,' Jack coaxed.

Anton started, as he felt a slight pressure on his hand. Then again, this time a little more insistent. 'Get the nurse, Annie. Quick!' he instructed, turning his attention back to Rachel. 'Good girl, Rachel. Come on, can you hear me? Just give my hand a squeeze. Come on, you can do it.' As he caressed Rachel's hand he was annoyed to see Jack, who'd been looking out the window suddenly join him at Rachel's bedside. Taking her other hand in his, Jack started to talk to her too.

'Come on, Rache. I know you want to come back to us. Just do it. Keep trying, please. We need to sort things out, right?'

Rachel's body jerked several times, her right hand twitched violently. It was very disconcerting and difficult to watch. A nurse rushed into the room, instructing everyone to move away from her patient. Anton obeyed immediately, but Jack refused to shift from the bedside. 'She's reacting to my voice,' he insisted. But the petite nurse was not to be moved.

'I'd like you to move aside, Sir, if you want to be of

any help. Otherwise you may hinder our efforts?' There was no other answer to that. Slowly, Jack acquiesced, clearing the space for two other medical staff who entered briskly.

Anton wanted someone to tell him what was happening, but understood the medics had to do whatever it was they needed to do, unhindered by the questions of loved ones. So, he stood quietly by the window, willing something, *anything,* to happen to indicate that Rachel was coming back from wherever she was.

§

I feel as if I'm being pulled, against my will, by the strong current again. I don't want to go with it. I must resist, try to pull myself out of its undertow, swim against the tide. I can hear someone asking me, very gently, to come to them. There's another voice too, but it's harsh, demanding. I want to tell them I'm here, to let them know I'm alright. But my thoughts are muddled and thick like treacle, and no words come.

Chapter Fifty-Two

Two hours later Anton and Annie were drinking their second cup of gloopy, machine coffee, more for something to do than from actual thirst. Jack was standing looking out of the window, and hadn't spoken to anyone since leaving Rachel's room. Suddenly, the door opened and a nurse came in, telling them the doctor had suggested they might like to return to Rachel.

'All of us? It won't be too much for her?' Anton asked, concerned. But she reassured him it was OK for all three to be there.

Entering the room Anton was delighted to see Rachel sitting up, supported by several pillows. She was pale, her eyes huge in her head, but he was happy to see a smile on her lovely face. Suddenly, Jack pushed past him, taking up a place beside the bed.

'God, Rache, you certainly gave me a fright. What were you thinking, haring off like that in such atrocious weather?' The man I know to be Jack is holding my hand. Then I hear another voice.

'About time too, don't you think, Rache? If you wanted a holiday you only had to ask.' I see Annie, freckly faced and smiling and I smile back.

'Hi, Rachel, lovely to see you're back with us. You had us all worried. Very worried, indeed.' I look at the speaker - a handsome, rugged-faced man standing quietly near the door. His voice is gentle, smooth like silk and there's kindness in his eyes. I smile back at him, and he turns away suddenly. Have I offended him in some way?

'I think I'd like to be alone with Rachel now, if you all don't mind,' Jack says to the room in general. I see Annie look at the other man and I get the impression they're not pleased. I'm hoping they don't go, it's nice to have them here, somehow reassuring.

'Rachel, are you up to talking? Would you rather some time to yourself?' the man asks.

'No, she wouldn't,' Jack says emphatically. And I just don't have the energy or the inclination to argue. They both obviously take my silence as acquiescence, because the next thing I know they both take their leave and are gone. Jack draws a chair noisily to my bed and takes my hand again. I look at him, wondering why I'm uneasy in his presence. He's my boyfriend, isn't he? I definitely heard someone say so. Who is the *ex* then?

§

The lights are dim when something wakes me. The nice nurse is hovering. She smiles down at me, straightening my bedclothes and plumping up my pillows.

'Your friends are very relieved to have you back in the land of the living,' she says. 'One, certainly more than the others,' this said in a teasing voice. 'Lucky you!'

I look at her and hear someone speak. To my astonishment, I realise it's me. 'I suppose so. Jack says he's my boyfriend. But I … don't know. You probably think that's awful of me. But I don't … I'm not sure …I can't remember… it just doesn't feel … you know?'

'Well, if it doesn't feel right, it probably isn't. Anyway, I wasn't talking about Jack!' she winks, leaving my room. I lie back, exhausted by this simple exchange.

§

I'm in a bright, airy room, lying in a bed as soft as a marshmallow. The sun streams through a large bay window, curtains held back by multi-coloured silken ropes. The walls are punctuated here and there with small pictures, landscapes mostly, in colours to suit the hues and shades of the rooms décor. It's a peaceful haven and outside, the sky is clear blue, seen through the leafy branches of an oak tree.

To my right a door opens and a man pops his head around, smiling warmly. It's the man from the hospital. 'Hi, Rachel. Ready for breakfast?'

'Anton. You're so kind,' I hear myself say. Anton – of course!

But then I'm awake again, and the bright, airy room has been exchanged for the utilitarian magnolia of my hospital room.

§

I've had a restless night. The friendly nurse, Bernie, offered some sleeping tablets, but I decided against them. Now, I regret my decision as I feel totally wrung out, as if I've climbed a mountain, but with none of the exhilaration. Chrissie, the tea lady, pokes her head around the door.

'A nice cuppa, Rachel?' she offers. I look at my watch and realise it's only six-thirty. I thank God there are still some small cottage hospitals left, with an old-fashioned tea lady, instead of those God-awful self-service machines.

'Great, thanks Chrissie. Just what I need to jizz me up. You must have had an early start though?'

'Well, I'm not doing my breakfast rounds yet. I was in a little early this morning and made a cuppa for a few of us. Bernie said you were awake so I just thought you might like one, too.'

'You're very kind, Chrissie. Dedicated to your work, too, it seems, to be in this early, if you don't need to be?'

'No, no,' she laughs. 'More a means of escape. I just couldn't face the usual row with the kids trying to get them up for school, feed them, make sure they've washed themselves, etc. etc. Tommy can deal with that this morning – just to let him see the war that's waged in our house every morning!'

It seems Chrissie's three children are little angels – after nine o'clock in the morning – before that, absolute nightmares. A tug of war usually ensues over school uniforms, at least half a cereal box ends up on the floor each morning, and she's almost suicidal by the time she reaches the school gate from the arguing and shouting that goes on in the back of the car. So, this morning it seems, it's Tommy's turn to be frazzled before he even starts work. Chrissie turns to go out, smiles over her shoulder, and says 'Enjoy your tea, Rachel. Oh, and by the way, I've given one to your friend outside as well.'

'My friend? Who?'

'The gorgeous Anton, of course! Half the nurses have been mooching around the Nurses Station for the last hour. I'm sure he'll be delighted to hear you're awake so he can escape from their attentions. I'll tell him when I go out,' she says, as the door closes silently behind her.

I'm stunned. Anton is sitting outside – at six thirty in the morning! How long has he been out there, I wonder? As I puzzle over this, the door opens and Anton peeps around the door.

'Feel like a visitor?' he asks, shyly, not yet entering the room.

'Of course, Anton. I didn't know you were out there. Why didn't you come in?'

'Oh, I didn't mind. I didn't want to crowd you, or intrude. But the lady who gave me the tea told me you'd woken up. How are you?'

I haven't seen Anton since the other day, when Jack insisted we have some time alone. He looks very drawn, as if *he* hasn't slept well either. He comes and sits beside me, on the hard, plastic hospital chair. His blue-black hair is beginning to curl slightly on his collar, as if it needs to be trimmed. But I think he looks gorgeous, just as he is. His eyes are tired, evidence of bags underneath them. They'd be any woman's nightmare, but on Anton, they seem to speak of fatigue, rather than age.

'Intrude, Anton? I would never think of you intruding. You've been so good to me lately. You've been an amazing friend. I'll never forget what you've done for me. Thank you – so much.'

'Oh, Rachel, there's no need to thank me. I …'

'I know, Anton. You would do it for anyone. But, believe me, it saved my life.'

'Yes, Rachel. We'd all do the same for a friend. But, speaking of that, I was hoping … I mean …'

Anton is interrupted as the door opens and the doctor walks in. He asks several questions, determining my progress, and, to my delight, informs me I can go home in the morning. I'm thrilled, until he tells me it's on condition that I have someone to look after me at home. Before I can reply, I hear Anton say 'She does, doctor. She can come back to my house and I'll keep my beady eye on her 24/7. If that's OK with you, Rachel? Unless you'd rather ...'

The doctor looks sternly at me, cocking his head on one side, waiting for my answer. 'I'm not letting you out of here without knowing you'll be cared for. I've spoken with your GP and it seems you've been through the mill lately. You've come a long way now, Rachel, and I don't want you having a relapse through sheer exhaustion again. You need to allow yourself to be pampered a little,' he says, smiling and I get the feeling he's saying this more for Anton's benefit than mine. I look at Anton and hear myself agreeing. At this stage, he takes his leave, saying he needs to go and make some arrangements, make some phone calls.

'I won't be sorry to see the back of you, young man,' the doctor says good-naturedly as Anton heads for the door. 'Maybe then my nurses will be able to concentrate on their work again.' Winking at me, he also heads out, confirming that I can leave after rounds in the morning. I can't wait.

§

Annie pops in later in the morning and stuns me with her news about herself and Henry. But she doesn't give me the details as to how exactly it all came about.

'No, that can wait until tomorrow, until you're home. Then we'll have a big catch-up.'

'Well, actually, I'm going to Anton's. He promised the doctor this morning that he'd look out for me. It was a condition of my discharge, that I don't do too much and that there's someone to care for me. I feel awful, Annie. I'm sure I'd be OK on my own. But he won't let me out otherwise.'

'And what's happening with Jack, Rache? He seems to be taking over, big time. What's the situation there?'

'Well, I've made my decision there, and I just need to talk to him. I thought I'd give him a call later, or maybe he'll call in this afternoon. I really need to have a good heart-to-heart with him.'

'Oh, no need to call, babes,' Annie says in her usual 'oh, it's him' voice, as we both turn to see Jack come through the door. 'Have to go,' she says. She can't get up quick enough in her haste to get out. She really can't stand him and it's been a huge problem in our friendship.

'Well, hopefully, you'll call round tomorrow then?' I ask, trying not to show my disappointment at her leaving. I was looking forward to a nice long chat with my friend.

'Try and stop me,' she says. 'I'll call round to

Anton's about two, is that alright? Want me to bring anything?' she says maliciously, and I know she's goading Jack.

'No, no, that's fine Annie. See you then,' and suddenly I just want her gone.

Before the door is even closed behind her Jack comes close to the bed, saying 'What's this about Anton's?'

Suddenly, there's tension in the room. Jack's looking at me a little belligerently, leaning over me. This is not the way I wanted to talk to him. I wanted things to be much calmer, less confrontational. But, perhaps, I'm fooling myself.

'I was going to call you and ask you to pop in, Jack. We need to talk. We need to sort things out. Don't we?'

'Absolutely. I've been trying to, for ages now. That was the whole point in coming to Wales,' he says. And my heart goes out to him. He looks like a little boy, desperate to make up with his best friend after a row, but not sure how. 'We need to make plans, Rache – for the future, right?'

§

I hate this. Why does this happen in love? The early

days of a romance are so wonderful, so *crazy*. It feels like you're walking on air, like you can achieve anything. Waking up every day is exciting, because it means you're going to see him, or her, again. Every minute spent away from each other is a wasted minute. I throw myself into love at the very deepest end – it's totally all or nothing, I'm incapable of any happy medium. Love gives us an energy, even when at our most exhausted; love gives us delight in the silliest things, and makes us tolerant of things we thought we hated.

I've seen friends, who were animal-haters, suddenly turn into slavering idiots over some tiny puppy. I've had a friend with a one-room studio apartment suddenly bring an Irish wolfhound home in an effort to impress the country boyfriend - needless to say, it didn't last long. Luckily, the hound was re-homed and is now deliriously happy in the Yorkshire Dales.

But, to my mind, love has its down sides, too. When it goes wrong, it seems to go disastrously wrong. Lovers go from being each other's beating heart to sworn enemies, dividing up the spoils of battle. Friends are trapped in the vicious circle of having to choose between 'him' and 'her'. Dinner party invitations turn into minefields, and the High Street of every small town a place to avoid until the dust settles.

'You're right, Jack. We both need to make plans, for the future. Why don't you sit down.'

§

Anton entered the cottage with a decided spring in his step. Things were looking up. He'd been given another chance. Another chance to show Rachel what she meant to him. Of course, he was unhappy that she was still unwell, but he'd make sure she was well looked after.

'Hi, Brad,' he greeted his friend on the phone, as he sat at the kitchen table of the cottage, mug of coffee in front of him. Annie was upstairs hogging the bathroom.

'Well, how's Rachel today?'

'Good news there. She's much better and is, in fact, being allowed home tomorrow. I've offered her a room at home, and she's accepted. So, we'll head down in the morning. Anything we need to talk about today?'

Brad heard the joy in Anton's voice when he spoke of this girl Rachel. He'd never known him like that before and was really pleased for him.

'Well, we've had several phone calls from Marty – he's back on his feet again - about those tracks you're going to lay down. People are getting a bit anxious, I'd say. It's such a huge thing, Anton, and I can understand – the music world is eagerly awaiting the next offering from The Manic Antelopes. What's the situation? When do you think you'll go into the studio?'

'Well, now with Rachel coming to Mill House I'll to be around a bit more. Don't worry, Brad,' Anton hurriedly assured him, 'I've given my word - they'll have them before April. It works out well actually. This way I can divide my time between the house and studio. Lucky it's just across the yard, eh?' he laughed. 'Will you give a call to Marty this evening and sort out a start date?'

Anton also asked Brad to get Frieda, his housekeeper, to spruce up Rachel's room, as he now thought of the bedroom overlooking the garden. He wanted several bouquets of flowers put in and to be sure everything was as it should be. He hoped Rachel would feel at home there again.

§

This was his second chance and nothing was going to stop him this time.

Chapter Fifty-Three

Aidan sat in the crowded restaurant, slightly nervous, but anxious to get things over with. Looking at his watch he noted Vee was a good fifteen minutes late – unusual for her, he thought.

It had been an eventful week. Both Henry and himself were extremely busy, trying to run the surgery without either Annie or Rachel. Thank heavens for Maura. Even though she wasn't with them very long, she was certainly a very hands-on woman, also extremely practical and down-to-earth.

He was very pleased to hear that Rachel was on the road to recovery. Annie had called that morning, saying she should be back in Norebridge the next day, as she felt there was no need for her to stay any longer in North Wales. Rachel was in good hands, and getting stronger each day, and returning home tomorrow.

Suddenly, Vee was there. 'Sorry I'm a little late,' she said casually, taking her seat at the table. 'The roads were bad, the usual idiots driving as if they're out for a

Sunday drive.' Aidan looked through the small bay window onto the clogged-up High Street.

'I know. All the more reason I appreciate you making the journey down, Vee. It's nice to see you.' There's that word, *nice*, again, Vee noted, silently. I'm fed up of it, if I hear it again I'll scream.

'Well, Aidan, you said you wanted to talk. So? Shall we?' Vee called the waitress over, ordered her peppermint tea, and sat back, arms folded across her slight chest. She'd done a lot of thinking over the last few weeks, deliberately not contacting Aidan, although she'd come *so* close on several occasions. If he wanted space, she decided, she'd give it to him – and she had.

After her disastrous trip to Norebridge she realised Aidan was in a state of confusion. She wasn't sure what about, but there had been a definite shift in their relationship since he moved. She'd been tormented with the idea that he'd met someone else – the reason which had prompted her to arrive, uninvited, at his new place of work. She hadn't picked up on any special 'vibes' between Aidan and the two girls who worked in the practice. But they were both very pretty, and it slightly worried her that he was surrounded by them all day. They certainly seemed to get on well – Henry, the owner,

Aidan and the two 'lovelies.'

'Yes, well, ... we haven't spoken for a while now?' Aidan had realised a few days ago that Vee hadn't been on the phone to him – every day – as before. It puzzled and intrigued him. And, when he *really* thought about it – it worried him. 'Have you been OK? Busy?'

'Very.' The silence was broken only by the waitress, delivering Vee's tea.

'There you go, love,' the elderly woman said, placing it gently on the table. 'Do you fancy a nice slice of Victoria Sponge? It's been freshly baked this morning – delicious. Can I tempt you – either of you?' she asked, sensing the tension at the table.

'No, thanks. Maybe later,' Aidan answered, becoming increasingly concerned at Vee's silence. *She* was usually the one chattering away, nonsensical chatter sometimes, which on occasion got on his nerves. But this was a different Vee. A more . . . disinterested, Vee? What was going on?

'Well, what've you been up to? Besides work, that is?' Aidan asked, tentatively.

'Oh, this and that, Aidan. The usual, you know? Mmm ... it's hard to quantify your time, when put on the spot. Work, work and more work, I suppose. Like you, probably?'

'Yeah. I've been really busy too. Rachel, one of the girls in the practice, had a bit of a breakdown, I suppose you'd call it. Break-up with the boyfriend, it seems. Then, she had an accident up in North Wales and he high-tailed it up there, so I assume it's all back on again. Annie, the other girl, took off up there to see her, too, so we've been extremely short-handed. And, the work's been piling on. Hopefully, things'll get back to normal soon.'

Then Vee realised why Aidan looked so wrung out. His eyes looked very tired, and he seemed a bit grey in the face. So, not out on the tiles every night then, she thought, surprised at how relieved she felt.

'Well, I treated myself lately. Took a trip to York two weekends ago. Bit of research for work. I'd never been before, and I loved it. It's an amazing place. I'd happily go again.' Aidan wondered if she'd gone alone, but decided he couldn't ask. 'Then, on Wednesday night last, I went out for dinner with Robert from work. A business meeting – about the project I was telling you about. It turned into a very late one, actually. Thursday was a little difficult. I haven't drunk that much wine in a long time,' she smiled.

Aidan was surprised, but said nothing. Vee wasn't a drinker and he found it hard to imagine her getting drunk. And, who was this Robert? Although he was sure she'd mentioned him before, but he hadn't paid much attention. Vee was still talking when, suddenly, the implication of what she was saying hit home.

' ... what do you mean, work in York?'

'I have the opportunity of transferring to the York office for a year. I went to see it when I was there. It's much more proactive than the set-up where I am at present. The client base is much wider and varied. It could be very exciting. I've . . .'

'Have you agreed to go?' Suddenly, Aidan realised he was holding his breath, not sure he wanted to hear Vee's answer.

'Not yet. I told them I wanted time to think about it. There'd have to be a little more incentive – financially – for me to make the move. It's a long way from home, and I really think I'd miss my friends – *our* friends. I wouldn't be able to just pop down to see them - it's about three hundred and forty miles, round trip. I can't see myself doing that very often.'

'And...me? Would you miss me, Vee?' Aidan couldn't stop himself asking.

Yes, yes! It worked! Vee thought triumphantly, looking coolly at her lover. 'I … suppose so, Aidan,' she said, 'but to be honest, the last few weeks have given me pause for thought. You haven't exactly been keeping in touch, have you?' Vee held up her hand, as Aidan started to protest. 'I understand you've been busy – you've just explained. But, a phone call doesn't take five minutes, does it? Even if it was just to say 'Can't talk right now. I'll call you later tonight.' Vee sat back, the ball was in Aidan's court now.

'No, nooo,' Aidan said slowly. 'But, I haven't deliberately been avoiding calling you, Vee. I really have been very busy. And, in the evenings I just want to collapse after grabbing something to eat, usually in the local pub. But, well … there *is* something, actually.'

Here it is, I knew it. Vee sat very still, trying her best to look casual, prepared for the hammer to fall.

'I've started, eh … fishing, again. Haven't done it in years. But I used to love it.' Aidan spoke quickly, as if he felt the need to get it out fast. '*And*, I suppose, I was at a loose end in the evenings when I wasn't entirely shattered. So … one thing led to another, *and* I caught my first fish in years the night before last,' Aidan beamed.

'*Fishing?* You've been *fishing?*' Vee almost spluttered her peppermint tea across the table.

'Yeah, I know,' he said looking, for some reason which eluded her, as if it was something to be ashamed of. 'Not something you'd have associated with me, eh?'

Vee laughed out loud – real laughter, laughter full of relief. 'No, definitely not what I was expecting, Aidan.'

'Well, actually, Vee, I think it was due to the fact that I was missing you. I know I haven't said it – well, not lately anyway. But I *have* missed you – very much. Perhaps, to be honest, I've only just realised it.' And, once he'd said it, he knew it was OK. Sure, Vee had her faults. But didn't he? He was no Mr. Perfect. He wouldn't be the easiest person to live with either. And, before he knew what was happening, he found himself taking Vee's hand across the table, asking his less-than-perfect girlfriend: 'Vee, will you marry me?'

A loud scream was followed by a very definite '*YES! YES!*' Then, having smothered Aidan with kisses, Vee called over the waitress. 'We'll have that Victoria Sponge now, please!'

Chapter Fifty-Four

I look at Jack's face and hate myself, but there's no going back now. My decision is made, once and for all.

'Jack, I really appreciate you coming up to Wales. I'm sure it wasn't easy for you to get away - with Jenny, and everything ....'

'I told you, Rachel, that's taken care of. She's heading back to the US tomorrow. You don't have to worry about her.'

'I'm not, Jack. I've done a lot of thinking recently. Foisted on me, I suppose, by everything that's happened. It's funny how things become very clear in your mind when you think you're going to die,' I say, wrapping up in a soft, fleecy blue dressing gown, which Anton brought me. I sit down opposite my once-adored lover.

'But you didn't. So, now we can get on with our plans, right?' Jack says, a little impatiently. 'I think the first thing we need to decide is where we're going to live. Your place is going to be advertised for rent soon, isn't it? If you don't mind me saying, Rache, I think you were a bit premature there. We could have just moved in there again. Now...Oh, well, never mind. There are loads of places. We'll find ---'

'Hang on a second, Jack. We're not ... I can't ...'

Jack looks at me slightly puzzled, then realisation dawns. 'Oh, God, Rache. Stupid of me,' he says, slapping his palm against his forehead. 'Of course, you don't want us to start again in that house. We'll just have to find somewhere else. You can always sell it, though.'

Why am I not surprised at Jack's certainty that we're going to start again – it's just typical of the man. And, I think it's this display of arrogance which finally gives me the courage to speak.

'No, Jack. I certainly do not want to start my new life in that house. But neither do I want to start my new life with *you*! We're done! Through! Finito!'

I won't say I didn't experience tremendous satisfaction looking at Jack's face - his mouth wide open - as I flounce out of the room as best I can in my weakened state. Outside in the corridor, my doctor along with my favourite nurse, are somewhat startled to find me punching the air, saying *'Yes, Yes!'* with a great big grin on my face.

'You go, girl,' Nurse Bernie mouths at me. Aloud

she says, 'Have you picked the right one?'

'Oh, yes. I have absolutely no doubt – at last!'

§

Anton arrives punctually at eleven o'clock, arms full of wine, chocolates and flowers for the nurses and other staff. How thoughtful. He also wheels in a wheelchair, balloons tied to the handles claiming 'Hurray! You're going home!' He's surrounded by five or six nurses, along with Chrissie the lovely tea lady, who suggests we might like a 'quick cuppa' before 'one of our nicest patients' leaves. They've all been so good to me, I think I'm going to miss them.

But I'm terribly excited - excited by the thought of going to Anton's, and am hoping I haven't made a huge mistake. I'm also feeling very shy in front of him this morning.

'Ready to go?' he asks.

'Just give me a minute. I want to check I've got everything from the bathroom,' and I head into the shower room, where I know I've already gathered all my belongings, but I can't resist having another quick look at my appearance. Checking my reflection in the mirror I note my hair badly needs a trim; my eyebrows are like bushes and, horrified, I see the hint of moustache on my top lip – oh, God! How could anyone possibly fancy me, looking like a female version of Poirot, the famous Belgian moustachioed detective. But there's nothing I can do right now.

'Let's go then,' I say to Anton, my voice a little muffled behind my hand. I'm so conscious of my hairy lip that my hand keeps flying to my mouth. *Get a grip, woman*!

'Are you feeling alright, Rachel?' Anton says, worriedly.

'I'm fine, really,' I say, dying to get under way, so I can make an emergency phone call to Annie – my most urgent requirement this minute is facial hair strips! Thirty minutes later, after lots of goodbyes, we're away. Outside, the sun is warm on my face, and it feels so good to be alive – and going home.

§

I doze several times on our long journey back to Norebridge, but finally, we're there and accompanied up the drive by a riotous Lucius, and a much improved Zebedee , who both refuse to let us in the door without lots of ear fondling and stroking of coats. Covered in slobbery kisses we eventually make it in, to be met by Frieda, Anton's housekeeper. Close on her heels comes Brad, and introductions are made. Apparently, he's heard a lot about me and enquires after my health. He seems genuine, his smile sincere.

Frieda shows me up to the same bedroom I was in before. Huge bouquets of lilies, interspersed with baby's breath, sit on various table tops around the room. 'Oh, how gorgeous,' I say, 'I've always loved baby's breath.' It reminds me of my maternal grandmother, who used it in every vase of flowers and even in small bouquets on the dining-room table. I even love the name, which suits the fragility of the tiny flowers.

'Anton's orders,' she explains. 'He said you loved flowers, and I was to fill the room to bursting with them,' she laughs.

'How sweet of him. He's been so kind to me, since I got ill. I hope you don't mind having me foisted on you. It shouldn't be for too long, I feel much stronger now.'

'It's absolutely no problem, Rachel. May I call you Rachel? Anton is delighted to have you here – and that's good enough for me,' she says, touching me gently on the arm before leaving me alone in this lovely room.

My bag is already on the bed, so I set to unpacking,

not that there's very much. And there's already a wardrobe full of my clothes here, since before I left for Wales. It's almost like coming home after a holiday away. I'm busy, so don't notice the door open, until I hear Anton's voice.

'Everything OK? Need any help? You're not to overdo things, remember.'

'No, I'm fine, really, Anton. Thank you so much. You have no idea how ... '

'Enough of that, Rachel. I'll extract payment for this, don't you worry. No such thing as a free lunch, isn't that what they say,' he teases. 'Now, what I came to say was, as soon as you're ready do you fancy a walk down by the stream? Only if you feel up to it, of course?'

'That sounds lovely. I'll only be five minutes. See you downstairs?'

I sit on the soft, luxurious bed and for the first time in a long while I feel a sense of peace and calm descend on me. My life has taken a much simpler turn since I finally saw that Jack had no place in my life. The awful uncertainty about everything has lifted – the worry that I wasn't good enough/pretty enough/interesting enough for Jack. Which in turn crept into an uncertainty in my working life too. I know Henry, my boss, rated me highly, but somehow discussing my work with Jack, seemed to fall on uninterested ears. This eroded any belief I had in myself, or that my working life could be of any interest to him or, indeed, anyone else.

Annie's antipathy to Jack was a problem too. This forced me into a loyalty to him that, perhaps, under other circumstances would have been questionable at best. I chose to believe that Jack didn't neglect me – because he told me so – not in actual words, but in some insidious, raising-of -the-eyebrow way when I expressed the slightest displeasure at yet *another* trip to the States. Jack succeeded, probably because I allowed him to, in creating a glass wall around just the two of us.

And, to be honest – this is that great *Be honest with yourself* moment – for a long time I felt happy inside my glass bubble. I could still *see* everyone outside it – friends, colleagues – so never had that feeling of being cut off from them. But slowly, I realise now, I was being distanced from them all – if Jack didn't feel at ease in their company then what was the point in going out with them? It was as if he was slowly turning the glass opaque, the figures outside becoming blurry. Why didn't I notice? I'm ashamed at how easily I was manipulated. And I wonder if Jenny was Jack's first betrayal – or just the first time he was caught? But I'm free now – thank God! Free to be myself, free to be with my friends and, dare I think it - free to find love again?

§

Anton is sitting out on the verandah. I catch a glimpse of him before I go outside. His side profile indicates someone in deep thought. He has such a handsome face and I want so much to stroke it. But I can't, Anton is a friend, a wonderful friend to me. He has given me a home once already, without asking any questions. And, here I am under his roof – again, unconditionally. His hand strokes Lucius, sitting motionless at his master's feet. He inclines his head towards me and it's obvious he's in absolute ecstasy. I would be too, in his position. He wags his tail, which alerts Anton to my presence.

'Oh, hi. Didn't hear you coming. Ready?' I nod, and we head down the incline towards the meandering stream. It's a perfect day – the blue sky is dotted here and there with gauzy clouds. A large, black cat, it's coat gleaming, washes its paws, then stretches lazily under the shade of a willow. The air feels warm on my face, despite the crispness in the air. Further down the bank I spy something spread out on the grass. 'What's that?' I ask.

'I just thought it'd be nice to relax by the river, so earlier I brought a rug and some cushions. Frieda brought the picnic basket, ice bucket and champagne,' Anton smiles down at me.

'How absolutely gorgeous,' I say, and that's exactly what it feels like – absolutely perfect. We head towards our picnic site, Anton helping me descend the sloping bank and we make ourselves comfortable on the rug. I lie back on the cushions, sighing with total contentment – and happiness.

§

'I was hoping we might have a chat, Rachel. Would that be OK with you?'

'Absolutely,' I say, but feel a slight frisson of fear. I don't want anything to ruin this. *Please, don't let him say anything that will spoil this day.*

'If you don't mind … I mean, I was wondering … do you think I could ask what the situation with Jack is?'

'Oh … no, of course not!' I'm completely taken aback at Anton's question. But then I realise it's perfectly rational for him to wonder at my situation. I haven't been very forthcoming with anyone about Jack and me.

'I mean ... are you and he...? Will he be coming round? I mean ... obviously, if that's what you want he'll be welcome. I was just wondering.'

'No, Anton,' I say, at last with total conviction, 'he will most definitely *NOT* be coming round. I've finally realised I don't want Jack in my life. It's taken me far too long to realise it, I see that now. But he's well and truly gone.'

'I'm so glad to hear it, Rachel. When did you give him the boot – if that's not being insensitive.'

'For the *last* time? Or the time before that?' I laugh. And it feels good to be able to laugh about it. 'This morning, at the hospital. There was a very defining moment when it all became clear – no doubts, no regrets whatsoever. It's over. And, I'm very happy that it is.' And I look at Anton, who's smiling broadly at me. Far too smugly, I realise. *He's* not getting off that lightly, I think.

'Well, never mind about me. What about that young girl of yours that day on our walk? Come on, I'm not the only one with a story to tell, I think?' I tease him. But I'm puzzled to see a sadness cloud his lovely face, and I almost regret asking. 'Sorry, Anton. Perhaps it's not something you want to discuss. Forgive me, I shouldn't have asked. It's none of my business.'

'No, Rachel. I'd like us to get everything out in the open before ...' he stops, unsure.

'Before what, Anton?'

'Look, that was an episode in my life which I deeply regret. It was before I really knew you.' I can see Anton is very uncomfortable, but he seems determined to relate whatever is so troubling him. He coughs, clears his throat, looks at me intently. 'Well, that girl you saw me with was part of a group my friends and I got to meet in the pub one night. It was in my wild, *stupid*, days. And, before you say anything I know, it was only a few months ago. But it seems a hundred years ago. So much has changed, so much has become clear to me.

'Anyway, we all got very drunk and headed back to my place when the pub closed. The next morning, I ... well, it seems ... I woke up and she was beside me in bed.' Anton puts his head in his hands, as if he doesn't want anyone to look at him. 'I'm totally and utterly ashamed. I can't seem to remember anything about it. The last thing I remember is conking out on the couch downstairs. All the others were still dancing around the place. How I got upstairs remains a mystery. I wasn't in any fit state to dance, never mind climb the stairs, so I'm puzzled as to how I ... you know. But it seems I took her to bed, that's what I'm told. And now she claims she's pregnant. Are you totally disgusted with me? I know *I* am.'

'Anton, why would I judge you? I've come to realise that sometimes we all do things that are absolutely and utterly stupid. But which seem perfectly reasonable at the time. I'm not saying jumping into bed with someone you've just met in the pub is a reasonable thing to do,' I say, smiling to take the rebuke out of my words. 'But I'm sure there was a reason for such ... unusual behaviour – drunkenness, loneliness, unhappiness? Who knows? But I believe there is always a reason why we behave in a particular manner.

'Can I explain why I went back to Jack after the betrayal? No, I can't. But I'm sure there was a reason – insecurity, loneliness, fear of being alone? Who can say? The main thing is we realise we're behaving in an unacceptable manner, and we pull ourselves up and cut it short. So, no, Anton, I do not feel in any way disgusted with you. I could never feel that. I think you're the most wonderful human being in the world –

you're kind, caring to humans and animals,' I laugh, in an attempt to lighten the mood. 'You're handsome, fit, and every nurse in the hospital fancied you to bits!' At this he throws back his head and laughs. Then, he looks at me – *really* looks at me to the point that I feel slightly uncomfortable.

'And what about *you*, Rachel? Do you think *you* could ever fancy me to bits?' And in the silence that follows I can feel the electricity in the air, crackling in the space between us. I become aware of birds singing overhead and the sounds of the river below. Suddenly, we're both startled as a silvery-gilled fish leaps high into the air, twisting and turning in the sunlight, landing with a resounding splash in the sparkling water. We both laugh out loud, and somehow it breaks the tension. Then I look at Anton, and am amazed at the look in his dark, fluid eyes – uncertainty, longing, pleading – and very definitely, love. And my heart leaps wildly as I realise what has been staring me in the face for so long.

'Oh, yes, Anton. I could certainly fancy you to bits. In fact, I think I already do!'

'Oh, Rachel. I didn't allow myself to hope you could. Do you really mean it? Do you really like me - maybe, even ... could you ever ... *love* me, do you think?'

And, again, I know something for sure. I know now, with absolute certainty that I love Anton Wickers-Stroppton. *'I love The Strop'* I want to shout out loud, for everyone to hear. And, as I laugh with happiness, Anton takes a bottle of champagne out of the cooling bucket and cracks the cork, terrorising a pair of loving swans cruising by the river bank.

'I didn't want to tempt fate. So, I couldn't open the bottle until you said 'yes.' You have said 'yes' haven't you?'

'To what,' I ask, totally puzzled.

'Oh, didn't I say? Rachel, will you marry me?'

And this time the swans flit wildly on top of the water, anxious to get away from the two mad things rolling around on a tartan rug on the river bank. Humans!

The End

Acknowledgements

A huge thank you must go to all my writer friends in the Bangor Cellar Writers' Group, for their encouragement and motivation, and for their constructive criticism, which at times none of us wanted to hear!

To my friend Margaret, fellow fan of the late Maeve Binchy, and ever-so-patient reader, who kept me buoyed up with her enthusiasm for the project.

To all the lovely staff of my local coffee shop where this book was written, who kept me fed and watered during the process – Llywella, Sharon, Julie, Dionne, Rhian, Llinos, Melissa, Gwenno and all the others, too numerous to mention but equally important.

Made in the USA
Columbia, SC
20 November 2018